DOROTHY
AND
AGATHA

Also by Gaylord Larsen

A Paramount Kill

DOROTHY AND AGATHA

Gaylord Larsen

A DUTTON BOOK

DUTTON
Published by the Penguin Group
Penguin Books USA Inc., 375 Hudson Street, New York,
New York 10014, U.S.A.
Penguin Books Ltd, 27 Wrights Lane, London W8 5TZ, England
Penguin Books Australia Ltd, Ringwood, Victoria, Australia
Penguin Books Canada Ltd, 2801 John Street, Markham, Ontario,
Canada L3R 1B4
Penguin Books (N.Z.) Ltd, 182-190 Wairau Road, Auckland 10,
New Zealand

Penguin Books Ltd, Registered Offices: Harmondsworth, Middlesex,
England

First published by Dutton, an imprint of New American Library,
a division of Penguin Books USA Inc.
Distributed in Canada by McClelland & Stewart Inc.

First Printing, December, 1990
10 9 8 7 6 5 4 3 2 1

Library of Congress Cataloging in Publication Data:

Larsen, Gaylord, 1932–
  Dorothy and Agatha / Gaylord Larsen.
    p.   cm.
  ISBN 0-525-24865-X
  1. Sayers, Dorothy L. (Dorothy Leigh), 1893–1957, in fiction,
drama, poetry, etc.   2. Christie, Agatha, 1890–1976, in fiction,
drama, poetry, etc.   I. Title.
PS3562.A734D6   1990
813'.54—dc20   90-34515
                                                            CIP

Printed in the United States of America
Designed by Nissa Knuth-Cassidy

PUBLISHER'S NOTE
This is a work of fiction. Names, characters, places, and incidents
either are the product of the author's imagination or are used ficti-
tiously, and any resemblance to actual persons, living or dead, events,
or locales is entirely coincidental.

Dedicated to:
SGT. CHESTER D. SAMPLE
(1893–1960)

AUTHOR'S NOTE

This is what is now popularly referred to as a "faction" book, carefully divided between fact and fiction. Dorothy L. Sayers and Agatha Christie—along with many of the supporting characters—were genuine enough, and we discover them in their natural settings with many of their real-life back stories in evidence. The fiction part begins about twenty-four hours prior to the action within these pages.

Although the two ladies were contemporaries, sharing an amazing number of parallels in their personal lives, I can't help wondering if the differences in temperament and outlook might not have been points of contention, to say nothing of the rivalry they must have sensed in their chosen field of work. We do know they collaborated—along with other members of the Detection Club—on several projects, both for publication and for BBC production, so they certainly must have known one another fairly well. Except for some rather mild derogatory comments attributed to Miss Sayers, however, nothing is known about how they felt toward one another.

I decided to explore the potential for conflict (and/or harmony) by dropping the two of them into the middle of a proper mystery of the period. And while the book should not be considered biography in any sense, I have, to the best of my ability, kept the ladies in character.

If you should happen to notice a distinct improvement in the quality of writing during the meeting of the Detection Club, it is understandable. Miss Sayers dearly loved the fun of the group, and I could not resist the temptation to lift, almost verbatim, her incantations and her initiation script.

The hesitant reader may be assured I have allowed no bodily harm to befall these two treasures of the mystery genre. And, as soon as my fictional tale reaches its denouement, I am careful to return "Dorothy" and "Agatha" to the condition in which I found them, so they might pick up the threads of their real lives unchanged. For after all, it's one of the Rules of the Game, isn't it?

DOROTHY
AND
AGATHA

1

"Calm and easy," Dorothy told herself. "Calm and easy." She touched the bare skin above her breasts to see if her heart was still racing. At the same time she watched the familiar sight of her cook busily scratching about in their garden. Only another quiet summer's day in Witham, she kept telling herself. Nothing to be alarmed about. Nothing at all.

When she was sure her voice could be relied upon, she began, "What on earth are you doing out there, Betty?"

At the sound of her mistress's voice, the startled cook cried out in surprise. She pushed herself upright with the aid of the potato fork in her grasp.

"Oh, Miss Sayers, you're home at last. Sorry I didn't hear the taxi. Well, how could I? Standing on my head that way." She gave a hearty Welsh laugh and brushed some wild strands of red hair away from her forehead with the back of her hand. "I don't know how I managed it, but I come away from me marketing a potato short. I was just sifting through our old potato rows to see if I could glean at least one more for the evening meal."

Dorothy L. Sayers shifted her heavy briefcase to her other hand and kicked at a wayward clod of English loam at the near end of the exhausted vegetable garden.

"I don't think there is much hope of that, is there? When old Albert finishes a potato patch, even Ruth and Naomi would be out of luck. To say nothing of Betty and Dorothy."

"Ruth and Naomi . . . Oh, like in the Bible." Betty

Cooperman burst out with more laughter. "Miss Sayers, you can make a joke out of anything, I declare." She put a free hand on the small of her back and got herself straight enough to walk. "I suppose you are right, though. I haven't found a trace. Not so much as a blinkin' eye. I'll just get on me bicycle and do what has to be done."

"Never mind. I'm sure we can make do with what we have. London was so hectic, I don't know that I am all that hungry anyway."

"Now, Miss Sayers, you always say that, but you know you enjoy a good meal all the same."

Dorothy chuckled, and patted her ample midriff. "You know me too well."

"Why, of course. You need to keep up your strength, what with all you been up to."

"Never you mind. Let's see what we can do inside, first."

Betty propped the fork against the small potting shed and the two ladies ambled toward the kitchen door. Their relationship spanned nearly a decade, and there was a good deal of trust and caring woven into it. It showed even in the way they walked, each allowing for the other.

"I think I'll draw a bath before dinner," Dorothy sighed. "Unless Mr. Fleming has beaten me to it. He is at home, is he?"

"Why, no, mum. Not since this morning. I haven't laid eyes on the Mister all day." Betty slapped at her forehead in mock punishment. "Oh, listen to me going on, would you. I forgot to tell you the other gentleman is in the house, waiting to see you."

"Gentleman? What other gentleman is that?"

"Why, the one what said you was expecting him. Oh, dear. You was expecting him, wasn't you?"

"What kind of gentleman? What does he look like? Oh, never mind, now. When was this? What time of day?"

"Oh, dear. A good half hour ago. I told him you'd be comin' home on the London train and to make himself to home. Then I completely forgot about him, what with the potatoes and all."

"Where did you put him? The sitting room is a mess."

"I made space for him at the dining room table. I hope that is all right. He seemed like such a nice-spoken . . ."

But Dorothy was already through the back door. She put her briefcase on the kitchen table next to her hat and Betty's grocery bundles, then she moved toward the dining room at a slower pace.

Betty closed the back door behind them, then sniffed at the air and whispered, "Oh, I meant to ask you, what is that strange odor? Would he be a pipe man?"

Dorothy didn't appear to hear the questions. She was standing dead still in the dining room doorway. After a few seconds she cleared her throat, as if to announce her presence. When this received no response she said, "I'm Dorothy Sayers. What can I do for you?"

Betty had started washing up at the kitchen sink, but when Dorothy didn't budge from her place in the doorway her curiosity got the better of her. She peeked over Miss Sayers' shoulder at the empty table in the adjoining room.

"Well, what do you think, mum? You don't suppose he's gone off with nary a word, do you?"

Dorothy only pointed toward the end of the room where her typewriter stand stood next to the bay windows. A middle-aged man in a brown tweed suit sat slumped over the typewriter. His head was cocked against the carriage at a strange angle, which seemed to contribute to the look of astonishment on his puffy white face.

Betty screamed into her mistress's ear, then drew back and held both her wet hands over her mouth. For a moment they both stood staring at the man, half expecting him to stop playing his childish game of making faces and to start acting his age. But he wasn't playacting. And he wasn't going to make any more moves on his own. Dorothy took two tentative steps forward.

"Is this the gentleman you let in to see me?" she asked.

Betty grunted a vigorous "yes" behind her sealed lips. Dorothy went over to the figure and reached for his dangling hand to search for a pulse. But she had no more than touched the wrist when she dropped it again and looked at her own fingers. There was blood on her thumb. Betty screamed again.

"Betty, please. That is not helping at all. We must think what to do."

"Is he dead? He looks dead. How could he be dead?"

"The body is warm, but . . . Yes, I think he is dead."

Betty swooned against the door frame and covered her eyes.

"Don't fall apart on me now, old dear. We need to think what to do."

Dorothy searched one end of the dining room table among scraps of disorganized material until she found some cotton gauze. She pulled a small corner of it free and took her time wiping her fingers clean. Then she turned back to the aberration that had manifested itself in their presence—and at her very favorite work station.

"Did he have a heart attack, or what?" Betty whispered.

"That wouldn't explain the blood, would it? And I think there is more blood up in the hair."

Because of the way the body was slouched forward, the nearest corner of his suit coat was nearly touching the floor. With one cautious toe Dorothy pushed back the coat front and exposed a large handgun lying on the floor beneath the chair.

"Oh, good heavens," Betty muttered.

"So much for the strange smell. Spent gunpowder."

"I think . . . I need . . . some air," Betty gasped.

Dorothy lifted the window near the dead man, as if working around bodies were something she did every day.

"Why don't you sit down, Betty? I'll ring up the police."

Betty nodded quietly and went back into the kitchen. Dorothy moved to the telephone in the front hallway. She kept the phone call very formal and to the point. Would they please send some one around to 24 Newland Street?

Yes, it was a police matter. There was a dead man in the house. Yes, the police would most certainly be interested. It was obviously an unnatural death. Thank you.

After hanging up the receiver she took a moment to check her reflection in the mirror, which she had hung next to the front door for last-minute's primping. Her round face was flushed and her eyes still held a startled expression. Today there would be no need to add color to her normally pasty complexion. The slight upturn at the corners of her mouth, which her mother had always insisted made her look like a guilty pixie, was still very much in evidence—an inherited quirk that most definitely projected the wrong image for the serious occasion. She made the muscles about her mouth tight and the pixie smirk turned into something a schoolteacher might wear after a chalk duster fight in the back of the room. She would have to remember that. So much to remember.

Without really thinking what she was about, Dorothy started gathering up some of the muslin material that was on the dining room table in an attempt to tidy up the place, but then thought better of her efforts. She had written of and read enough about police investigations to know she shouldn't be touching things. The house was in such a shambles it really didn't matter. Picking up one armload of confusion wouldn't make much of a difference in the attitude the police were going to take about the appearance of things. She dropped the material back on the table, made space for herself in the Queen Anne chair next to the entryway, and plopped herself down with a sigh.

Why now, she asked her private self, when everything seemed to be going so well with her new career? Why did this have to happen to muddy the waters?

But no sooner had she thought such negative thoughts than she stiffened with resolve. This was no way for her to be acting. She had work to do. No time to be feeling sorry for herself. It was time to buckle down and do what had to be done. She found her prince-nez on her bodice, reeled out the string, and snugly positioned them on her nose. Then she picked up the seventy-odd pages of script from the lamp stand nearby and tried to get busy. She had promised the cast of her play that line changes would be made and in their hands before their next rehearsal. If she was going to keep that promise she would have to get busy. No police investigation could stand in her way . . .

Try as she might, she could not concentrate on the written word. The script might just as well have been written in Mandarin Chinese. She looked at the clock in the hallway, then closed her eyes and put her head back against the antimacassar. She had been on her own for all of her adult life. She would have to see this business through on her own as well. Husbands were supposed to be good, stalwart, dependable rocks in times of trouble, but she had long since given up any hope of seeing Mac in such a role. Since he had lost his steady employment with the newspaper two years before he had become increasingly unreliable and irritable in moments of need.

She forced her mind over the events of the last half hour and wondered if there had been anything she had overlooked. Or anything she should have done differently. No doubt she had taken the wrong actions, but there was no turning back now. No time for regrets. Her course was set and she would have to live by it, whether she liked it or not.

Fourteen minutes had ticked off the hall clock from the time she had telephoned when Dorothy heard the crunch of gravel under car tires coasting to a stop in front of the house. Strange, she thought, how very formal and orthodox the noise was. As if she knew the tires carried omnipotent authority, like the Almighty Miller, come to grind down some spurious grain and sift the flour for signs of truth.

"Betty, they are here," she called toward the kitchen. "Why don't you come out? I know they'll want to question us both."

Dorothy got to her feet, slightly hitched up the skirt of her dark dress and gave two firm tugs to the trailing edges of her foundation garment before she opened the door.

2

The two uniformed men who came in the door did not look very omnipotent. In fact, since Dorothy had slipped quietly into her mid-forties, authority figures had taken on surprisingly youthful appearances.

They asked immediately to see the body, but Dorothy took the time to make proper introductions. Inspector Petry, the taller of the two, did most of the talking. With his visored hat removed, he took on an almost comical appearance. His straight blond hair was parted severely over his left eye, in the manner of a Gilbert and Sullivan bobby. The Inspector's partner was Sergeant Harry White-comb. A squat, thick bulldog of a man, he looked older and more experienced than his fellow officer, but his manner of speaking belied the fact that he had progressed about as far as he was likely to go in the local police force.

Betty made a slight curtsy when introduced, but held back against the wall rather than speaking out. When Dorothy introduced herself as Mrs. Fleming she detected an extra movement of the Inspector's head, but she didn't volunteer more to satisfy his curiosity.

Then she led the way into the dining room and stood to one side. The policemen went over the body, touching it and checking pockets, but not moving it from its unique position. The Inspector put his hand on the neck, search-ing for traces of a heartbeat. Finally satisfied the man was indeed dead, he gave a solemn nod of his head to his sergeant, who turned to the cook.

"Mind if we be using your phone, mum? We'll be needing to call the station. Won't take a minute."

Betty dutifully led the way to the telephone in the hall, where the policeman made his call, consisting of two short sentences. Apparently the station had been alerted and would soon be sending the appropriate people right along.

"I do hope we won't have to have all sorts of people traipsing in and out of my house," Dorothy said.

The Inspector cleared his throat, "No, mum, we're a very small station here. But we will have to look things over carefully before moving the body. I'm sure you understand." Then he took a pencil out of his pocket and tried to pick up the gun on the floor by running the pencil through the trigger loop.

After several spins and false moves, Dorothy cried nervously, "Be careful, there, Inspector. That thing is no doubt still dangerous."

The Inspector finally gave up and used his handkerchief to get the gun on the table.

"Humm. If I didn't know better I would say that is an old military blunderbuss. Wouldn't you say, Harry?"

The other policeman took a superior glance at the weapon and nodded agreement. "Very good, sir. Looks like a Berten-Wellar, .44-caliber. Haven't seen one o' those since the Great War. Military people say they had a fierce tendency to jam."

This got a nod in return from the Inspector who then took out a small notebook and tapped it with his pencil. Dorothy was getting the firm impression the two men didn't know what they were about. Mysterious gunshot deaths were hardly common occurrences in quiet little Witham, and they were valiantly trying to act their parts.

"Now, then, Miss, ah, Mrs. Fleming," the Inspector began in a formal tone, "would you be so good as to tell us the dead man's name and his relationship—"

"His name? How should I know his name?"

The Inspector blinked in surprise. "This is your house, is it not?"

"Yes, of course. My husband and I live here. And Betty, of course. But I still don't know . . . You see, I just returned home from London this afternoon. Betty, please tell the gentlemen—"

"Tell them what, Miss Sayers?"

"Tell them how we came in the house together and found the body . . ." She made hand signs to Betty to continue.

"Yes, that's right, sir. I was in the garden, don't you see, when the Missus come home from London. And we got to talkin' and come in the back way. And we found him like that."

"I see." The Inspector wrote something down, then stepped toward the kitchen for a better look into the backyard garden. Then he came back, rubbing his pencil against the side of his face.

"Excuse me now, but am I to understand that neither of you know how this body came to be in your house?"

"No, no. We didn't say that. You must learn to be more discerning about what people tell you," Dorothy lectured. "You see, Betty here, let him in. Did he give you his name?"

Betty blushed. "Oh, dear. I suppose he must have, but you know how I am with names."

"But why did you let him in in the first place?" the Inspector asked.

"He said he come to see Miss Sayers. He said she was expecting him, and I says she isn't here right yet. She would be comin' with the afternoon train from London. So he says he would be happy to wait. He spoke so well and all. And Miss Sayers knows so many people I never laid eyes on, I didn't think a thing about it."

"And he gave no other indication of what his visit was about?"

Betty thought a bit, then shook her head. Her hazel eyes were beginning to get misty. "He spoke just like a gentleman. I thought it would be the proper thing to do. How was I to know . . . "

Dorothy put a comforting arm around her. "Of course you had no way of knowing what would happen. You did exactly the right thing." Dorothy turned to the Inspector, using her firm authoritative voice. "Wouldn't it be much easier to look through the man's pockets to find out who he is?"

"He has no identification on him. Not in his usual pockets, anyway."

"Nonsense," she said. "How did he get here, then, if he has no identification—a wallet or whatever men carry?"

"That is what we would like to know." He turned back to Betty, "So you did not leave the premises at all after you let the man in?"

"Leave the premises . . . No, I was here, like I said. Here and in the backyard."

"Now I want you to think very carefully, Betty." The Inspector pointed his pencil at her, which didn't help her nervousness. "Are you sure you didn't go down to one of the shops in town or to the neighbors' while the man was here waiting?"

"Inspector," Dorothy interrupted, "she says she didn't leave the premises. What is so important about where she was? What are you getting at?"

"It appears the gentleman took his own life by shooting himself in the head. Now if that is in fact the case, I would like to know why no one heard the shot. Those old handguns are pretty noisy. Right, Sergeant?"

The Inspector looked for and got a quick nod of agreement from his sergeant. Dorothy decided they made a great pair of nodders.

Betty and Dorothy looked at each other for explanations. Then Betty spanked her forehead again.

"Oh! You are right, you know. I did step out of the house for a minute. I went next door to the Masons'. She's doing her first bit of tomato preserving and asked me to help with the boiler. But look here . . . "

Betty went into the front hall and stopped at the open window right next to the umbrella stand. "I opened this window before I went next door. That way I can listen for Miss Sayers' telephone while I'm in the Masons' kitchen. See, right through that hedge out there. That's the Masons' kitchen door. I've done it before when Miss Sayers was away and she might be calling me about dinner plans and such."

The Inspector looked out the window for himself. "And you say you can hear this telephone ringing when you are across over there?"

"Oh, yes, sir. Many a times I've done it. And if I could hear the telephone bell, wouldn't I be able to hear a gunshot?"

"Humm, yes, you probably could. Strange you didn't think of your trip to the neighbors before, isn't it?"

Betty took this as a joke. She tried to smile, then found a handkerchief in her apron pocket and dabbed at her moist eyes.

The Inspector went over his brief notes. "The doctor will be along in a few minutes. Let's see now if there is anything else I should be . . . "

"Shouldn't you be asking what time the deceased arrived?" Dorothy suggested.

The Inspector cleared his throat. "And what time of day was it when you let the gentleman in?"

Betty checked the hall clock, which had just ticked past five-thirty. "Why, I'd say an hour ago. Maybe just a bit more. I didn't really pay much attention. I'd just come home from me marketing when I heard the front doorbell ring. Let me see . . . I put my bundles down and then . . . the potatoes . . ."

Something troublesome was going on in Betty's mind. She scowled heavily and blinked her eyes back and forth between her mistress and the Inspector.

"And then . . ." the Inspector repeated, trying to help her memory along. Betty's eyes filled up again and she shook her head.

"Inspector," Dorothy interrupted, "would it be all right if I answered the rest of your questions? Betty has had quite a shock to her system."

He scratched at his sideburn again. "I suppose that would be all right. You won't be leaving the premises, I presume."

"No, sir. I'll be right here in the kitchen."

"Very good."

The Sergeant, who had been hovering next to his superior's elbow, touched a finger to his forehead in a thank-you salute and stepped out of Betty's way. "We'll let you get back to your potato peelin'," he smiled.

"Potato peelin'? I've not been peelin' no potatoes," Betty declared, as if she had been insulted. The gentlemanly tones from the Inspector had her tongue tied a moment before, but now the common, more familiar speech patterns of the Sergeant seemed to loosen her up again.

"Oh, really?" the Sergeant said. "Thought I smelled raw potato when we come in."

"Nonsense. Miss Sayers says that was spent gunpowder. And she ought to know." Betty marched into the kitchen, muttering something about rude complaints from strangers about smells in people's houses.

Inspector Petry turned back to Dorothy. "She called you Miss Sayers, but you introduced yourself as . . ."

"Mrs. Fleming. That's right."

"But you are the mystery writer lady, aren't you?"

"I've published several mystery novels in the past."

"Yes, I'd heard you lived here in town. Very pleased to make your acquaintance. I wish it could be under better circumstances."

"Yes, I'm sure."

"My wife is a big fan of yours."

"But you are not, I take it."

"Well, no. Perhaps it's the subject matter. Murder and mayhem. Busman's holiday, don't you see."

"I understand . . . About the name, Inspector. Betty was with me when I was single and she can't get out of the habit. And Sayers is still my professional name even though I am now married to Major MacDonald Fleming, although he goes by Mac. Sorry to be so confusing."

Petry nodded and made an entry in his little book, which troubled Dorothy.

"Inspector Petry, I wonder if you would mind using only my married name in your report?"

"I beg pardon?"

"Mrs. Dorothy Fleming. Please use that name. After all, it is my legal name now."

"Why don't I simply mention them both? Since you are better known by your maiden name I thought . . ."

"That is precisely what I am concerned about. Perhaps I am too well known. The publicity this ridiculous matter is likely to create may be blown totally out of proportion. You see, I am in the midst of preparing a new play for production. I really don't have the time to be fencing with a horde of reporters just now."

"Oh, I see. I was wondering what all this fabric was doing lying about. Doing your own costumes, are you?"

"Friends of mine. I'm letting them use our house."

"Is this going to be for a local amateur group?"

Her back straightened. "Hardly an amateur group, Inspector Petry. It is part of the program for the Canterbury Cathedral Festival."

"Is that so?" He sounded impressed. "You mean it will be like the play that American poet did?"

"T.S. Eliot? Yes. I presume you mean *Murder in the Cathedral*."

"My wife tells me that was a very impressive production."

"Yes it was. And Archibald MacLeish was commissioned to do a production. And now it is my turn."

"That all sounds like quite a change for a mystery writer."

"If everything goes well, it could be quite prestigious. A nice step up and a new direction for my career. But none of that is likely to occur if I am not allowed to give my full attention to the production. And since it is for the church,

I really don't know how they would take it to have one of
their festival authors involved in a messy . . ."

Out of the corner of her eye, Dorothy had been nervously watching the Sergeant move about the room, poking about the play costumes and other paraphernalia.
When she saw him trying to peek behind a Chinese screen
standing in the corner, she barked, "Sergeant, may I help
you?"

He jumped and smiled. "Oh, just looking about, Miss
Sayers . . ."

"You mean Mrs. Fleming, don't you?"

"Yes, of course. Mrs. Fleming. Hiie!"

When the Sergeant moved the screen, he had inadvertently bumped a large dress mannequin standing behind
it. The top-heavy mannequin began to topple, and he had
to act fast to grab it by one feathery wing before it hit the
ground. He fumbled about some more, trying to get it
back on its narrow base. With two huge white wings
strapped to its back and no head, the dummy looked
something like a life-size version of the *Winged Victory*
sculpture.

"Be careful," Dorothy cried, "that is Archangel Gabriel's costume you are grabbing so carelessly there."

The Sergeant managed to get the strange figure upright,
but in the process several white feathers came loose and
either clung to his dark uniform or fluttered silently to the
carpet.

"Sorry about that, mum. It doesn't seem to be on too
sturdy a base."

"It was perfectly secure until you arrived on the scene."

"Oh, yes. Sorry about that."

"And I'll thank you to return my feathers, if you please.
We're running short of them as it is."

Dorothy and the chagrined Sergeant started plucking
his uniform and returning the wayward plumes to a sack
on the table. The Inspector finally got into the act and
helped retrieve some feathers from the carpet.

"This appears to be the molting season for archangels,"

he smiled, very pleased with his joke, until he caught Dorothy's steely glare.

"If you have any practical suggestions," she snapped, "as to how we might attach these damn things I'd be happy to entertain them."

"No. I'm afraid this is a little out of my line."

"It's out of my line, too, Inspector, but someone will have to do it. This will be the last play I write without giving careful consideration to each and every aspect of production pitfalls. Writing for the church is twice as difficult as writing for the commercial theatre. Make no doubt of it."

"Yes, mum." He dusted his hands as the last loose feather floated into the sack. "I assume you are not doing all this work by yourself."

"I thought we had covered that. The Festival committee has supplied a staff that works with me. I certainly couldn't manage a major production on my own."

"No, of course not," he said. "And I assume a great many people come in and out of your house during the course of your preparations."

"Oh, I see what you're getting at. You think the stranger was one of the production people involved with my play."

"Exactly."

"No, he was not on staff. I know the entire team quite well, and he was not part of our group."

"Perhaps someone had to drop out and he was a re-placement. Or perhaps he was with a newspaper, here to do a story—"

"Highly unlikely. But I certainly don't want to interfere with your investigation. Please pursue that if you wish. I'm sure you understand by now why I must insist on your using only my married, legal name."

"Well, I will see what we can do."

At the sound of another car pulling to a stop in front of the house the Sergeant looked out the window. "They're here," he called and went to open the front door.

One of the local doctors, whom Dorothy recognized, and another policeman came in. The policeman carried

with him a collapsed stretcher that looked as if it were
army surplus. It had been twenty years since the Great
War, but the sight of those old litters still did something
chilling to the sensibilities of the people who had lived
through the experience. That, and the pressure of the
current situation made Dorothy gasp for air like a floundering swimmer.

"If you don't mind, Inspector, I think I'll see how Betty
is doing, while you . . . do what has to be done in here."

"Of course," he said. "This shouldn't take long."

Betty was sitting at the kitchen table, snapping the
stems off a basketful of garden string beans. Dorothy's hat
and brief case had been removed from the table and
placed on a chair next to the dining room door. Dorothy,
for something to do with her hands, sat down and took a
handful of beans and started to work on them.

"What are they doing in there now?" Betty whispered.

"Removing the body, I presume."

"Oh, dear. I don't know if I can continue to work in this
house."

"What on earth are you talking about?"

"Every time I'd go into that room I think I'd see that
awful sight. That staring puffy white face."

"You've seen dead bodies before. Didn't you help lay
out your uncle for his wake not two months ago?"

"I know, but this is different."

"What do you mean, different?"

"Uncle Orville was eighty-one and he had a growth. He
was ready to go. But this man . . . shot right in our house.
I think I best be looking around. My brother wants me
back in Wales, doing for him . . ."

"You'll do no such thing. You're staying right here. I
couldn't possibly do without you now, with the production less than three weeks away. Whatever put that idea
into your head?"

Betty found her hankie again and wiped some more
tears. "I just feel it would be best . . ."

"Nonsense. This will pass. You'll see."

They snapped beans in silence for a while. Then they listened to the grunts of the men in the next room, hoisting the fourteen-stone body from the typewriter chair, then lowering it onto the litter, which creaked under its load. Then there was some mumbling in quick quiet breaths among the men. The next thing Dorothy knew, the Inspector was in the kitchen doorway with a three-by-five card in his hand.

"Mrs. Fleming, may I have a word with you again? In the dining room, here, please."

He back-stepped into the dining room and waited. Instead of looking at her, he was busily reading over and over again some typing on the card in his hand. The other men were tending to the body and covering it with an army blanket in a way that would keep the arms from dangling over the side of the narrow litter.

When the Inspector had maneuvered Dorothy to one side of the dining room where they might have a bit of privacy he said, "I would like to take this opportunity to ask you again about this man. We'll just forget about what you said earlier. I'm sure you have been greatly shocked by what has happened and you may just have said some things you wish now you had not said."

"What on earth are you talking about, Inspector?" she boomed in full voice.

The other men in the room were keeping to their work over the body, trying to look as if they weren't listening.

"This dead man"—the Inspector waved the card for emphasis—"are you absolutely certain you have never met him before?"

"Isn't that what I told you?"

"Yes it is. But I have reason to think otherwise, now."

Dorothy snatched at the card. The Inspector, who moments earlier had seemed so comical and unsure of himself, flipped the card out of her reach with style. "Is there something you want to tell me in private, Mrs. Fleming? Perhaps if we step outside where . . ."

"There is nothing I wish to discuss with you in private,

Inspector Petry, either outside or inside. Now if you would be so kind, that looks like one of the note cards I use for my rehearsals. May I see it?"

She reached out her hand. He somewhat reluctantly moved the card into her reading zone, but kept a firm grip on the edge of it.

"When we moved the body," he explained, "we found this in the typewriter carriage, under the man's head. Please bear in mind this might very well be evidence for the inquest."

"There's no need to lecture me on what may or may not be evidence, Inspector . . ." Dorothy got her pince-nez into place and read the typed message:

> Dorothy, darling,
> I can't go on any longer. The pangs of guilt I feel
> are too much to bear for a lifetime. Please try to
> understand and forgive. I love you.

When Dorothy's troubled eyes had finished scanning the note and had returned to the Inspector's grim face, he asked, "Now, is there anything about your statement you would like to change?"

Dorothy stared hypnotically at the khaki blanket covering the body. "No. Nothing I can change . . . about my statement . . ."

Dorothy's complexion, still rosy just moments ago, had now turned ashen. Her lips, which had not floundered over words since she was sixteen months old, suddenly lost their rhythm. She reached out and gripped the edge of the Chinese screen to steady herself.

The Inspector persisted. "You know of no reason why this man would write such a note to you?"

"I don't understand. Don't understand . . . at all."

Sergeant Whitecomb and the other constable hoisted the litter between them and started toward the front door with their heavy load. The Inspector went ahead to open

the door for them, then saw to it that the body got into
the back of the paneled lorry without too much difficulty.

When he came back into the house to talk further with
Dorothy L. Sayers, he found the formidable lady sprawled
in the corner of the room in a dead faint. It was unlikely
she had injured herself. The Chinese screen and the molting white wings of the Archangel Gabriel had no doubt
cushioned her fall.

3

Dorothy awoke and found herself lying on the couch in her own sitting room. When the men put her there they apparently had not bothered to roll up the bolts of yardage draping the couch, but had simply placed her on top of the gold lamé, which the drama committee was thinking of using to dress one of the titled characters in her play. Just like men, she thought. Then she heard her husband's abrasive voice, booming in anger, in the adjoining room. The familiar sound must have been what woke her. As she struggled to sit up someone reached out to restrain her.

"Why don't you rest for a bit, Mrs. Fleming?" It was the doctor who had come in with the litter. A damp washrag fell off her head as she sat up. The good doctor retrieved it from her lap and put it in a nearby basin. "You must have fainted as a result of all the business in the other room. Just a bit of rest and you should be good as new."

"I assure you, I'm perfectly all right."

The arguing that was going on in the next room rose to a fever pitch. Dorothy got to her feet and started toward the front door.

"Damn it all, man, I live here," Mac Fleming was explaining in no uncertain terms to the Inspector. "What are *you* doing here might be a better question."

The two men were standing chest-to-chest and nose-to-nose in the narrow entryway discussing common law regarding a man's castle, as it is practiced in the British Isles.

"Mac, listen to me," Dorothy called. "Something quite dreadful has happened."

Mac finally backed off long enough to consider his wife's countenance. And to brush at the corners of his mustache.

"But this chap here wants to question me on my own doorstep," he barked.

"He has every right to be here. A man has shot himself here in our house."

"Our house. Why, how dare he? Who? Who has done such a thing?"

"Oh, Mac, do please quiet down. Everything will be explained to you in due course. Won't it, Inspector?"

"Of course." The Inspector readjusted the drape of his uniform jacket, hoping to return a bit of decorum to the situation. "But if you don't mind, I would like to explain the situation in my own way."

"Yes, of course."

Mac started pacing about the dining room and looking into the sitting room. The doctor came out of the sitting room and introduced himself as Dr. Endicott. Mac didn't bother to take his extended hand in greeting, but continued his visual search of the premises.

"The body has already been removed, if that is what you are looking for, Mr. Fleming," Dr. Endicott told him.

Mac grunted in response, then carried his weathered squire's hat and muffler to their accustomed place in the entryway umbrella stand. Mac was not a tall man, standing only five feet eight, but there was a certain thickness to his body that gave him the appearance of size. He had broad shoulders and heavy muscular arms. Only recently had his stomach started to precede his chest. And even that he could still suck in when he wanted to. Like right now.

Dorothy could tell from his erect military bearing that he had been visiting a pub, for after hoisting a few, his stiff back loosened up and the aches and pains of advancing years were forgotten. For a little while, at least, he would feel he was in charge of something again. Too bad his swagger stick was packed away upstairs with his uniform. He looked as if he could make good use of it about now.

"Now then, tell me what this business is all about," he ordered.

The Inspector cleared his throat. "We are not very far along in our investigation. We were rather hoping you might be able to shed some light on things for us."

"Me? How could I? I've been gone all day."

"For the record. You are Mr. MacDonald Fleming, are you not?"

"*Major* Fleming," he corrected. "Now I want to know who the blighter was, and what he was doing in my house."

Sergeant Whitecomb came into the house from the back way, startling Mac all the more.

"Godfrey Daniels, the Huns have us surrounded. Who the devil are you?"

"Sergeant Whitecomb, sir," the Sergeant touched his forehead in introduction, then turned to his Inspector. "I could hear you and the Mister here, quite distinctly from the kitchen across the way, sir."

The Inspector nodded wisely and made another entry in his small book.

The Sergeant smiled at Dorothy. "Glad to see you are back on your feet, ma'am. Feeling better?"

Dorothy would have said something back to the Sergeant, but Mac was blinking his red eyes at the exchange.

"Will somebody please tell me what in bloody hell is going on around here?" he cried. "What's wrong with you, anyway, Dorothy?"

"Oh nothing." Dorothy brushed down a few strands of Mac's thinning hair so he wouldn't look quite so disheveled. "I simply passed out for a moment from all the excitement. Nothing is wrong."

"Fainted at the sight of a lifeless body, eh? I would have thought there was more backbone in you than that, old girl, after all those bloody stories of yours. It's a good thing you weren't in the war. Why, we had bodies all over the place after the second gas attack at Simes. You couldn't muck your way through the mud without stepping on some poor devil . . ."

Dorothy put a restraining hand on his arm. The same arm he was using to show how the bodies were spread about in his story. "Why don't we let the Inspector ask us what he needs to ask?"

Mac jerked free of her and faced the inquisitor in the dark suit. "Aren't you a bit young to be an inspector, young man?"

The Inspector only cleared his throat again and tapped his pencil on his notebook. "You say you have not been on the premises all day, Major. Where—"

"That's correct. I haven't. The Missus and I had some words this morning before she was to leave for London. But I beat her to it. I was out of the house before her and didn't return until, well, until I came to the door and found you blocking my way."

"And where did you spend the day?"

"In my motorcar, if you must know."

"And where did you travel?"

"Is that really pertinent? The point is I was not here. Isn't it?"

"Were you with anyone? Or did anyone see you in your travels?"

"I say, look here. This is beginning to sound a good deal more like another kind of investigation."

"Oh, do you think it is?"

"You're bloody well right, it is. I didn't spend ten years of my life with the Fleet Street boys without picking up on your slippery police inuenenos—inuenos—ways."

"You are quite observant, Major Fleming."

Mac nodded his head in agreement. When his body kept on swaying after his head stopped nodding, he steadied himself with the back of a dining room chair. Dorothy tried to counsel him by whispering in his ear, but he only shrugged her off.

"I will ask you," the Inspector said, "to come outside and take a look at the body in the lorry. Perhaps you can help us make an identification."

"Can't identify the bugger, is that it? Be happy to give you a hand, although I hardly see how it could be any of my acquai—chums. All my chums have better things to do than go about killing themselves in somebody else's house. Lead on, MacDuff."

Dorothy was right at her husband's side as the party moved toward the front door, but before they went very far the Inspector stepped in her way. Mac went out the front door with the Sergeant and the two other men, while the Inspector and Dorothy continued to dance an excuse me two-step in the hall way.

"Mrs. Fleming, if you don't mind, I would like to have a few words with your husband in private."

"Inspector, my husband is not himself right now. I don't want his condition taken advantage of."

"I duly recognize his condition, ma'am, and assure you I will be the soul of discretion."

"Just the same, I think I should stay with him. He is liable to say or do anything . . ."

"Mrs. Fleming, we are either going to have our little talk with your husband here or down at the police station. Now which shall it be?"

"I beg your pardon. That is no way to address a loyal subject of the crown. I'm not someone walking through town, I'll have you know. My father was rector of St. Bartels, Oxford."

"I will do my best to remember your high standing in the community, ma'am. Now if you will excuse me for a moment." He went out, making sure the front door latched behind him.

Dorothy went into the sitting room and pushed back a shutter so she could see what was happening in the front of the house. Mac was already halfway into the back of the vehicle, and the Sergeant had pulled back the blanket from the dead man's face. Mac took his time examining the face, but finally pulled back out of the lorry, shaking his head very seriously all the while. She thought she could read his lips: No, I do not know the man. The Inspector was talking most of the time, although Dorothy could only guess at what he was saying because he had turned so that his back was toward the house. He took something small out of his pocket and showed it to Mac for his inspection. Without quite seeing it, Dorothy knew it was the three-by-five card from the typewriter. Mac took out his reading glasses and took his time focusing on the item. He and the Inspector exchanged a few short words.

Then Mac became angry and started thrusting his arms into the air. The police tried to calm him, but he was in no mood to be placated. He made a lunge for the card, but the Inspector managed to keep it out of his reach. Then Mac started lecturing the Inspector, waving a very menacing index finger in his face.

Dorothy closed the shutter and flexed her fingers nervously next to her mouth.

"Oh, that man. What's to be done with him?" she muttered to herself. "What's to be done?"

She wandered aimlessly about the house until she found herself at the dining room table, where she started folding up material in a futile effort to make the place look a bit neater. Before long Mac stormed into the house wearing a heavy scowl on his face. He charged his burly way up the stairs to the bedroom without a word. She called after him, but his heavy steps on the wooden stairwell continued without pause. Dorothy went to the foot of the stairs and called again, but got no answer.

The silhouette of the Inspector fell across the lace curtain on the front door. It was quite obvious he was there, but Dorothy still jumped when he twisted the front door ringer. As Dorothy was on her way to answer it, Betty came to the kitchen doorway, wiping her hands on her apron. "Will the Mister be eating the evening meal with us, mum?"

"Honestly, Betty, you can ask the most mundane questions at the most inappropriate times."

"Yes, Miss Sayers. I'm sorry . . ."

"Oh, it's not your fault. It's mine. I don't know. I'll try to find out."

"Yes, ma'am." Betty disappeared again, her feelings hurt.

Dorothy opened the front door for the Inspector. He didn't move to enter, but removed his hat instead. "Just wanted to let you know we will be off now, Mrs. Fleming. We may need to come back for another look around. If that would be all right."

"Inspector, what did my husband say to you?"

"Say to me?"

"I saw you showing him the card. What did he say about it?"

"We really don't wish to be involved in any family problems— "

"But you don't mind starting them, do you?"

"Yes, well, perhaps you should ask your husband what he said."

"Now listen to me, young man. I've been more than cooperative with you, in spite of your highhanded tactics and your indiscreet way of handling this matter. Now I think it is not going to hurt you in the slightest to grant a bit of help when I ask for it. What did my husband tell you, please?"

"He suggested that the dead man must have been a fan of yours and held some sort of unnatural attraction toward you because of your mystery writing. And he chose this melodramatic way of taking his own life to somehow associate himself with you."

"I see. Yes. That seems possible, doesn't it?"

"Does it? Seems rather farfetched, if you ask me. I expressed the same to the Major and he took it very personally. Said I was accusing him of being a liar."

"I take it he did not identify the dead man for you, did he, Inspector?"

The Inspector tilted his head and looked at her out of the corner of his eye, as if he were questioning the motive behind the carefully enunciated question. "No, he said he did not recognize him. Were you expecting him to say anything different?"

"No, of course not. I have no reason to think that he might know him."

The Inspector sighed, and scratched at his sideburn one last time. "No, I don't expect you would."

"Thank you, Inspector," Dorothy started to close the door on him. "That wasn't so hard for you, now was it? Good-bye."

Dorothy leaned on the door and breathed a sigh of relief. When she opened her eyes she found she was looking at her own image in the hallway mirror. The pixie smile was in place again. It seemed to have a mind of its own. Blast. She must be careful about that.

The fingers came up to her mouth again in a prayerful supplication of some kind. "What to do . . . what to do . . ." she asked herself. But as usual it did not take her long to decide on a course of action. She went up the stairs at a hurried clip and into the spare bedroom. She went down on her knees in front of the large chiffonnier in the room and pulled out the lower drawer. It was filled with Mac's army uniforms and memorabilia. Dorothy removed the belt and sash from his parade dress uniform, along with the leather leggings and straps, and put them on the floor so she would have more room to run her fingers around in the back of the drawer amongst the khaki material. But she came up empty. That drawer she closed with a bang and then tried the next one up.

Before long Mac opened the door to see what she was doing. "Am I to have no place in the house I can call my own? Is every inch of this place destined to look like a cyclone had gone through it?"

"I'll put everything back," she promised.

"Perhaps if you told me what the devil you're looking for, I could point you in the right direction."

"The way you came back into the house after your little chat with the police, I got the impression you were incommunicado."

She started restoring the contents of the two drawers. When she was too casual with the shoulder strap he protested.

"Be careful how you treat that old leather," he warned. "You can damage the facing very easily, folding it that way."

"Mac, would that be such a crime if I did? What use is the thing, anyway? This uniform is twenty years out of date, for heaven's sake."

"Yes, it would matter a great deal. There are certain things a military man holds sacred. I don't expect you to understand." He took over the chore of putting the drawers right himself. The woman was beyond understanding anything, the shake of his head seemed to say.

"I meant no offense, Mac. Sorry if I upset you." Dorothy got off her knees and moved toward the door. But something was still bothering her.

"Mac, did the Inspector show you the gun?"

"Gun? No, he did not show me any gun. Why?"

"Nothing. I just thought he might have done so."

Dorothy started down the stairs. But Mac was soon on the steps behind her.

"So that's what you're looking for. You thought it was my gun that was used. I say. I say, old girl, that is just a bit much, don't you think?"

"Whatever do you mean?"

"You think I killed the blighter, don't you?"

"I don't think any such thing. You're jumping to conclusions. Why don't we talk in the morning when you have a clear head?"

"There is nothing the matter with my head. I can think rings around you or any policeman any day, with a load on or not."

"I see. Perhaps you wouldn't mind telling me where that old handgun of yours is, then."

"Yes, I would mind. I can't see that it is any of your concern. Poking your nose into other people's business. I do mind a great deal."

"Mac, please. I knew we would end up arguing. Can't we talk after dinner?"

"I would like to get this matter cleared up here and now."

"Very well. The handgun we found on the floor looked very much like the one you showed me. The one you used in service."

"I see. Are you an expert on handguns now?"

"No. I most certainly am not. In all probability it does not look at all like yours. The police called it a Berten something or other, .44 caliber. I simply wanted to know if someone had got into things here in the house."

At the partial mention of the gun's name Mac Fleming turned pensive and missed his turn at the argumentative interchange. He headed toward the entryway and his hat.

"Mac, what is it? Mac, where is your gun? Do you still have it?"

He turned on her savagely. "I will not be badgered in this manner, as if I were some wayward schoolboy. I left this madhouse this morning to find a bit of peace and quiet on the open road. And now I come home and find a dead man in my house and policemen coming and going making all sorts of silly charges which they have no business . . . I will not have it. This play business is going to be the death of me. Or the death of this marriage."

He jammed on his hat and headed for the front door.

"I don't want you on the road in your condition, Mac."

"Thank you. So very nice of you to take my welfare into consideration. It is a shame you didn't do the same when this place was still a quiet home for—"

Betty dropped something in the kitchen and momentarily interrupted the diatribe. Mac pointed his angry finger in the direction of the kitchen.

"And if that woman calls me 'Mr. Sayers' one more

time, so help me I just may do some shooting of my own."

With that he stormed from the house, slamming the door behind him. Dorothy waited for the sound of his ancient Belsize coupe to grind to life. He shifted gears clumsily, and drove away in a roar. Dorothy slumped down in a chair and rubbed at her temples.

"Miss Sayers . . ." Betty began.

"Betty, you know I've asked you countless times to call me by my married name."

"Yes, ma'am, but I get thinking of other things and forget."

"Yes, dear, I know. But I do wish you would try a little harder. You know how it upsets Mr. Say— Fleming. Fleming. Good heavens, I'm doing it myself."

"Yes, ma'am. I'll try."

"What was it you wanted, Betty?"

"I just wanted to be sure I understood. The Mister won't be eating with us tonight?"

"I think that it is a safe assumption to make."

Betty made a clicking sound with her cheek. "Then all my worrying about the potato business was for nothing, wasn't it?"

Dorothy laughed and sighed at the same time. "Yes, dear. All your worrying about the potatoes was for nothing."

4

Three days later the June meeting of the Detection Club was being held in its usual digs, a small set of upper-story rooms at 31 Garrard Street in the Soho district of London. It was a casual locale where food could be ordered in and the members' garrulous activities could be performed in privacy. Normally they were a very lively group, but by eight-thirty it had become obvious the evening was not progressing well. The main course of the dinner had already been served, but there was still no sign of Dorothy L. Sayers. It never seemed quite the same when she was not present. She was one of the two founding members of the organization and as such had been instrumental in setting the tone of the club right from the start. She always knew how to deliver just the correct amount of tongue-in-cheek seriousness to the proceedings.

Another sorely missed member—from the club's past—was G.K. Chesterton, the well-known Christian moralist and lecturer, and author of the Father Brown mystery stories. With him at one end of the dinner table and Dorothy Sayers at the other, they had, like two giant literary bookends, dominated the effusive exchanges of many a meeting. But a year earlier, Chesterton had gone to his reward, no doubt resting with his fellow saints in Catholic heaven.

He had been president of the Detection Club at the time of his death, and it had been assumed that Dorothy would take over the post, primarily because she was the only one with girth enough to do justice to the black robe

31

Chesterton had left behind. But Dorothy, because of other pressing obligations, had declined the high office, retaining only the post of Chief Initiator of New Members, since that was where most of the fun came in. Anything involving incantations and high-sounding pledges and sacred oaths was her meat. She had written nearly all of the club's ritual rigmarole and loved reciting it in her formal Oxfordian tones.

In fact, an initiation service was scheduled for that very evening. The members had been spending time in other endeavors, hoping Dorothy would show herself before the Moment of Truth.

The evening's conversation, as usual, was slanted toward the lighter literary efforts of its members. Last month they had made a concerted study of bad grammar, each participant concocting his own most blatant examples in a sentence designed to fit into descriptive passages of a badly formed mystery story. Tonight they had returned their attention to the common limerick form, a frequent vehicle for their games, and were entertaining one another with their efforts. It was Alan Milne's turn. From his slouching position at a window seat he found a crumpled slip of paper in his coat pocket and offered the following:

> "There was a young puppy called Howard,
> When at fighting was rather a coward,
> He never quite ran
> When the battle began,
> But he started at once to bow-*wow*-hard."

He coyly brushed back some long strands from his receding hairline and waited for judgment. It wasn't long in coming.

"Still entertaining the children, I see, Alan," E.C. Bentley declared. "Is that rich vain of gold now to offer yet another branch employing the lowly limerick?"

Bentley had just cause to ridicule the limerick form. He himself was the master of a short, four-line poem form designed for caustic comments on the people and manners of the day. But the pattern of those four lines was so difficult to master that the other members had outlawed its use at their gatherings, thus depriving Bentley of much of his style. That restriction, however, did not mean he was unwilling to wallow in the mud with the others. From his breast pocket he took out his own offering, tweaked at his greying Edgar Allen Poe mustache and recited the following:

"I'm bored to extinction with Harrison
His lim'ricks and puns are embarrassin'
But I'm fond of the bum
For, though dull as they come,
He makes me seem bright by comparison!"

He smiled as he returned his offering to his pocket. "Since we have no Harrison in our present gathering, please feel free to substitute without reservation."

This challenge generated groans from most of the others and a general rustle of clothing and papers as other gems were made ready. It was the president's turn next. Anthony Berkeley cleared his throat with aplomb and delivered his limerick from memory:

"A bather whose clothing was strewed
By winds, that left her quite nude,
Saw a man come along,
And, unless I am wrong,
You expected this line to be rude."

General applause and laughter. "Shades of Dorothy Sayers," Alan Milne called out good-naturedly.

Dirty limericks were not as a rule permitted. About the only member who broke this understanding was none other than the lady, Sayers. Most of the group could still recite from memory her aisle-clearing rendition of:

> A certain young sheik I'm not namin',
> Asked a flapper he thought he was tamin'
> "Have you your maidenhead?"
> "Don't be silly!" she said,
> "But I still have the box that it came in."

After that, efforts were made to keep Dorothy from too many cups of refreshment. When they were successful, poems like that one were generally avoided. When she was out with friends, Dorothy did enjoy her ale and the camaraderie, but not all the Detection members shared her free and easy lust for life.

The laughter had just died away after Alan's comment when the door to the Garrard Street stairwell opened up and the lady herself stepped into the room. Dorothy was dressed to the hilt: under her large fur coat she wore a Chinese brocaded jacket and a black pleated skirt that fell, not to her knees, but to mid-calf. On her feet, hand-knitted socks and sturdy brogans, which looked as if they had toured Scotland more than once. On her head, an old parson's hat with an exceptionally wide brim. And in her hand, a long walking stick, sturdy enough to part the Red Sea. Once seen, the lady was not soon forgotten.

"What's this I hear?" she cried, gasping for breath. "First the mention of my name, followed quickly by the sound of unseemly laughter?"

"We were heavily into a round of limericks," Anthony Berkeley explained, "and we only mentioned how much you were missed."

"Limericks, you say? How appropriate." Dorothy proceeded to plop her large handbag on the middle of the dining table and began rummaging through its interior. "It so happens that I have brought a bit of the truth in rhyme with me."

She looked about the table for the right face. "Ronald Knox. Very good. You are here. You greatly disturbed me at our Gathering of the Faithful. Did you or did you not offer the following as your bit of agnostic wisdom for our little group to ponder?" She took out a small notebook and read:

> "There once was a man who said, 'God
> Must think it exceedingly odd
> If He finds that this tree
> Continues to be,
> When there's no one about in the Quad.' "

"Are those or are those not your sentiments?" Dorothy demanded.

Ronald Knox got to his feet and raised his right hand, as if being sworn for testimony. "I cannot tell a lie. You have made obvious reference to traces of my brilliance in the field of modern philosophy."

"Good. I don't want to be accused of quoting you in error."

"I believe you have me measured word for word. Which as I recall, did not sit well with Your Eminence."

"Indeed it did not. Your god is too small, my friend. And I apologize for being so tardy in getting back to you with my rebuttal." Dorothy turned a page in her book and began:

> " 'Dear Sir, Your astonishment's odd,
> I am always about in the Quad,
> And that's why the tree
> Will continue to be,
> Since observed by Yours faithfully, God.' "

She snapped her book closed theatrically and bowed to the applause of her friends, including Ronald Knox. "It took me the better part of a one-hour tub-soaking to come up with it. But I think it was worth it."

Space was made for Dorothy at the table, but she refused the offer of a clean plate, saying she had only stopped by for a few moments. "I'm in the midst of another troublesome meeting regarding my play and I must be flying off again, just as soon as the initiation is completed. It is still on, is it not?"

"Why don't we get started with that right now, then?" Ronald Knox asked.

Anthony Berkeley cleared his presidential throat. "We do have one more member who has as yet not participated in our poetry round. Why don't we hear from her first?"

All eyes in the room turned to Agatha Christie, who had been sitting quietly at a corner of the table, away from most of the action. She looked surprised to be recognized and began shaking her head. "No, I . . . why not pass me by?"

"Come now, Agatha," Berkeley encouraged. "Earlier I saw you jotting something down."

"Well, just a little something I remember from my youth. It's not anything to compare . . ."

Agatha Christie was a contemporary of Dorothy Sayers in age, but the two women had no personality traits in common. Self-effacing in public, with very conservative manners, she seemed out of place among the other extroverted members. She had a pale complexion, which turned pink very easily, such as when called upon to recite poetry. Still she could be called a handsome woman, with large doe eyes and an aquiline nose, although she seemed in a rush to make herself into an old lady, judging from her deportment and the matronly clothes she chose to wear.

Anthony Berkeley was an old friend who seemed to know just how to draw her out. Finally, she agreed to participate.

"Well, it's just a little something. I don't know if I made it up or maybe my brother made it up about me." She adjusted her reading glasses and read:

"Agatha-Pagatha my black hen,
She lays eggs for gentlemen,
She laid six and she laid seven
And one day she laid eleven!"

Deathly silence.

"You see," Agatha explained, "I think we had a hen, in my childhood, which I called Agatha Pagatha . . . " Sensing she had made an error, her cheeks turned crimson and her eyes and hands returned to some needlework in her lap, which only seemed to make the moment all the more embarrassing.

Agatha was something of an anomaly for the other members. Most of them considered the Detection Club and mystery writing in general a lark, a mental release from headier endeavors in fields of real literature. Even Milne's children's stories had a more lofty standing than the little mental exercises. But Agatha, with her literal and unliterary mind, was another matter. What made her presence even more disconcerting was that Agatha's books sold so very well. She seemed like a ripe candidate for ridicule, especially among a group such as this, with so many sharp pens. But strangely enough it did not happen. Perhaps it was because the lady kept quietly to herself for the most part and harbored no illusions about her abilities beyond those of an intricate puzzle-maker. The fact that she looked like everybody's favorite old maid aunt probably worked to her advantage as well.

Anthony Berkeley mercifully cut short the pregnant pause that had descended upon the room by clearing his throat again.

"I think the time has come to move on. Dorothy, we have in our midst this evening a young man who considers himself worthy of membership in our society, by virtue of having published . . ."

He went on with a lengthy preamble expounding on the great value of the membership to which the applicant aspired and to the applicant's shaky qualifications. The "young man" stood and took his medicine. He was thirty-five-year-old Colin Breen, or C.C. Breen, as it said on the dust jacket of the thin volume he presented in evidence.

Dorothy lifted the mystery book, as if evaluating it by weight, then sought for and got a grudging agreement from the other members that the man's application should indeed be taken seriously. Then the members rearranged themselves, getting ready for the ceremony. The lights were turned off as most of the members moved enmasse out of the room. The befuddled Colin Breen was told what to do and where to stand. Soon the group came back into the darkened room, marching to their own pontifical humming of the Largo from Handel's *Xerxes*. They made a strange sight, since there were more people in the procession than were left in the audience. Dorothy led the ensemble, of course, carrying before her on a large black velveteen pillow a human skull affectionately known as Eric. His innards had been hollowed out and he now glowed ominously from the small battery-powered light inside the brain cavity. It was virtually the only light in the room. Dorothy was followed by torch bearers with papier-mâché torches, two sergeants-at-arms, official witnesses, and other personages of high office.

By the time the solemn members had circled the dining table once, the dirge hummers had slipped badly off key. Mercifully, they stopped in front of the applicant. The group placed the somewhat shaky Mr. Breen in a chair on top of the table and Dorothy prepared to read the rites by turning Eric's mouth toward her scroll so that she could see to read.

Anthony Berkeley called out from the back of the room in a deep trembling voice, "What means this untimely darkness, these secret ceremonies and this illumined reminder of our mortality?"

Dorothy answered in kind, introducing the applicant to the world of the mystery spirits and to all the live spirits assembled. She asked him if he still sought admission to their midst. Mr. Breen thought that he did. He was told to close his eyes and cross his arms before his chest in a dead man's pose as the oath was administered.

"Do you promise that your detectives shall well and truly detect the crimes presented to them, using those wits which it may please you to bestow upon them and

not placing reliance upon nor making use of Divine Reve-
lation, Feminine Intuition, Mumbo Jumbo, Jiggery Pokery,
Coincidence, or any hitherto unknown Act of God?"

"I do," Breen pledged.

"And do you solemnly swear never to conceal a vital
clue from your reader?"

"I do."

"And do you promise to observe a seemly moderation
in the use of gangs, conspiracies, death rays, ghosts,
hypnotism, trapdoors, Chinamen, super-criminals, and lu-
natics, and do you utterly and forevermore forswear mysterious poisons unknown to the world of science?"

At this, Breen hesitated. "You are asking a great deal.
But for the sake of the Club and the good of the genre, I
do so swear."

Dorothy upbraided him. "There is no need for flippant
responses, sir. We intend to hold you to each and every
promise."

It was not always easy to tell when Dorothy was joking
and when she was totally serious. Breen decided not to
take any more chances with her, and the rest of the oath
was administered in a sober fashion. Finally, Breen became a full member with all rights and privileges, whatever they might be. He was allowed to open his eyes and
rest more comfortably as Dorothy administered the Final
Warning, a severe hex to be placed upon him, just in case
he was thinking of backsliding.

"If you fail to keep each and every promise you have
made here this evening, may other writers anticipate your
plots, may your publishers do you down in your con-
tracts, may total strangers sue you for libel, may your
manuscripts swarm with misprints and your book sales
continually diminish. Amen."

A final Dirge of Retreat, sounding suspiciously similar
to the processional, was hummed and The Mysteries faded
into the anteroom. The lights were turned on again and
they all congratulated themselves on another job well
done. Dorothy extinguished Eric the Skull and returned

him to the glass bookcase where he resided between pa-
rades. Then she reached for her fur coat.

"Must you leave?" Bentley asked. "I believe there are to
be raisin crumb tarts for desert."

"Don't tempt me. I'm late as it is. Details with my play
will be the death of me yet."

"Speaking of death," Alan Milne said, "what's this I
hear about a body appearing at your house in Witham?"

The general chatter in the room ceased with this bit of
news and all eyes turned to Dorothy. She tried to chuckle.
"Where ever did you hear that?"

"Oh, my wife gets the Witham paper for the local flower
news and she happened to run across your name in the
metro columns. Your married name, that is. Mrs. Dorothy
Fleming. That was your house, was it not?"

Dorothy slowly took off her greatcoat again and came
back to the table, leaning forward on her hands.

"I have a large favor to ask of you all. I know this is
quite an imposition, especially for those of you with print-
er's ink in your veins, but I do ask it most sincerely.
Please, please don't let this conversation go beyond these
walls. Right this moment I should be on my way to a
meeting with two bishops and a handful of Church law-
yers who have some serious questions about my religious
play. The Church simply does not tolerate notoriety very
well, and I don't want to rock the boat in any way. The
success of this play is very important to me."

"I think I can speak for all of us," Berkeley said. "We
most certainly will honor your privacy, if that is what you
wish."

"Thank you. I felt I could count on you all."

"But you mean to say," E.C. Bentley began, "there
really was a body found in your house? How extraordinary."

"Yes, my feelings exactly. It appears the poor fellow
committed suicide."

"But who was he? And how on earth did he happen to
get into your house?"

"Oh, he talked my cook into letting him in. That's

about all we know about him. I don't believe the police know yet who the man was."

"Why, how extraordinary."

Her friend Alan shook his head. "Dorothy, I think you are missing a golden opportunity for a little publicity. Think what a bit of notoriety of this kind could do for your mystery sales."

Dorothy shook a finger back and forth. "I don't care to take that chance. This project I'm working on means too much to me. To do serious work for the Church has always been one of my dreams. Now that I have that chance, I don't want to muff it."

"I only wish there were something we could do for you."

"There is. You can all plan on attending our opening two weeks from next Friday—if I manage to survive that long. Sorry to be so short, but I really must dash. Good-bye, Mr. Breen. I hope you will have as many happy experiences with this shameless group of eccentrics as I have had."

Colin Breen shook her hand and said he hoped so, too. The members called out their good-byes and saw her out the door.

But the fascinating and somewhat ghoulish topic of conversation lingered after her departure. E.C. Bentley had to say once more that he thought the discovery of a body in Dorothy Sayer's house was extraordinary. Alan was asked for more details from the newspaper article he and his wife had read. He brought out the facts that the man was well dressed, possibly from the upper class, and that he had done himself in with a rather exotic old handgun. Alan went on to repeat he felt Dorothy was silly to avoid the natural publicity that could result from such an event. Freeman Wills Crofts, who hadn't been heard from for some time, spoke up now with the opinion that Dorothy was really worried needlessly, that the Church would most certainly understand, under the circumstances, and that such an "accident" could happen to anyone and it would not reflect badly upon Dorothy and her religious play effort.

Dessert was served, and other things were talked of for a time. But the group's thoughts consistently drifted back time and again to the questions surrounding the unclaimed body.

Then, in mid-sentence, President Berkeley was suddenly struck by a brainstorm. He got to his feet, rapping a table knife on a nearby glass.

"May I have your attention again, friends? The thought has occurred to me that we might be missing a golden opportunity as club members. As you know, in years past we have undertaken projects on behalf of our club with a good deal of success. Our joint-venture book, *The Floating Admiral*, while it did not sell too briskly, did help to pay the overhead for our meeting rooms here. And our other short story efforts and scripts, in conjunction with our friends in the BBC, have certainly given us all many pleasant hours of enjoyment. Both for those of us who contributed articles and for those who only critiqued our efforts, I think it is safe to say we have all grown closer and gained a good sense of camaraderie out of our projects."

"You have a plot for a new book up your sleeve, Mr. President?" Freeman Wills Crofts asked.

"No, I don't. I think we are all too busy to undertake another project like that. But I think there is something presenting itself to us that we might very well take advantage of. Something that would lend itself to our common interests, those of criminal investigation and detection. Something which we might undertake to the benefit of someone quite dear to us all . . . It should not be too time consuming. Perhaps a weekend or two for each of us . . ."

"Good heavens, man, drop the other shoe," Crofts demanded. "You have us all primed and at the ready."

"Why don't we undertake as a Detection Club project to determine the whys and wherefores of this suicide case that happened in Dorothy's house? The lady says she wants it kept quiet, and I think we would be in an excel-

lent position to carry on an investigation with a good deal
more secrecy than the police would. I realize, of course, it
would not be quite as exciting and demanding as investigating a murder. But then a suicide with lots of juicy
unanswered questions might be a more logical place for
us to try our wings."

He paused to let the idea germinate. Alan nodded and
leaned forward on his elbows. "You know, I think we
might have something, here. An opportunity for us all to
get a bit of practical experience in the very kind of work
we should be expert in. I for one don't know the first
thing about how to establish the identity of a person."

"There is a national Missing Persons Bureau," Agatha
Christie put in, quietly. "One would assume the Witham
police had already notified them."

Agatha had reason to know about the missing persons
bureau. During the twenties, when she was experiencing
the agonies of the breakup of her first marriage, she went
through something akin to an emotional breakdown and
was actually missing herself for several weeks. Every police agency in the nation was fully alerted, to say nothing
of the newspapers and the wireless services. This was still
not a subject she chose to discuss in public, and her
reference to Missing Persons was something of a surprise
to the other members.

"What is your point, Agatha?" Crofts asked.

"I mean, one would assume that the police are already
doing everything possible to establish the identity of this
poor unfortunate soul. Somewhere or other there is a
husband missing, an employer or employee not turning
up for work. It would seem to me that it would be only a
matter of time. I don't see what there is that we could do
to help."

The others thought on that a bit.

"Of course it has already been three days," Edmund
Bentley commented. "You would think by now that a
match could have been made. We are assuming, of course,

that the local police in little Witham are operating on modern standards."

"Personally," Crofts snorted, "I have my doubts about the efficiency of some of these locals. If the man who died wasn't from their own town, they might have a tendency to lose interest in the case."

"You mean they might bury the man's remains in a pauper's grave and be done with it?"

"Oh, they would probably keep the case open, but no real work would be done on it."

They thought some more. Finally Edmund chuckled aloud. "You know, it would be rather a lark to see what we might turn up. After all, we certainly wouldn't be hurting anyone. And it might turn out to be a quiet favor to Dorothy. After all, she has done so much for our organization. It might be a rather nice way of paying her back."

This generated calls of "Hear, hear" from the others.

"Then it is agreed," Anthony Berkeley intoned. "The Detection Club will give it a go? We will try to find out who this poor chap was, and why he happened to take his life in Dorothy's house in Witham."

Rather than taking a vote, he looked about him for head nods. When he had counted enough, he said, "Now then, I suspect we should need a bit of organization, so we all don't go off in a haphazard manner, duplicating each other's work. What would you say to appointing a chairman . . ."

There were no volunteers until Alan put up his hand.

"Very good. Alan is volunteering."

"No, no. Not me. I only wanted to put Agatha Christie's name in nomination."

Agatha looked up from her needlework. "Me? Heavens no. I could never do—"

"Oh, but I think you could. You are the logical choice," Alan argued. "From the very first, when Meg read the Witham article to me, I've thought of how similar this whole scene is to the opening episode in your bestselling book, *The Body in the Library*. I mean, it is all there—the appearance of an unidentified body in the home of inno- cent, well-respected people in a village setting. Agatha, you have already done so much of the work we would have to do. You are the logical choice to be our leader, with your analytical mind. And you do know the village scene so well. I really don't see how you can refuse us."

"Oh, dear . . ." Agatha fidgeted, looking for a reason- able excuse. But the others seemed to agree with Alan. Gradually she began to soften.

"Well, my husband is off to Iraq on an archeological dig, right now . . . and Roseland is at riding school . . . I should need a good deal of help," she insisted.

"Of course," Berkeley agreed. "That goes without saying. We will be at your beck and call."

"Well, I simply don't know what to say . . ."

Berkeley turned to Freeman Wills Crofts, who had not been helping the cause but rather had his nose buried in his notebook. "Freeman, are you with us?"

"Agatha," Crofts called out, "may I read what I have just written?"

"Certainly you may, Freeman."

Crofts arose and cleared his throat for attention.

> "A gentle young lady named Christie
> Found a body quite lacking a history.
> Though the lim'rick's beyond her,
> All the clues she will ponder
> Till her little grey cells solve the mystery

The members clapped and Agatha blushed.

"Oh, my. How very clever. Now I suppose I shall have to accept, shan't I?"

They all agreed, she would.

5

Bright and early the following Saturday morning, Agatha and a contingent of three other Detection Club members met at Victoria Station, ready for their journey to Witham. Edmund C. Bentley, in an attempt to establish the right spirit for the excursion, appeared in a tweed cape and matching deerstalker hat. Alan Milne and the new member, Colin Breen, saw to getting a private first-class compartment for the four of them, so they might make a few plans as they traveled.

They were barely out of the station when Agatha took a small notebook out of the large carpetbag she was using for a purse.

"I was wondering," she began, tentatively, "if any of you have given any thought to how we might proceed, once we are in Witham."

The three men looked at one another for someone to lead. Finally Breen moved eagerly in his seat opposite Agatha and cleared his throat. "I was thinking it might be well for one or two of us to make contact with the police, first off."

"Yes, of course that is a must," Alan said, getting a pipe ready for the ride. "But first I think it behooves us to pay a courtesy call on Dorothy. Just to let her know what it is we are up to."

"Yes, I totally agree," Agatha nodded. "I have already tried calling her several times, but her phone was either busy or the operator couldn't get through. Why don't I tend to that myself? I'll call at her house. Unless any of you would prefer—"

"No, no. Ladies talk and all that," Edmund said, "I think you would be the logical one."

"Very well then." She made small printed notes to herself. "And Mr. Breen—"

"Oh, please call me Colin."

"Very well. Colin. Since you mentioned the police, perhaps you would like to make contact there and find out how the formal investigation is proceeding. They may have completed an inquest by now—"

"I say," he interrupted, "they really are not apt to bare their souls if I just wander in off the street. What do you say I make some sort of official claim? A job title with Missing Persons in Glasgow or something like that."

She shook her head. "Oh, I don't know."

"Shame on you, Agatha," Edmund chided. "This is exactly the kind of stunt your two young detectives, Tommy and Tupance, would try to pull."

"Why yes, I suppose it is. But this is quite different."

"How is it different?"

"Well, for one thing, this is real life. I realize this is little more than a game for us, but remember there are laws against impersonating an officer of the law. And I dare say it would not take much questioning by real policemen to expose such an outlandish story. Have you thought of that, Colin?"

Colin could not say that he had. "But there might be subtle ways of implying things without having to produce credentials. It's just that I'm looking for some little edge . . . Perhaps, Mr. Bentley, you could come along and we could refer to one another as Captain or Inspector. Things like that."

E.C. Bentley thought that was a capital idea. Agatha looked suspiciously at Edmund's deerstalker cap resting in the overhead rack and sighed.

"Well, as you wish. But do please be careful."

"And what is my assignment, Madam Chairman?" Alan asked.

"I rather thought one of us should look into the transport question," Agatha said.

"What transport question is that?"

"We know the dead man was a stranger to the community, so it stands to reason he arrived in Witham by some mode of transport other than on foot, since the one and only newspaper article about the death noted that he was well dressed. That leaves us to assume he arrived by car, by train, or possibly by bicycle. I don't know if there is river traffic through Witham or not. That also might be a possibility, but since it is rather remote, I think we should investigate that last."

Alan combed his fingers through his long hair and scowled. "Well dressed . . . I don't recall the Witham article mentioning that the dead man was well dressed."

"Yes, it did, Alan." Agatha said, matter-of-factly. "I was able to find a copy of the Witham paper your wife had read from and it did mention he was a 'well-dressed gentleman.' " She retrieved the copy of the paper in question from her large bag and passed it around. "If he arrived by motorcar or bicycle, then it stands to reason the vehicle would still be standing about and would most certainly be noticed in a small town, where no doubt everyone keeps track of other people's business. No, I think our best possibility will be the train.

"Now then, the timing will be crucial, of course," Agatha continued. "I have brought along a railroad timetable." She brought out of her bag a dog-eared rail schedule. "It is a bit dated so we will have to double-check these times. The afternoon three-ten train looks most promising."

"Excuse me, but am I missing something here?" Alan asked. "What's so important about the railroad timetables?"

Edmund laughed aloud. "It appears we men have come on what we thought was going to be a lark, while Agatha here has definitely decided to take the matter seriously. Correct me if I'm wrong, Agatha, but I think the importance of the Witham train schedule is that we might back the train up and find out where the mystery man came from."

"Yes, exactly. If the man did arrive on the three-ten, for example, there is a good possibility that he boarded the train somewhere in the Lake District. A concerted effort could then be made to find out if anyone is missing from that area."

"I say, very good. Why didn't I think of that?" Colin said.

"No doubt the police already have," said Agatha, "but mentioning it to them may be a way of striking up a conversation. It has been my experience that if you can get on the good side of people and get them talking, they have a habit of sharing more than they intend."

Colin Breen slapped his knee and laughed. "You are marvelous. You sound just like the character in one of your books. What's her name? Miss Marble."

"Miss Jane Marple, you mean."

"Yes. That's the lady. With her didactic but provincial mind working for us, this could turn out to be a piece of cake."

"Oh, I doubt that," Agatha said. "I have already exhausted all my ideas on this matter. People assume that if a person can write a mystery story, one ought to be good at solving real mysteries or puzzles. To tell you the truth, I am terrible at word games and puzzles. You see, I write my stories backwards. I already know who the guilty party is before I put one word on paper. Don't you do the same?"

Most of the rest of the trip was spent in shoptalk. The four storytellers discussed how they created their red herrings and the oblique ways they hid the crucial clues that pointed to the guilty party without giving too much away.

As they stepped down on the small platform at the Witham station Agatha had some last minute advice. "Don't hesitate to talk to the townspeople. They may know more than they realize. And don't forget to take notes so the other Detection Club members can be kept fully informed."

Agatha thought she sensed a slight bristling amongst the men after all the instructions she had presented. She decided it was time to be diplomatic. She deferred to the oldest male in the group.

"Have we overlooked anything, Edmund?"

Edmund Bentley pointed with his walking stick to a distant tea room that appeared to be in good order.

"Why don't we plan on meeting over there for lunch? That should give us ample time to wander about a bit and we should all have something to report by then."

That sounded good to all. Alan headed for the station-master's office, Colin and Edmund went out front and looked for a taxi. Agatha had on her walking shoes and started toward the main part of town on foot.

She ended up trying three different shops before she found a proprietor who could tell her where Dorothy Sayers lived. It was more of an experiment than anything else, since she had the address to the Major MacDonald Flemings in her purse all along. The lady in the stationery shop, where Agatha purchased two greeting cards, said she did not know the "mystery lady" well, but that she had come into the shop "on occasion" when she had run low on some of her letter writing material.

Major Fleming was a different story, the stern-faced clerk informed her. He was quite well known, primarily because of his questionable driving habits. The town council on more than one occasion had advised the constable to issue the man warnings. The common understanding was that the man drove while under the influence of spirits. Agatha thanked the opinionated clerk and went on her way.

It was a long way to the Fleming house, but Agatha was in a mood to stretch her limbs. She enjoyed watching life in charming English villages and the brisk walk past the quaint, well-kept cottages and shops picked up her spirits as usual. There was one slight drawback to the outing—

two nights earlier a major storm with accompanying heavy winds had caused damage to a few of the front yard flower gardens.

Finally Agatha reached the Fleming residence. The large brick house was situated in a nice residential area but quite near a busy highway that skirted the town. Agatha walked up the drive and turned the small bell crank in the front door. After waiting several seconds she was in the process of turning the crank a second time when a red-headed woman, wearing an apron over her workdress, came through some bushes bordering the neighbor's property and crossed the yard toward Agatha.

"The Flemings are not to home, ma'am. Is there anything I can be doing for you? I work for them."

"Oh, I see. You must be Dorothy's cook.

"Yes, ma'am. Betty's my name. I was just over to the neighbors'."

"Nice to meet you. I'm Agatha Mallowan. I'm a friend of your mistress's. We belong to the same club."

Agatha was not sure why she used her married name. There was no reason to keep secrets from Dorothy's faithful cook. But that was what had come out.

"I'm sorry, but Miss Sayers is off to London. She didn't say just when she would be getting back. And the Mister is out, too."

"Oh dear. That's such a shame. And here I've come all this way." Agatha leaned on the white pillar by the front door and massaged the instep of one foot, hoping Betty would show some mercy and let her inside for a nice visit.

Betty finally took her cue. "Do you have a stone in your shoe?"

"Oh, no. It's just this terrible bunion. The doctors say I should stay off it. But what else can you do? When you have to walk, you have to walk. If I could only get off it for a little while, just to ease the pressure."

Betty hesitated. She wanted to help, but the memories of last week's adventure were still fresh in her mind.

"You say you are a club member . . . What club would that be?"

"The Detection Club, which Dorothy helped found. We meet down in London nearly every month. Hasn't Dorothy mentioned us?"

Betty nodded. "Would you like to come in a minute and put that foot up? I was just going to put the kettle on."

"Oh, may I? That would be very kind of you."

Betty pushed open the unlocked front door and led the way into the house. Betty made excuses for the appearance of things as she made space for the guest by clearing off some advertising handbills from a dining room chair.

"Oh, please don't bother with that," Agatha said. "Why don't I just sit over here by the window?"

"Oh, no. Not there, please."

Betty's anxiety about the empty typewriter chair made Agatha suspicious. Then she noticed traces of chalk marks outlining the area. "Oh, I see. That's where the poor man . . . You have been through a terrible time, haven't you?"

"You know about what happened?"

"Yes. Dorothy confided in us at our last club meeting. I'm so sorry you had to be a witness to it. It must have been a terrible experience."

Betty nodded agreement. "I'll just put the kettle on," she said, then disappeared into the kitchen.

Agatha got up from her "bunion rest" to rubberneck, without a sign of a limp. The typewriter stand was surprisingly clear of the theatrical paraphernalia that littered the rest of the room. Almost as if it still held some aura of the fearsome event. Agatha had already experienced some theatrical success of her own, and though she had never turned her home into a workshop, she felt very much at ease among the trappings. She picked up a playbill from a stack on the dining room table and quickly scanned it.

THE ZEAL IN THY HOUSE

by

Dorothy L. Sayers

A Play of Conscience

With one eye on the open kitchen doorway, Agatha folded the playbill and dropped it in her large bag. Then she sat down in the chair that had been cleared for her and raised her foot onto a nearby parcel of string-tied books. Betty came in carrying a tin of store-bought biscuits and put them on the table.

Agatha decided to take a flyer, to get Betty talking. "I spent a good deal of my time during the Great War working in hospital. One would think that being among the dead and the dying all the time one might get used to it. But I never did, I can tell you." Betty only nodded in agreement. "Were you alone here when the man shot himself?"

Betty frowned. "I don't know."

"Oh, I'm sorry. I suppose it is still too painful to talk about, isn't it? Honestly, that was very thoughtless of me."

"No. It's not that. They tell me it is good for me to talk about it. It's just that we don't know when he shot himself, you see."

Agatha nodded, but didn't speak.

"Miss Sayers and I came in together and found him, you see."

"You came in together?"

"Yes. From the backyard, don't you see. It's hard to say when he shot himself. None of us heard the gun."

"Why how strange . . ."

"Yes, isn't it? I don't think the police even know. Miss Sayers, you see, had just returned from her day in London, and we came in the back way. I had been in the garden. And we found him there." She looked at the typewriter with resignation.

"Miss Sayers had just returned from London, you say?"

"Yes, that's right."

"Did she take a taxi from the station?"

"I think so. She usually does. She's not a great one for walking when she can ride."

"Why, how extraordinary."

"What's that, ma'am?"

Agatha got up and hobbled to the front door and looked out through the curtains, then came back to Betty. "If the taxi driver let her out in front of the house—which I assume he did, since there is only the steppingstone walk leading around to the back of the house—doesn't it stand to reason that Dorothy would have come into the house by the front door?"

Betty didn't answer. But her eyes grew round and watery. She looked as if she wanted to say something, but it wasn't coming out.

"Or, perhaps I'm wrong," Agatha sighed. "Maybe it *is* her custom to come around to the back of the house and enter that way. Some people do, I know. Was it . . . her custom?"

Betty found a chair to sit on and bobbed back and forth for a moment, looking like a chicken searching for pecking grain. Suddenly she burst out in a rush of words, almost too fast for Agatha to follow.

"But that's just it, don't you see. She never comes in the back way. Never. That's why I was so surprised to see her. I was out back, scratching about for an extra potato for dinner and the next thing I know, there she is. I was so surprised. She never comes about that way. And I ask myself, of all the times to come in the back way, why should it be that day? I don't want to say bad things about her. She's been so good to me. Like a big sister, she has. Such a wonderful woman. But I ask myself, why that day?"

"And the hat she wore to London that day. There it

was on the kitchen work table. When we come in together, there it is."

Betty lost control of herself and cried, with great emotional sobs, into her apron. "I haven't told this to a soul. Not even to the police. How could I? With Miss Sayers standing right here beside me all the time. I don't want to hurt her. What am I to do?"

Agatha wanted to reach out and comfort this poor woman, but her upbringing in a proper English household made her hold her place.

6

Agatha spent some time quieting the troubled cook as best she could, finally persuading her to lie down on her bed for a bit. Before Agatha could tiptoe out of the house, Betty had managed to cry herself into a morning nap.

Agatha let herself out, then spent more time looking about the neighborhood. Little came of her efforts, except she did manage to meet the Masons, an elderly couple who lived next door. It appeared Betty did a lot of the heavy work about the kitchen for them, merely has a favor, so they spoke very highly of her, but they knew next to nothing about the "mystery writer lady" and her husband. Only a few generalities that Betty had passed on to them. Such as how much the Mister drank and how difficult he was to get along with at times. At least the town gossip was consistent. Village life had its liabilities as well as its advantages, Agatha remembered, as she headed back downtown.

She was the last club member to arrive at the tea room for their appointed luncheon. The others had already seated themselves in a small window-lined alcove, separated from the other diners by a screen and several feet of space. Agatha was thankful for the isolation. She had spent most of the walk back worrying about just how she would be able to break her news about Dorothy's lie. She didn't relish the thought of enduring eavesdroppers from the other tables. And the last thing in the world Agatha wanted was to appear catty. There had never been bad words exchanged with Dorothy Sayers, but she had sensed a certain formality, if not hostility, between them. Perhaps it was because they were the two dominant women in their chosen field and a natural sense of competition was bound to develop. But she didn't wish to aggravate the situation by speaking badly of the lady behind her back. Perhaps the discreet thing to do would be to avoid mentioning the matter altogether. After all, it did not prove anything conclusively. Perhaps the poor thing only wanted company when the body was officially discovered. But as soon as Agatha thought that, she knew it was not right. Not right at all.

She was surprised to find the men in a quiet mood when she arrived. The excitement and good-natured kidding that had started at Victoria Station that morning had vanished. As soon as their plump, very pleasant waitress had taken their orders and departed, Agatha opened her mouth to speak. But when she didn't know quite how to begin, Colin Breen jumped into the silence with both feet.

"I say, we came up with some rather startling news on our little safari. It appears we may not be looking at a suicide case at all. It may very well be we are looking at—he lowered his voice for dramatic impact—a murder case . . ."

"Now, we don't know that, do we," Edmund corrected his young friend. "That hardly seems a fair statement to make."

Colin was hurt. "Really, Mr. Bentley, I don't see what other interpretation you can place on it. The officer said so himself."

"He said it was a possibility. Meteorites falling to earth and ruining our lunch is also a possibility."

While the two men went on arguing about the wording of their report, Alan Milne touched Agatha on the elbow.

"Agatha, you look quite peaked. Aren't you feeling well?"

She drank some water from her glass and tried to smile. "It must be the sun. I think it may have been a bit warm for me to have walked so far. I'll be all right." She turned to her old friend Edmund, with her usual quiet serious-ness. "Why don't you tell us from the beginning what it is you found out?"

"Of course, Agatha. We took your advice about striking up casual conversations. It happens we found someone out behind the police station who was actually part of the investigation." Edmund looked at his notes. "A Sergeant Whitecomb. Very pleasant chap. He was having trouble with the station's car and Colin, here, was able to give him a hand—"

"Just a distributor coil that had come loose," Colin snuck in.

"—then we got round to the topic at hand, without having to resort to any grandiloquent lies."

Colin took over. "It seems that Dorothy didn't tell us quite everything about the man's death." He smiled at Agatha like the Cheshire cat and waited for her and Alan to beg him go on.

"You mentioned murder," Agatha said. "I don't think this is the time for levity, Colin."

"Sorry. I suppose you're right. I just felt the whole thing was so very interesting." Colin Breen was the only one who hadn't lost his enthusiasm. He leaned forward in his chair to get closer to Agatha. "The Sergeant says there were no gunpowder burns on the man's face, as there ought to be, if in fact the man did shoot himself. No powder burns at all."

"Really," Edmund huffed. "I do wish you'd let me tell this in my own manner."

"But you weren't getting to it."

"The lady asked to have it told from the beginning. That bit of news didn't fall out until nearly fifteen minutes ago."

Agatha intervened. "Perhaps he held the gun behind his coat or something."

Colin had taken over again. "Then there would be holes and burns in his coat, wouldn't there? And even if he held the gun away from himself as far as he could, there would still be traces of spent gunpowder about. No, it does appear that the man was shot from a distance."

Edmund slapped his kid gloves on the table in anger. "I don't like this. I don't like this one small bit. Dorothy is a very dear friend of mine. You are making this whole business sound as if she is involved in a murder. I did not come on this outing to be a party to some sort of witch hunt. To start spreading rumors about one of the most upright, god-fearing people on earth."

"Good heavens, man," Colin scoffed, "I'm only repeating what an investigative officer has told us. I hardly consider that spreading rumors. Perhaps you are letting your feelings for Miss Sayers effect your objectivity, which is the last thing we should permit ourselves to do, if we are going to have any kind of meaningful investigation."

"This whole damn thing was a lark. Pardon me, Agatha. A very unwise lark. I wish to heaven we'd never started it."

"I'm afraid I don't follow, Edmund," Alan said. "Whether it is a suicide or a murder, I really don't see how it besmirches Dorothy's reputation in the least. After all, she only supplied the man's final resting spot, so to speak."

Now Colin shifted his upper body in Alan Milne's direction. "I think what Mr. Bentley is most concerned about is . . . another matter. Something that complicates things somewhat. You see, there was also some sort of mash note left behind, supposedly written to Dorothy by the dead man."

"Mash note?" Alan asked. "You mean a love letter?"

"Yes," Colin smiled. "Something about, 'I can't go on. My guilt is too great. I love you, Forgive me,' et cetera."

"You had to say it, didn't you?" Edmund frowned. "I think it should be pointed out, it was typed on Dorothy's typewriter with no signature, so anyone could have written it."

Alan massaged his temples. " 'My guilt is too great.' What the devil is that supposed to mean? This is getting more strange at every turn."

"Did the policeman say anything about theories they were working on?" Agatha asked.

"Yes, he did. They think the man may have been shot someplace else and then brought to the house at a later time."

"What on earth makes them think that?" Alan asked.

"Because no one heard the gunshot." Edmund said.

"But the newspaper article noted that the cook let the gentleman in. That would seem to imply the cook is lying," Agatha put in. "Why on earth would she lie?"

It was Colin's turn again. "They think there may be some sort of link between the cook and the husband. Possibly romantic. The town gossip says that Dorothy and her husband don't get on all that well together. The husband has no job at the moment and he stays at home quite a lot, while Dorothy is off to London almost every working day. That could certainly throw them together . . ." He finished the suggestive thought by raising both eyebrows.

Agatha ran over in her mind the performance that Betty had put on for her benefit. She couldn't help but feel it was genuine. The woman had cried real tears . . . Of course, it was while she was accusing her mistress of coming into the house without telling anyone.

Edmund's voice brought her back to the discussion. "Agatha, what did Dorothy have to say when you told her what we were up to?"

"She wasn't at home, I'm afraid."

"I see." He shifted uneasily in his chair. "You know, I really don't like this business. We are, in effect, operating here behind Dorothy's back. I wonder if that is what we should be doing."

"I'm sure she would understand that it is not by choice," Alan said.

This didn't satisfy Edmund, but he didn't have a ready answer for the problem either. Agatha tried to change the subject.

"Did you learn anything from the stationmaster, Alan?"

"Yes, I did. But in light of the police report I'm almost afraid to tell you what I've learned. The three-ten train schedule is still accurate, and it did make a stop here at Witham, although no one could remember seeing our man get off the train. Then I went over to the taxi stand and talked to the old fellow who operates the green taxi." Alan looked out the window to see if he could spot what appeared to be one of the few cabs in the small town. "He's a crusty old chap named Bantam Lapwood. He didn't take the dead man anyplace, but it turned out he did take Dorothy home after she arrived on the four-thirty London train. He said that Dorothy balled him out for being so slow. And hear this—she told him she had someone waiting at the house to see her. The way he talked, it seemed that Dorothy was expecting the dead man."

Alan looked across at Edmund, who was shaking his head. "I'm sorry, Edmund. That's what the taxi driver told me. We can locate the man and you can hear it for yourself, if you like."

Edmund said nothing.

"Has Mr. Lapwood told his story to the police?" Agatha asked.

"No, he has not. Apparently he has some sort of running grudge against the police of the town and, since they haven't asked him any direct questions, he hasn't volunteered anything and is not about to."

"Oh, oh"—Colin shook his head—"I don't like this . . ."

"What's the matter, Colin?" Alan asked.

"This means that we are now in possession of vital evidence in what may be a murder case. Could we be accused of withholding evidence if we don't take it to the police?"

"I hardly think so," Edmund said. "If my early legal training still serves me, anything the taxi driver may have told you about a conversation he had inside the cab could be considered hearsay evidence. Which brings me to an important point. You all remember at our last club meeting how Dorothy pleaded with us not to publicize this business? I do hope we are still planning on respecting her wishes. There is no reason why any of this need leave this table."

Their food arrived and they each sat in brooding silence as the jolly waitress put things before them. She finally caught sight of their faces.

"Is there anything wrong with the food?"

"No, my dear," Agatha assured her. "We were thinking of other matters."

"Oh, well, I'm sure you will all feel better when you have something under your belts."

Her cheery laugh seemed totally inappropriate, and they were relieved to have her retreat and leave them to their morbid thoughts. The foursome picked at their food in silence for a time. Then Alan Milne dropped his fork on his plate and leaned back in his chair.

"Edmund, I'm sure none of us here would want to hurt Dorothy Sayers. But on the other hand, there is a dead man. And I for one feel a certain sense of civic responsibility."

"You've never cared for her, have you, Alan?" Edmund said bluntly.

"She has never been one of my favorite personalities, I admit. I find her mysteries disappointing and her theology stilted and dogmatic. But that most certainly does not mean I have some vendetta against her."

The two men exchanged hard looks, until Alan went back to work on his plate of pig's trotters.

"There is no reason for the two of you to be at odds," Agatha said. "After all, we know that Dorothy came home on the London train at four-thirty or so. And if the police now believe the man was shot somewhere else and then brought to her house, that certainly would exonerate her, would it not?"

"It would seem to," Alan said.

"What do you mean, 'it would seem to'?" Edmund demanded.

"I am not through with my account of my morning activities," Alan said. "I also had a chat with the postman who delivers to Dorothy's part of town. Remember, Agatha asked us to find out if there were any unfamiliar vehicles about on that particular day. I thought the postman would know, if anyone would, since he covers the streets daily. He said he saw only a boy's bicycle lying about the neighborhood, which he knew belonged somewhere else, but no motorcars."

"Good heavens," Colin marveled, "these people keep track of bicycles in their town, do they?"

"Not a bit unusual," Agatha said. "I grew up in a small town not unlike Witham. What little the townsfolk don't know would surprise you."

"That certainly bears out the rest of my story," Alan went on. "It seems the postman lives with his sister down by the river. And the sister returned from her housekeeping job rather late on the same night that the body was found. She couldn't swear it was her, but the postman said his sister saw a woman of Dorothy's description down by the footbridge, throwing something that looked like a man's wallet into the river." He looked at Edmund for his reaction.

"Really now, Alan." Edmund's mustache bobbed nervously as he marshaled his thoughts. "You said yourselves that you know these small-town types. Most of them are jealous of anyone from the big city who could be considered successful. Especially a woman with a university education, such as Dorothy. I suppose you are thinking she threw the dead man's wallet away. But when would she have had opportunity to take the wallet? Didn't she find the body with her maid or cook? And then they telephoned the police together . . . "

It was Agatha's turn. She related to the group as dispassionately as she could what Betty had told her. That Dorothy probably did, in fact, go into the house alone before she came around to the back and reentered with the cook. "I'm sorry, Edmund." She patted her old friend's hand. "I don't think we can dismiss this as only so much small-town gossip."

Edmund scowled at his plate for a time, then finally shook his head. "I think you are probably right. I think there must be something more to it. But I don't think Dorothy . . . poor Dorothy."

"Yes, poor Dorothy," Colin echoed. "If she isn't involved, then why all the strange moves?"

Agatha had a bracing sip of tea, then touched at the corners of her mouth with her napkin and looked out at the town's main street.

"I heard some time ago that Dorothy had settled in a small town. And I remember wondering to myself at the time, why would she do that? She always impressed me as being so . . . cosmopolitan. She worked for several years in an advertising agency. Even now with her play and other activities, everything seems to be centered in London. And it appears she has made very little effort to make friends here. What would be the attraction?"

"It is rather an easy commute to London from here," Colin pointed out.

"Yes. At the same time it is rather isolated."

"You mean you think . . . she desired isolation?" Alan asked.

"I don't know. What other reason could have drawn her here?"

"I say, I hardly think this amateur psychoanalyzing is fair to Dorothy," Edmund said. "It sounds a bit more like gossip to me."

"Gossip or not," Alan smiled, "I still feel a sense of notoriety or intrigue can work wonders. It certainly won't hurt an author's standing with the reading public."

"Hear, hear," Colin said. "It certainly did wonders for Agatha, didn't it?"

In unison, Alan and Edmund both made under-the-table moves toward Colin's shinbones. Agatha's "problem," although ten years in the past, was still not a proper topic of conversation in her presence.

Always the lady, Agatha had developed the ability to turn a deaf ear to such outbursts, and she practiced it now, continuing to eat her light lunch without a hair on her head out of place.

After a polite interval she said, "I, for one, have often felt that deep dark secrets can help one write ever so much better. Oscar Wilde is a case in point. I have no doubt that *The Picture of Dorian Gray* benefited a great deal from Wilde's personal troubles."

Alan looked at her with surprise. "Funny you should happen to mention that. I was just thinking along the same lines."

"About how a person's problems can strengthen their writing?"

"No. More about Wilde . . . I was wondering if Dorothy might not share something of his . . . shortcomings?"

Colin snickered. "You mean misplaced sexual interests?"

"Well, it's all there, isn't it?" Colin shrugged his shoulders. "I mean she has the traits. The short, man's-style haircut. The deep, piercing voice. I've heard she even dresses in men's suits on occasion."

Edmund was on his feet. "Have we stooped to rumor-mongering now? There is no evidence whatsoever to support such implications."

"You are absolutely correct," Agatha said, trying to calm him. "We should not be implying—"

"And I will thank you, Agatha, not to encourage comparisons of such a nature."

"Comparisons? Edmund, I assure you, I meant no such comparison. Oscar Wilde is one of my favorite writers. I merely meant to make an innocent point."

Suddenly, without seeming explanation, the other two men got slowly to their feet. Alan's face had gone ashen and he said, almost in a whisper, "Dorothy . . ."

Agatha turned to follow the line of his stare and found Dorothy L. Sayers behind her, in the act of pushing the dining room screen to one side. She was dressed in a black skirt and what appeared to be a man's suit coat, tie, and white shirt. Her face was dressed in a dark scowl.

"What's the meaning of this auspicious gathering, may I ask?"

"Dorothy, we're so pleased that you are here," Edmund pulled out his chair for her, but she didn't move. "Did you just arrive? I didn't hear a train."

"I've just come from my house. What on earth are you people up to? You've roused half the town."

Alan moved from foot to foot like a schoolboy. "It's a Detection Club activity, actually."

"Indeed."

"Yes. After you left the other evening we decided it might be good sport to help you sort out this mysterious death that took place in your—"

"Have I done or said something that gave you the impression I wanted help with 'sorting out,' as you put it?"

"No, you certainly did not," Edmund said. "But we couldn't pass up such a golden opportunity. We thought you would be pleased."

"Pleased? I begged you repeatedly to let the matter drop."

"We have no intention of having our findings publicized."

"Oh, you don't. With the authors of *Winnie the Pooh* and *Trent's Last Case* walking the streets of little Witham, just what do you think is going to happen? Who authorized this activity anyway? Who's in charge?"

Three sets of nervous male eyes suddenly shifted uneasily in Agatha's direction.

Agatha gulped to clear her pallet . . . or her thoughts. "Why, I was. I was asked to chair the investigation."

Dorothy moved to get a better look at Agatha, who remained seated. "I see. I wasn't expecting such an action from you."

"Well, they promised I wouldn't have to make any speeches," Agatha tried to joke.

"This is the thanks I get, after my defense of you in the Club."

"Defense?"

"Yes. I came to your rescue and spoke on your behalf more than once. And this is how you reward me. *Et tu, Brute?*"

Agatha sat with her mouth open. She wasn't sure what Dorothy was talking about. The waitress poked her nose in and asked. "Oh, one more for lunch? Should I bring another chair?"

"No, don't bring another chair," Dorothy commanded. "I wouldn't want to be responsible for what I might do with it."

Agatha, completely overwhelmed, blinked and stammered. "We had . . . best interest . . . your best interest at heart I assure—"

"Yes. I'll just bet you did. After all my pleading to the contrary. Why wasn't I notified about this?"

"We tried to call, but we couldn't reach you," Agatha said.

But Dorothy had her mind made up. She pointed an angry finger at Agatha. "What is it? Jealousy? Your chance to attack a person when they are down? I should think I would have better treatment from the watercress sandwich division of our profession. But I can play vicious, too, if that is what you like. Your irresponsible book, *The Murder of Roger Ackroyd*, broke the basic rules of detective fiction. It should never have been published and you should have been drummed out of the Club when it was. I intend to bring the matter up at the next session."

Agatha got up from her chair, on the downwind side away from Dorothy. "Excuse me, I . . . please excuse me."

With her carpetbag grasped tightly before her, she started backing away from the table. First she bumped the screen, for which she apologized, and then she bumped into a stout man at the next table trying to eat his soup. She finally turned round the right way and headed toward the ladies room.

"Awkward Agatha," Dorothy said. "Almost as graceful afoot as she is with a pen."

Fifteen minutes before the departure time for the London train, Agatha finally came out of the ladies room of the tea room and quickly crossed the square with her head down. Going immediately to the train, she found an empty compartment and hid herself in one corner.

About ten minutes out of the station, the sliding door of her compartment opened and Alan Milne poked his head inside.

"Oh, here you are. We'd almost given up on you."

Agatha was busy with her knitting and didn't look up. He sat down next to her.

"We were afraid you's missed the train. I didn't see you get aboard."

"No," she said, between needle clicks.

"So sorry about that outburst. It was really most uncalled for."

"Please, I would rather not discuss it."

"Of course. I understand." He drummed his fingers on his knees for a bit. "What is that you are working on?"

"It's to be a scarf. For my daughter or husband. I've not decided which, yet."

"You do nice work. One of them will be very fortunate."

Agatha started weeping. She finally had to stop work and search out a hankie.

"I've never been spoken to like that before. Never. So humiliating. I shall never be able to show my face again."

He patted her carpetbag, no doubt intending to comfort its owner. "We must remember that Dorothy is under a terrible strain right now. I'm sure she'll think better of her words after a bit of time has passed.

"But all the same, the others and I," Alan stammered, "because of the situation, have decided the Detection Club had best drop this whole matter. It wasn't turning out to be the jolly time we had imagined anyway, was it?"

"No. It wasn't. After all, murder seldom does turn out to be a jolly time for anyone, does it?"

"Whatever do you mean by that? Are you so certain, then, it was murder?"

She didn't answer. She had gone back to her knitting with a vengeance.

7

When Dorothy got home she found Mac's car already in the drive. "That man," she mumbled to herself as she hoisted her bundles for a better grip and let herself in through the front door.

Her friend Muriel Byrne was in the dining room with two of her staff, putting costumes on traveling racks in preparation for their trip to Canterbury. She was a pert young woman with bobbed hair, a pencil over one ear, and wearing the very latest style in glasses with large round lenses. When she saw Dorothy, Muriel took a half-dozen pins out of her mouth and came over to give her a hand.

"Honestly, you didn't carry all this from town, did you?"

"Yes. There was no one to help," Dorothy puffed. She went into the kitchen and put her bundles down, then fumbled in one of the sacks until she came up with a spool of thread. "There is no gold thread in the entire town. The closest I could come was this yellow-orange. It was the best I could do."

Muriel took it and scolded, "Honestly, Dorothy, you should not be bothering with things like this. That's what my staff is for."

"It's all right. I was full of nervous energy and I wanted to do something. We want everything to be correct. Val Gielgud of the BBC hasn't phoned, has he?"

"No. Oh that reminds me. The telephone company called while you were out. Apparently the storm the other night put down the London phone line. That's why we haven't been able to get through all this time."

"That's a relief. Mac has been accusing me of wearing out the blasted instrument. How is the packing going?"

"Oh, first-rate. We should be all ready by the time the lorry gets here."

"Dorothy!" Mac called out in his loud angry voice, the sound filling the house. Dorothy went into the hallway to see what the trouble was. Mac was standing on the stairs in his shirtsleeves.

"It's about time you got home. Where is my lunch? You know I have to have my meals on a regular schedule."

"Why don't you put on your coat and come down to the kitchen? We are all going to have a snack down here before the lorry comes for the costumes."

"With a pack of women? I think I'll have a tray in my room." He turned on his heels and went back upstairs.

Dorothy came back into the kitchen and started preparing a sandwich.

Muriel stood in the doorway with her hands on her hips. "What is it you are up to?"

"I'm preparing my husband his lunch."

"Where is Betty? Can't she be doing this?"

"It's her afternoon off."

"Honestly, Dorothy, I don't see how you put up with that man. You'd think he could be just a little considerate, what with all we have to do."

"He was gassed in the war, remember. His stomach lining can't seem to tolerate disruptions in his routine. He has to eat regularly."

"And what about the alcohol? What does that do for his stomach lining?"

"He says he needs it from time to time to control the pain."

Muriel grunted a sarcastic, "Um-hum."

"And while you are busy passing moral judgment on a man you hardly know," Dorothy said, "would you be good enough to also pass me that tray next to the drainboard over there?"

Dorothy took a sandwich and a pot of tea upstairs to Mac's room. The door was slightly ajar and she pushed it open with her backside. He was seated at his desk, apparently making some notes about the contents of an old photo album. When he realized she was there he closed the album.

"Where do you want this?" she asked.

"Right here in front of me."

She set the tray on the desk, as ordered.

"I would think the least you could have done was come downtown and help me with my bundles," Dorothy chided.

"I didn't know you *were* downtown. I came right upstairs when I got home. I didn't talk to any of that crowd of yours downstairs. Had I known, I would have helped."

She turned the album toward her and opened the first page to check the contents. It was Mac's collection of regimental photos.

"What on earth are you doing with this old album?"

He took the book out of her hands and closed it again. "It so happens, ah, if you must know, we are planning a regimental reunion and I was only . . . getting some names right."

"Are you sending out invitations?"

"Yes, er, no. We're telephoning, mostly."

"Where is it to be?"

"We haven't chosen a site as of this date."

"Doesn't sound to me to be very well organized. I do hope it isn't going to interfere with my play schedule."

He slapped his pencil down on the desk. "If you weren't so busy with that play of yours you might at least know what I'm up to. As it is, I can handle things here on my own."

She put a peacemaker's hand on his thick shoulder. "Would it help the tension around this house if I were to tell you I don't have the foggiest notion what that typed note was all about? It made no more sense to me than it did to anyone else. Honestly."

His reaction surprised her. He only patted her hand and said, laconically, "I know, dear. I know."

She didn't know quite what to make of that. Soft answers were not a specialty of Mac's. She decided to leave well enough alone and get back to her business downstairs.

The four ladies had barely finished their kitchen snacks when the doorbell brought Dorothy out front. Through the curtains she could make out the silhouette of Witham's youthful police inspector, and her already frayed nerves took another jolt. What now? She squared her shoulders and put on her schoolteacher face.

As she swung the door open for him he tipped his hat politely, as usual. Then he opened his little black notebook.

"Sorry to disturb you again, ma'am, but I wanted to let you know we have a pretty definite name to go with the man who died in your house."

"Oh, do you?"

He waited a second, expecting to be let inside, but Dorothy held her ground and a tight grip on the front door handle.

"Yes, ma'am," he said. "It appears our description matches that of a missing man from the Lake District. A Mr. Thornton Matthews. He was a dean of something or other at Harcroft Public School for boys." He stopped long enough to check Dorothy's face for signs of recognition, but her schoolteacher face held firm. "It appears he disappeared the same day our gentleman appeared on your doorstep. One of the other staff people at the school is on the way over to identify the body. But everything matches. We're quite certain this is our man.

"Can you think of any reason why a dean from some school about sixty or seventy miles distant would be wanting to appear on your doorstep, Miss Sayers?"

"You mean Mrs. Fleming."

The Inspector didn't seem as willing to be corrected this time. "Can you help us out, ma'am?"

"No, Inspector, I'm afraid I can't."

She started to close the door on him.

"Don't you even want to know if he was a family man?"

"Was he a family man, Inspector?"

"Yes, he was. A wife and two children. Ages fifteen and eleven. Certainly makes one wonder, doesn't it? Neither the wife nor anyone else at the school know of any reason why the Dean would be visiting little Witham. Don't you find that rather remarkable?"

"Yes, Inspector Petry, I certainly do. Now if there is nothing else, you must excuse me. We are very busy right now. It is costume-moving day, you see."

She finally managed to get the door closed on the man. Moving away from the curtained window, she drew a heavy breath and let it out slowly.

Muriel backed out of the sitting room, pulling the winged figure of the Archangel Gabriel with her.

"I think this is the last of it. Can you give me a hand with this muslin covering, Dorothy?"

"Please get one of the girls. I don't feel very close to winged creatures of any description right at the moment."

"You're simply having an early case of opening night jitters. Don't worry so, dear. Your play is going to be a smashing success."

"I wonder." Dorothy dropped wearily into her favorite chair and rubbed her tired eyes. "I wonder if anyone in their right mind can presume to speak for the Church. To speak about righteousness. What was it the Apostle Paul said? 'The very things I ought to do, I do not do. And the things I ought not, those are the things I do.' I feel so unworthy. So . . . unclean."

"Why, Dorothy . . ." Muriel took Dorothy's nervous hands and held them still, against her own body. "This isn't like you. I've never seen you so upset. What is it, dear?"

Dorothy was on the verge of tears, and maybe ready for girl-talk confessions. But just then the lorry horn sounded and the moment of reflection was lost in the flurry of activity that followed.

8

The following morning a brief article appeared in the *London Times*, page seven, about the strange death of Dean Matthews of Harcroft School. Agatha would have missed it altogether had it not been for the article's proximity to the Sunday crossword puzzle. It was the last thing in the world she wanted to be reminded about at the beginning of a fresh day. But there it was. There was no getting around it. She read it through twice before she finished her morning coffee.

Well, at least now it can be over with, she told herself. All the ambitious actions of the Club were for naught. The matter will certainly be taken care of by the authorities. It was a silly idea to think the Club could do anything in the first place.

Agatha had gone to bed the night before with a heavy sleeping draught and the firm conviction that she would not spend time thinking about such matters anymore. She knew from experience that upsetting her daily routine with anything out of the ordinary always threw off her concentration for writing, and then heaven only knew how long it would be before she could get back to it.

Now this article had appeared and she was right back in the fray. Wasted emotional thoughts. If she weren't careful it would be days before she could think properly again. She would have to get in her Morris and have a good long drive in the country. Away from the servants and the telephone and the notebooks she should be filling with story ideas. It was the drone of the engine or the

beautiful English summer countryside, or maybe the constant motion, but a good long drive always had a restor-
ative effect. And that was most definitely what was called
for now.

She was in the habit of keeping the old Morris filled
with petrol for just such emergencies. A quick word to the
cook about not holding lunch for her and a note for
Nancy, her faithful secretary, that she was not to worry,
and Agatha was off.

The direction and the choice of roads was of little concern, but Agatha had learned from unfortunate experience
that she should not get lost. And that she should avoid
narrow dirt roads at all cost. That was how her troubles
had started before. She had tried, without success, to blot
that ugly memory from her mind. Although it was ten
years ago, still hardly a week went by when she didn't
find herself reliving that terrible time.

Now that she could think back on it with some sense of
objectivity she had come to the conclusion that it had
been a genuine mental breakdown. So many things had
piled on top of her that she simply could not face. Her
poor mother's death and then the death of her favorite
Scottie. She was already in a desperate state, and the
news about Archibald's unfaithfulness had been just too
much to bear. Agatha had always thought of herself as a
strong person, but that only seemed to apply to her physi-
cal stamina. She could outwalk and outtalk most men, for
that matter. But the cruel truth was, she was still a child
emotionally. Protected in a loving cocoon of Victorian
upper-middle-class living where none of the hard edges of
life could get at her. Always nannies and grandmamas
and cooks about to tell her how a young lady should act
in each and every circumstance. A lovely upbringing, to
be sure. So many happy memories. She wouldn't change
it for anything on earth. But there was nothing in it to
prepare her for the overpowering feelings of rejection and
loneliness that the divorce brought upon her. No one was

there to tell her how to face her problems and make some decisions.

When the car had gone off the road and gotten stuck in the mud, the beautiful world she knew had come to an end. Even now there were long stretches of time for which she could not account for. How she had gotten herself to the hotel and checked in—and the days, even weeks of . . . of what? What was it she had been up to? She could remember coming to her senses in the hotel room, looking at her own reflection in the mirror over a strange washbasin and wondering to what kind of person that troubled face, with its pale cheeks and wild vacant eyes, belonged.

And even then it wasn't over. The notoriety. The terrible things the press had said about her. That she had intentionally stolen herself away and turned the searching nation on its ear for her own advantage as a writer.

If only she had been stronger. If only she had not been so alone in the world. If only she had had some guidance and sound advice. Some clue that life could turn without warning into something mean and heartless.

A farmer driving a horse-drawn hay wagon suddenly appeared out of the hedgerows on her left. Agatha was forced to swerve the big car across the road, perilously close to a ditch, in order to avoid striking the lead horse. She looked down at her speed indicator and was shocked to see she was traveling at nearly fifty miles an hour. And on a country road, too. She eased up on the pedal and caught her breath.

She must not allow herself to linger over old problems. It wasn't healthy. She must get her car back onto a main road and get her mind onto more pleasant things.

Unfortunately, the first thing that came to Agatha's mind was a mental image of the playbill for Dorothy Sayers' religious play that she had purloined from the Sayers' dining room. What an odd thing to be thinking about. She remembered scanning the playbill to see if she might discover some insight into what made the woman tick. The subject matter authors select could sometimes be very telling, she felt. The play, according to the brief description, dealt with a historical character, one William of Sens, an architect who had built part of the ancient cathedral. It seems he suffered from the sin of pride, which had led him into trouble with his construction work. Not much to go on there, as far as insight into Dorothy. Perhaps one of her mystery books . . . *Gaudy Night* was said to be Dorothy's most autobiographical work. Let's see . . . it involved an academic setting. Some of the professors colluded to suppress a body of work that conflicted philosophically with their own. Not a bad theme for a mystery. If she knew more about the academic world, Agatha wouldn't mind using that herself.

It went without saying that Dorothy was an accomplished liar. No, that was unfair. Capable of lying. Mystery writers had to be, Agatha felt, in order to be successful. The murderer lies, of course, in order to cover his or her crime. If you are going to have two or three decent red herrings, they, too, had to be lying about something, if only to confuse the detective. And now Agatha was certain that Dorothy was lying about some part of her involvement. But why? To what end? If the Dean was her secret paramour, why did he write such a strange note? Certainly he must have known other people would eventually see it and expose the affair. And if exposure was what he wanted, why choose such a circuitous method of getting it? Unless the poor man was deranged. A lover gone mad. No, no. That didn't fit. Perhaps with a young, attractive femme fatale, but not with abrasive Dorothy Sayers, who leaned to the portly side. Men did not choose fourteen-stone women for lovers.

Why was she thinking about this? Agatha asked herself. It was not as if she could do anything about it. Better to be spending her time thinking about the things she could control. The scarf she had been knitting was definitely going to be for her husband, Max. She could see, now that she had gotten into it, that it was going to be much too manly for Rosalind. Not her type at all. Yes, it would most definitely be for Max. Maybe for an extra Christmas present, wrapped up and tucked into his mantel stocking.

She passed an ancient roadside advertisement, done in fading black and white letters. An add for Guinness stout malt liquor. There was some sort of bird to one side, looking over a poem:

> If I can say as you can
> Guinness is good for you
> How grand to be a toucan
> Just think what two-can do!

Fifteen years earlier Dorothy Sayers had made quite a stir in the advertising world with that silly poem. And now all that was left was this weathered reminder, in the middle of some farmer's cornpatch in the middle of nowhere. It seems there was to be no end to it. Agatha was destined to think of Dorothy Sayers whether she liked it or not. What people saw to laugh about in that ad was quite beyond Agatha. The silly thing still didn't make sense. The bird was supposed to be a toucan. That much she knew. But why the fuss over such a simple play on words? It was as silly to Agatha as . . . as the lady herself.

Oh, very well. Think of her she would, and try to make some sense out of her dilemma. If Dorothy knew the dead man, and he was not her lover, what earthly reason could she have for denying him at the moment of death? It just did not make sense. And her desperate appeal to the Detection Club. What of that? It seemed unreasonable, as Alan Milne pointed out.

Agatha couldn't seem to shake the image of Dorothy's angry face, glaring down on her in that claustrophobic little tea room in Witham. She had looked near the brink of hysteria. Poor soul. A husband who no doubt was hard to handle at best. A play grinding through its final preparation period. Then a man shot to death in her house, with all the ensuing questions. No wonder Dorothy was in such a state. Such a state . . . such a state . . .

What state? Did she dare think it? Dorothy in the same state that Agatha had found herself in those many years ago? She thought of the face in the hotel's washbasin mirror, and then compared it to the face from the tea room. Two desperate women, alone in a world suddenly too big for them. Could it be that Dorothy was as desperate, in need of a friend?

But that thought was ridiculous. In view of the way Dorothy had treated her, the very idea of Agatha Christie being a close friend and helpmate to a troubled Dorothy Sayers was ridiculous. It was almost laughable. Not that Agatha carried a grudge against her because of all the harsh words, but because Dorothy had too much pride. Too much stature in the world of literature and the Oxford academic community. She would not be of a mind to accept help from a humble puzzle-solver.

A large lorry sounded its angry horn directly behind Agatha's car, which made her jump. The noise forced her to bring her thoughts back to the road and what she was supposed to be doing. Another check of her speed showed that she was now traveling at thirty-three miles per hour. If it wasn't one extreme it was the other. Instinctively she pulled over onto the first lay-by she came to, allowing the restless driver plenty of room to pass.

Where was she, anyway? Judging from the position of the sun and the time of day she must be traveling northwest. The road had most definitely improved. It seemed to be a major highway, and it was running parallel to a rail line. She drove on a few more miles and soon found some road signs that helped: CREWE, 12 MILES   CHESTER, 35.

Agatha drew in her breath. She was startled—not because she had come so far from home—but because of what she had done. Without realizing it, she had been following the rail line that led away from Witham. She was backtracking on the line that the dead Dean must have traveled on his way to his death. Now why on earth would she be doing a thing like that? Perhaps Dr. Freud and his subconscious business had something to say for himself after all.

At Crewe she pulled into a petrol station. While the tank was being filled she asked the elderly attendant about the condition of the road to Chester. He assured her it was in good repair. Then he asked if she was going up to the match to see her son play football.

"What match would that be?" she asked.

"Why, the finals match up at Chester between Benson-Ford and Harcroft. It should be very exciting."

"You mean, Harcroft, the school for boys that lost its dean last week?"

"I don't know about that. But it's the only Harcroft I know."

Football was hardly Agatha's favorite pastime. But she decided she might take in the activity just the same. If she could isolate a staff member or two and strike up a conversation in the casual setting of a sporting event, she might be able to gain some insight into the man's personality and a reason for his death. When she paid the attendant she also got directions to the field where the match was to be played.

After a bite of lunch in Chester, she found the field near the host school, Benson-Ford. But isolating a member of the visiting staff was quite another matter. The players and coaches did not come onto the field until very shortly before the game was to begin. Even then there were only three older men and no women in the crowd. Really no one with whom Agatha could feel comfortable striking up a conversation. The men all had their blood up and were terribly excited about the game, first shouting angrily at the boys, then pleading with them to play well. She marveled at how men could get so worked up about such a minor event. What great difference did it make if a ball passed into a net or not? And try as she would, she could not bring herself to approach them in the heat of battle, as it were.

Finally, five ladies who could pass for mothers and older sisters of the players came out of a school van and began watching the boys do their warm-up exercises. Agatha sauntered over next to a lady she thought nearly her own age and waited for an opportunity to open a conversation.

"Lovely day for a match, isn't it?" she began.

Perhaps "match" wasn't the right word. Or perhaps the lady simply didn't want to talk. Whatever the reason, she only received a cold glance for her efforts. She decided to stand in silence for a time, pretending she knew just what the boys on the field were up to.

"They should have canceled the game, you know." It was the lady with the cold glance, biting off her words in short disapproving sounds. "Not proper, after so short a time. I only came down because Timmy insisted. It's my only chance to see him play, you understand."

Agatha nodded her understanding. "Such a shame about the Dean, wasn't it? How is his poor wife taking the shock?"

"Still under the doctor's care, I understand. Totally distraught. You'd think they would have canceled out of respect for her, if nothing else."

"I suppose they went on because it is so many days since he actually . . . died. I did wonder why it took them so long to identify the Witham body, didn't you?" Agatha cooed.

"Perfectly understandable," the other lady assured her. "Since he traveled so much for the school the wife simply thought she had misunderstood about his travel plans. Then, after a few days when he didn't telephone home, naturally she got worried."

"Oh, I didn't know he normally traveled."

"Of course. Visiting former students on fund-raising trips and seeing parents from time to time, when it was necessary."

"Then he must have been on such a trip this last time."

"No one seems to know."

"Ladies, please!" A game official with outstretched arms came toward the cluster of women. "You are liable to be in the way if you stay here. Visitor's gallery right this way. See the underclassmen just beyond the rope. If you please."

The ladies were herded toward a small bleacher area that had been erected for spectators sympathetic to the visiting school. It was already quite crowded with lowerclassmen from Harcroft. At least, Agatha assumed they were. They all wore dark green jackets and small green and white caps on their tousled heads. As the ladies moved into the area the boys backed up higher in the bleachers, allowing the ladies to have the ground-level seats. Agatha moved right along with them, as if she belonged.

But the mother she had started with had found some friends and moved away from her. Soon the game got under way and she lost the opportunity to corner anyone, since they all seemed quite intense on the action.

The ball moved up and down the field several times. Agatha paid little attention until one team started to get near the other's goal. When that happened, the pitch of the spectators' voices grew higher and more intense. She knew something important was about to happen. She should at least pretend to be interested.

When one of the better players for the Harcroft team suddenly fell hard on the ground, several of the young men sitting behind Agatha started shouting at the officials to call for a foul. Then one particular voice called out, "You bloody well can't see, can you?"

Agatha turned with a start and searched the stands behind her for Dorothy Sayers. It was her voice, no doubt of it. The same piercing quality, demanding justice and retribution, like a wounded warrior. But Dorothy was not to be seen. Only the jumble of snickering schoolboys in various sizes and shapes.

Perhaps her imagination had gotten the better of her. She was experiencing Dorothy-Sayers-on-the-brain, no doubt of it. But when the Harcroft team intercepted a pass at a critical point and started toward their opponent's goal, Agatha thought she heard the voice again over the din of the yelling boys. She turned about and watched the boys' faces. One in particular, a narrow-faced, dark complected youth, had his hands cupped about his mouth and was shouting unintelligible encouragement for his team. He was cheering louder and longer than the others. His voice rang out with an uncanny familiarity to it. He didn't look at all like her, but the voice was unbelievably close to Dorothy's. Agatha studied the boy until the action on the field waned and her undo attention to him was beginning to be noticed.

She waited until Harcroft scored its first goal. In the ensuing excitement, she moved closer to the youth, clapping happily like the others all the while.

"Marvelous shot, wasn't that?" Agatha called out in the boy's general direction.

"Yes. Oh, yes," the thin-faced boy cried. "That was Ben. He's in our dormitory wing."

"Is that so? How exciting for you."

"Oh, you bet. He's our best forward. That'll take the wind out of their sails."

He appeared to be thirteen, maybe fourteen, to Agatha's eyes. But he couldn't be a son. Dorothy had been married only a little less than ten years. Maybe a nephew. Or could it possibly be only coincidence, an apparition brought on by Agatha's overactive imagination?

Play resumed on the field and Agatha tried to keep the youth within earshot, occasionally making some comment about the players. That was difficult with her limited knowledge of the game, but she did make sure that each time the player "Ben" did something well that she gave proper recognition to the boy's dormitory wing.

Finally, a time out was called, and Agatha extended her hand to the boy.

"Mrs. Mallowan is my name. I don't think we have met before, have we?"

The startled boy took off his cap and shook her hand.

"No, ma'am, I don't think we have."

"And your name?"

"I'm Anthony Fleming, ma'am."

She shook his hand and tried desperately not to show her excitement. She would leave it at that. There was no reason to put the youth on the spot. She did not make any further inquiry, but returned her attention to the playing field and the game at hand. Then, as soon as was possible, she edged away from the other spectators and back toward her waiting Morris auto.

It was beyond the realm of coincidence now. The voice, the name, and the little upturn at the corners of the mouth. And the dead Dean who visited the Fleming house nearly seventy-five miles away for no apparent reason. Or so they all thought.

Agatha pushed the self-starter button in the big green car and drove slowly away from the playing field. She was looking forward to the long ride home. There was going to be a great deal to sort through along the way.

Once on the main highway, she wiggled herself into a comfortable position and set her mind to work. Her very first thought was of her fictional detective from little St. Mary Mead. What would Miss Jane Marple have to say about all this?

Five miles out of town Agatha spotted another of the old Guinness advertisements. This time only the last two lines of the poem were readable:

> How grand to be a Toucan
> Just think what two-can do!

9

The Archbishop had just finished conducting his brief tour of the church office's quadrangle, all the while describing in great detail to his two guests the name and history of each sedate flower bed. Dorothy and Val Gielgud, her BBC producer, had walked slightly behind, trying their best to show appreciation for the Archbishop's homilies on the properly tended English garden.

"I do so enjoy an orderly life, don't you?" he asked Dorothy.

"I wouldn't know. I've never had one."

"Oh, come now. Your father was a man of the cloth. Surely you must have grown up in a fine reserved home."

"I managed to keep the household in a state of constant turmoil, as I recall.

"Excuse me if I do get back to our topic, Your Eminence, but we do have a play to stage. I've looked over your written criticisms and find that if we are to make the changes your committee has requested we will be taking the very heart out of the drama. I'm sure Mr. Gielgud will confirm that judgment."

Val Gielgud nodded his long aristocratic head in agreement. "If the dramatic impact is lost, the value of the play as a radio vehicle for the BBC will be very doubtful. Very doubtful, indeed."

The Archbishop only nodded and touched the tips of his fingers in front of his expansive waistband. He sighed.

"I am not unsympathetic to your need for dramatic conflict. My reservation is strictly theological. You have your main character punished for his sins by having him fall from church rafters and seriously injure himself. Whether this is with or without the aid of your play's archangels is somewhat confusing to me at this reading. But my point is, I wonder if the Church wants to project that cause-and-effect kind of theology upon our people."

"But illness and death are in the world as a result of man's sins, are they not?" Dorothy asked.

The Archbishop squinted an eye, as if focusing in on a distant platitude. "Yes, well, Scripture tells us the ancient Hebrews certainly did blame their misfortunes on their sins against the Almighty. But I wonder if we wish to be so literal. I mean this particular punishment for that particular sin—er, shortcoming. We must leave space for grace and God's great forgiving nature, don't you agree?"

"I agree that we must represent the nature of our Creator as accurately as we can. And in my study of the scriptures I have learned that he is a God of justice."

The archbishop waved a finger. "Who loves mercy. Let us not forget. Who loves mercy."

A church secretary with a very serious face approached the three. "Please excuse me, but we have an urgent message for Miss Sayers."

"Yes, Miss Manning, what is it?" the Archbishop asked.

The secretary took Dorothy's arm and led her toward a nearby stone bench. "I'm sorry, but there has been an accident."

Dorothy had barely sat down when she jumped back up. "Yes, what is it? What's happened?"

"I'm afraid it's your husband, Miss Sayers. He has been in an auto accident."

"Dead? He's been killed? I knew it. I knew something dreadful was going to happen."

"No. He's alive, but they don't know at this time how serious it is. They just called from Shaftesbury—"

"Shaftesbury? Where the devil is that?"

"They did not say. I only have the address . . ."

Dorothy snatched the slip of paper from her hand. "Excuse me, Your Eminence."

The archbishop raised his hand as if to comfort her, but before he could speak she was already hurrying out of the quad.

"A very troubled woman, there, Mr. Gielgud." the archbishop marveled. "I hope for her sake her husband is on the mend."

"For her sake?"

"You may think me soft on my theological points. But I've seen this condition hundreds of times. Calamity befalls a family and the most religious of the clan begins searching their souls to see what sin they have committed to bring the tragedy about. I must say, it is not a healthy prospect." He sighed and shook his head sadly. "There are times when I envy the convenience of the Catholic confessional."

Dorothy came away without so much as an overnight bag, but she was able to make fairly quick train connections to Shaftesbury, a small town on the line to Exeter, southwest of London. She arrived at the hospital late in the afternoon. She had wired ahead and a staff doctor was able to meet her at the door and fill her in on her husband's condition as soon as she arrived. The doctor was an older man with a gentle manner. He led her to a quiet corner of the only waiting room in the antiquated facility and sat next to her while he reported his findings.

"He is still unconscious, Mrs. Fleming. We really won't know the extent of his internal injuries until he comes 'round. We do know that he broke a collarbone, but no other major bones seem to be broken."

"I see. And when do you expect he might waken?"

"That is very hard to say. Head injuries are unpredictable at best. I'm sorry."

"I understand he was in his car. What happened? Do you know?"

"The car was found overturned in a ditch. The ambulance people said that, judging from the marks in the dirt and the car's distance from the road, he must have been traveling at a high rate of speed. That is really all we know. The car was brought into town. I understand it's in our local repair garage, if you care to see it."

"If I never see it again, it would be fine with me."

"Yes, I understand."

"Can you tell if he had been drinking?"

The doctor ran a hand over his receding hairline. It appeared he had not intended to get into that question. "His blood-alcohol level was rather high, yes. I think you should know . . . since the car turned over . . . and since it was an open roadster, we may have to assume the worst about his injuries."

Dorothy drew in a jagged breath and covered her face. After a bit, the doctor had to excuse himself and get back to work, leaving her alone with her thoughts.

After several minutes, Dorothy became aware that she was being observed. A young woman stood in the hallway, intently watching her. At first Dorothy tried ignoring the rudeness of her stare. Finally, the girl disappeared from view and Dorothy returned to her lonely vigil. Twice in the next hour hospital staff people dropped by to check on her and to let her know she had not been forgotten. At the first sign of stirring in her husband they promised to let her know.

Then, around six-thirty, the staring young lady reappeared in the doorway. This time she came across the room and held out her hand.

"Hi, there. You're Dorothy Sayers, aren't you?"

Dorothy scowled at the girl. "Have we met?"

"No, not yet. My name is Wanda Barton. I'm a great fan of yours."

"Indeed."

"Yes, really. I've read just about everything you've ever written. I'm very pleased to meet you."

"Young woman, I am in no mood to be talking about my writing."

"I saw you on the platform in London and I simply could not believe my luck," the girl gushed. "You see, I'm an American— "

"Yes, I know."

"—and I've come all the way to England to see you. Well, not really just you, but all the mystery writers I could interview."

"Dorothy rolled her eyes. "Is it the custom in America to approach worried strangers in hospital waiting rooms and strike up conversations with them?"

Wanda laughed. "No, it isn't. Not really. It took me a long time to do it. You see I was so shy on the train ride, I didn't dare."

"Timidity can be an appealing virtue. I advise you to cultivate it."

Wanda laughed again and patted Dorothy on the forearm.

"No, now listen. Please be serious. Do you know H.L. Mencken, the famous American newspaper man? He started *Black Mask* mystery magazine? Mystery writing is very big in America, right now. Well, he's offered to publish anything I can come up with, like a feature article on English mystery writers. Well, not just anything, but anything good I can come up with. And I just got off the boat last night. Can you believe it? My first day in London and bingo. I'm in the big depot you have there, trying to find out how to get to where Agatha Christie lives, and who should walk right by me, but—" She extended her arms toward Dorothy. "Isn't it a small world?"

"Young woman, stop chattering. It so happens my husband has been in a very serious accident. He may very well be dying. And I am most certainly not in a mood to be listening to your gibberish. Now please, take your leave."

"Husband? Oh, you're married to the Fleming man who was in the accident? Oh, I get it. I was wondering what you were doing out this way. You live on the other side of London, don't you?"

Dorothy got to her feet and went out to the nurse's station.

"Sister," she called to the first white uniform she saw, "is there somewhere else where I might wait? There is an unbelievable pest in the waiting room."

"Oh, Mrs. Fleming, there you are," the nurse smiled. "I was just on my way to find you. Your husband has been stirring. I knew you would want to know. He's not awake yet, but his feet have been moving about in the bed. That's a very good sign."

"Yes, I understand. May I go in and see him now?"

"The doctor thought that might be advisable. Why don't you come this way?"

Dorothy looked to make sure she was leaving the American pest behind, then she followed the nurse up the main staircase to the first landing and into a crowded hospital room.

She hardly recognized Mac. His head was swathed in white gauze, and they had shaved off his great bushy mustache because of a cut on his left cheek. His eyelids were partly open, but the eyeballs were up in his head, somewhere out of sight.

The nurse moved some of the instruments surrounding the bed so Dorothy could sit down. Then the nurse instructed her on how she might talk to her husband and rub his free arm, hopefully stimulating him to wake up. Dorothy had never been one for promoting tender loving care, but she played the part the nurse had given her.

It wasn't long afterward that she, too, noticed his feet moving under the covers. She stood over her husband and spoke loudly into his ear. "Mac, are you with us again?"

His eyes fluttered. "Mud's too thick. We can't move out—place—gas shells—can't get out. Don't open up. We'll die if it opens . . ."

"The war's over, Fleming. Wake up, Mac. It's me, Dorothy."

His eyeballs came down and stared at her. It was a

vacant stare. He was still dying somewhere in the trenches of France.

"Wake up, Mac. You've been in an accident. Do you remember the accident?"

"He was just . . . boy," Mac whined in a thin voice.

"Who was just a boy?"

"Boy in the window . . . just a boy. Car window . . ."

"Mac, the war is over." She shook his arm and he started blinking his eyes, as if he were coming to his senses.

"What happened? Is this—field hospital?"

"This is the 1930s, Mac. The war's over. You've been in a car accident."

"Oh, yes. The car. Had to go off the road."

"You had to go off the road? Why?"

"Boy. There was a boy."

"Where? A boy in the road? And you had to swerve into the ditch to avoid hitting him? Is that it?"

"The car—forced me in the ditch."

"Was there another car?"

His eyes refocused on Dorothy. Then he focused on different objects about the room. She could tell he was coming all the way back. "Where are we?" he whined.

"We're in a small town on the Exeter road. Shaftesbury, I think it's called. What were you doing out this way?"

"I was coming in from Plymouth."

"Plymouth? What in God's name were you doing in Plymouth?"

He considered the question, then squirmed about in the bed, groaning from pain.

"You'd better not thrash about." Dorothy went to the door and got a passing orderly to get word to a nurse. When she came back to Mac's side she noticed he was beginning to sweat.

"Try to rest, Mac. There'll be somebody here in a minute. Are you in a lot of pain?"

"No. Not bad. Not like the war."

"Can't you get the war out of your mind? What was it you were doing in Plymouth?"

"I thought you told me to get the war out of my mind."

"What's that supposed to mean?"

"Oh, nothing. Rattling on as usual." His eyes rolled across the ceiling, as if looking for a painless spot to rest them.

Two nurses were in the room in the next second, taking pulses and blood pressure readings. They asked Dorothy to step outside, which she did. In another five minutes one of the nurses came out to her, wearing a big smile on her face.

"You can relax a bit I think. All his signs are bouncing back beautifully. It looks like only a concussion. The doctor is on his way to make sure, but all the good signs are there. Mrs. Fleming, you don't look very happy. Don't you understand what I'm saying?"

"Yes, I understand. I was only wondering . . . if God is taunting me."

10

E. C. Bentley was in the process of returning two large historical volumes to their proper place on the shelves in the reference room of the public library, when he happened to spot a familiar female figure seated by the great windows in the reading room. He walked quietly to her side and peered at her reading material.

"Boning up on the particulars of the Great War, are we, Agatha?"

Agatha Christie sat up quickly and covered the book with her arms.

"Oh, Edmund, you startled me. So nice seeing you again."

He noted her secretive manner, but made no reference to it. He sat opposite her and spent time putting on his kid gloves.

"I was just finishing up some research of my own when I noticed you in here all by yourself. Back to work, are you? I take it you have recovered completely from our ill-fated journey to the provinces."

"Oh, yes, that. I've been so busy I've completely put it out of my mind."

"I wish I could say the same," he said. "I still wonder if we are doing the right thing by dropping the matter."

"What else could we do? She repeatedly asked us . . . as I recall all too vividly."

He chuckled a library-soft chuckle. "I thought you said it was out of your mind."

"Yes, well, almost out of my mind."

"Still, I feel we club members have a responsibility to Dorothy. It's almost as if we were standing on the shore of a great turbulent sea and one of our friends were floundering in the deep, with waves crashing over her head, yet here we are safely on the shore, doing absolutely nothing to save her."

"Perhaps we are extending her the greatest favor by doing precisely that—nothing."

Agatha picked up her writing paper, which she had filled with notes, then quickly closed the reference book she had been using. But her moves were not quick enough to avoid Edmund's curious eyes.

"Doing some research on the Old Regulars for a new mystery book, are you?"

"Yes, yes, that's it. A new mystery."

"I always thought it was an unusual name for a regiment."

"It was a nickname only."

"Oh, really? I didn't know. What was their official designation? Can't say as I recall, offhand . . ."

Agatha got to her feet. "You really must excuse me now, Edmund, or I shall be late for . . . something."

She had started to make her exit when Edmund suddenly slapped his hand on the table, startling Agatha and several other library patrons in the process.

"By Jove, Agatha, what is it you are up to?" he called after her.

"Why, whatever do you mean?"

He hurried to her side. "I mean, what is it you are doing? I just remember Dorothy once told me that her husband had been a member of the Old Regulars."

"Oh, really? How very unusual."

He took the liberty of stepping in front of her intended path, which surprised Agatha.

"Why, Edmund."

"Too unusual for coincidence, I should say. You are investigating this matter on your own, aren't you? I'll not have Dorothy hurt in any way."

"Edmund, do you really think that I would intentionally hurt Dorothy?"

"I would like to think you wouldn't. After the Witham
incident you'd certainly have reason to, wouldn't you?"

"I'm going to be late, Edmund. May I please pass?"

He stepped aside and apologized. "It's only that I'm
very concerned. If any further investigation is to be done,
I think the entire Detection Club should be involved."

She suddenly turned on him, gripping his arm. "No,
Edmund, that is precisely what we should not do. You
know as well as I how everyone in the group talks. If you
have any deep regard for Dorothy Sayers, and I sincerely
feel you do, then this matter must be kept from the Club.
This is a matter . . . that must be handled with the greatest discretion."

"Don't you think I qualify as a discreet friend?"

She started sidling by him. "You most certainly do.
And if there is anything anyone can do to help, you'll be
the first person I call."

"Call about what?"

"Please don't ask."

A librarian, who just happened to look a good deal like
Dorothy Sayers, complete with pince-nez, came toward
them with a finger pressed to her lips. "Let us all remember where we are, shall we?"

"Yes, we shall be quiet," Agatha assured her. "I was
just on my way out. Good-bye, Edmund. Now, not a
word to anyone. You promised."

"I did? What word?"

But she had taken up her large purse and was moving
toward the door.

Instead of following, Edmund stepped to one of the
great windows next to the entrance and watched as
Agatha hurried down the front steps and hailed a cab.
He fidgeted with the corners of his small mustache and
scowled.

"What on earth has gotten into that timid soul?"

                    *   *   *

The ancient, beetle-browed butler placed a small personal card on his somewhat tarnished tray and stepped into the master's study. The General was busy trimming his fingernails over the business section of yesterday's *Times*. He didn't like being caught at such a mundane act while among all his books and memorabilia, so he pretended to be intensely interested in the prices of South African gold bullion. The butler, Crippings, stepped forward to his spot and gave his little cough.

"Oh, Crippings. Have you seen the price on Johannesburg gold?"

"No, sir, I have not had that pleasure . . ."

"There's going to be another war. You mark my words. Another war."

"Very good, sir. But if I may, there is a lady to see you, sir."

"A lady, at this time of day?" He squinted at the mantel timepiece. It was approaching eleven in the morning. "Who comes at this time of day?"

Crippings already had his eyeglasses in place to read the card again. "A Mrs. Agatha Christie, sir."

"Christie? I don't know any Christie."

"She said to mention she was the wife of Captain Archibald Christie of the Royal Flying Corps."

"Oh, yes, of course. The hero. Good man. You say his wife? What the devil would his wife be doing here?"

Crippings sighed, under his breath. "She says it is about your military exploits. Shall I say you are not at home, sir?"

The General grumbled unintelligible noises. "No, we better not do that. For all I know her husband could be with the War Office." He folded up his own newspaper, then stood up and reset the front of his smoking jacket. "I suppose you had best show her in. I do hope she's not expecting lunch. I cannot abide unexpected people for lunch. Especially women."

"Might I suggest I bring coffee and some of last night's

crumb cake in here? That should serve as an adequate hint that lunch will not be forthcoming."

"Yes, good thinking. Very good. Is the place presentable, Crippings?"

"If I may suggest, sir, it is a bit close."

Neither Crippings nor anyone else close to the General had the nerve to tell him directly about his lingering problem with halitosis. Crippings merely opened the French doors to the garden on his way out of the room. The General used the waiting time to wave his breast handkerchief across the small picture frame that housed his important service medals, then positioned the case for easy viewing for anyone coming in from the hall.

His small home bordered an army training camp, and the distant strains of a military parade tattoo drifted in through the garden doors, triggering memories of happier days. For the General there was nothing quite as exhilarating as the sight of a properly disciplined regiment passing in review. By the time Crippings opened the door again the General was ramrod straight.

"General John Dana Pike," Crippings intoned, "Mrs. Christie."

Agatha was dressed in a light summer coat and the small hat she liked to wear while driving, since she could keep it on in the car without getting her hair bumped out of place. She quickly crossed to the General and took his hand formally.

"So very good of you to see me, General. I've read so much about you."

"Indeed? Indeed. Nice meeting you. Please sit down. Crippings, what say we have a little something in here, for Mrs. Christie. Coffee, perhaps, and a little something?"

Agatha nodded a thank you and Crippings disappeared.

"Now, then, tell me, how is that splendid husband of yours?"

"My husband? My, ah, husband is fine, thank you, General."

"Never had the privilege of meeting him, but heard so

much about his exploits. Country can't have too many heros, I say."

"General Pike, I've come here hoping you might be able to give me some insight on a military matter. It involves the regiment you served with during the Great War."

"Of course. The Old Regulars. Top fighting force. What can I tell you?"

"I certainly don't expect you to remember all of the officers, but I was wondering if you could trace two men for me? I've drawn a blank at the military library in London."

"What are the names?"

"The first is a Major Mac, or MacDonald Fleming."

"Fleming? Don't recall any Major Fleming."

"I believe he was a gas casualty. Still living, of course."

"Then he would have been in the Quartermaster Company. They were the only ones who came under gas attack. At Simes it was."

The General rose and removed a large leatherbound volume from the bookshelf behind his desk.

"Here were are. Company B. Even have pictures of the regular officers before we shipped off. Maybe we can recognize the chap."

Agatha looked over the double-paged picture of a group of very serious men in new British Army uniforms, squinting into the sun from parade rest. Very quickly Agatha put a finger on a young man in the second row. A stocky, broad-shouldered, scowling man. One could guess from the posture he was all military.

"There he is. Yes, I'm sure of it. That's Major Fleming."

The General looked at the man, then ran his own finger along the descriptive guide for the picture.

"You are absolutely right. Forgotten all about him. But it's *Captain Oswald* Fleming. Not MacDonald. That's why I could not place him. Lost track of him after the second German charge at Simes. I suppose it is possible he made upgrade, later. But that name difference . . . You say he was gassed?"

"That is my understanding."

"Nasty business, that gas attack. Never should have happened, you know."

"We all feel it was most inhumane, I'm sure."

"Don't mean what the Germans did. There's no accounting for those blighters. I mean the casualties. Never should have happened. General Reed's men had already sustained an attack down in Puysatier Valley, and our men should have been thoroughly prepared and checked out with the masks long before the attack at Simes. But because they were so far behind the trenches, they no doubt felt they could put it off. But the Jerries lobbed the artillery canisters too far over their target at the front and hit our Quartermaster Company. At least that's what we decided must have happened. Bad management all around. Lost over two hundred. Terrible way to die—that mustard gas. Terrible."

Agatha's eyes widened. "Who's fault was—who was in charge of the training? Was it Captain Fleming?"

"Him? Heavens no. He was in charge of supply, as I recall. Keeping the laundry going. That sort of thing. No, no. Training was in the hands of the senior officers. Too important a matter for lower-grade officers."

"Was the officer in charge of gas mask training, by any chance, Thornton Matthews?"

"Matthews, a very common name. What grade was he?"

"I don't know his rank."

The General started thumbing through another book from his leatherbound collection.

"Matthews . . . would have to be a major or colonel. All gentlemen at that grade. Not the type to go about changing their names or claiming a higher grade. Memory's not what it used to be, but seems I would remember a senior officer, name of Matthews . . . No. No Thornton Matthews listed. And this covers all our senior officers from 1910 to 1930. You know what the chap looked like?"

"Well, I do have a more recent photo . . ."

Agatha retrieved a news clipping from her purse and handed it over. The General made use of the magnifying glass from his desk.

"No, I don't recognize . . . Why, this is an obituary notice. The man's dead."

"Yes, I know. He died in rather unusual circumstances and we are trying to determine—"

The General, who had continued reading, interrupted. "Says here Matthews was a Lieutenant Junior Grade in His Majesty's Navy during the war. He wasn't in the Army at all."

"Yes, I read that. I thought perhaps there had been a mistake."

The General scoffed and handed back the clipping.

"Good heavens, woman, that's from the *London Times.* The *Times* doesn't make blunders in their obituary columns. Chamberlain may be leading our government into appeasement and shame, but some of our institutions are still in order, I'll have you know. Whatever gave you the idea he was Army?"

Agatha squirmed under the General's bombast. "Because of the weapon. The inquest records indicate that it was a very unusual gun that was used. It was a Berten-Wellar pistol. I believe your regiment was the only regiment . . ."

The General's face hardened. He tossed aside his magnifying glass and retreated behind his desk in a defensive maneuver.

"Yes, I know the weapon. What about it?"

"It is my understanding from the London Museum that your regiment was the only group ever to use that—"

"It had never been properly field tested. Had we known that we never would have allowed its adoption. As it was, only a few of the officers who used side arms selected it over the standard issue revolver. Blasted thing jammed with the slightest bit of dirt in the mechanism. In the laboratory, you couldn't ask for a better weapon. Naturally, in the muddy conditions in the trenches, the thing proved to be completely unreliable.

"You see, the developer, Reginald Wellar, was once connected to the regiment—through marriage, actually—and we thought it a good gesture to give his new side arm a try. Don't see how we can be blamed for that. Do you?"

"Blamed? Why, no, I suppose not."

"Good. Wouldn't want a thing like that to stand out on the record."

"General Pike, do you have any idea how many officers were issued the automatic?"

"Only a handful as I recall. Word got around in a hurry. Something of a collector's item, now, of course. Why all the interest at this late date? Was this Matthews fellow firing the weapon and the thing blew up on him? Is that it?"

"No, General. But Mr. Matthews was killed by one, either by his own hand or by someone else. The inquest did not attempt to make a judgment. Is there any way of knowing which men selected the automatics?"

He scratched at the side of his rather bulbous nose and thought a bit. "Not at this late date, I'm afraid. Regiment wasn't required to keep minor equipment records for more than five years after the Armistice. You might check with company files. Some of those might still be on hand."

"If Captain Fleming was in charge of clothing supplies, would he have records of who received the special side arms?"

"No, not likely. Weapons were not issued by the Quartermaster."

"How about the gas masks?"

The General was becoming uneasy from the rapid questioning. "Yes, possibly. I suppose they were to be issued through the Quartermaster. Can't really swear to it at this late date. I say, is this all that important?"

"I'm not sure. I'm just trying to gain some understanding."

"By you, you mean . . . just you. You aren't here on behalf of your husband?"

"Why, no."

"Christie isn't in the War Department?"

"Christie? Why no, he left the Army a good many years ago. Are you under the impression I am currently married to Archibald Christie?"

"Of course I am. That's what you told my butler."

"Oh, I beg your pardon. I told him that I *was* married to Archie. Not that I am."

Crippings must have been listening at the door. As if on cue, he came in carrying a heavy tray.

"Crippings," the General barked, "did you or did you not tell me the lady was married to Captain Christie?"

"Indeed I did, sir. 'Was married,' as in the past tense."

The General grumbled to himself.

"I'm most dreadfully sorry," Agatha said, lamely, "I thought surely you knew."

"Knew? How was I to know? You mean the man's dead?"

"No, General, not dead. We were . . . we have been . . ."

"Not divorced?"

Agatha nodded her head.

"Good God. First the Prince of Wales chasing after that divorced American trollop. And now, even our heros. Is nothing sacred anymore?"

"I'm most dreadfully sorry. I thought everybody knew. After all, it was in the *Times*."

"I'm not in the habit of reading that section of the paper."

"Oh. Well then, that explains it, doesn't it?"

"Explains? Explains what? What exactly is it you—"

"When you talked about my husband, I thought you were referring to Max Mallowan, the famous archeological explorer."

"Mallowan? Then why the devil do you still call yourself Christie?"

"That is because of my writing. I write under that name."

"Write? Write what?"

"Why, murder mysteries. I write murder—"

"Murder? You mean as in fiction? Those trashy little things the enlisted men read?"

"I beg your pardon? Yes, I suppose—"

"Fiction? *Fiction?*" he barked, as if the word were tainted. "Why am I talking to you?"

"It's about the man's death. I think it is somehow connected with the regiment, your regiment. I ah—"

"Crippings, what the devil are you hovering about like that for?" the General shouted at his man. "Can't you be doing something useful?"

"I was wondering," Crippings said dryly, "if you wanted me to pour." He held the coffeepot aloft.

"No, I don't want you to pour." The General rose from his desk chair and brought his smoking jacket to attention. "As a matter of fact, we are finished with our business here and the lady is just leaving. Weren't you, Mrs. whoever-you-are?"

"Oh, yes. I see." Agatha got slowly to her feet and gulped at the lump that had been forming in her throat. "Well, I don't think I could eat a thing, really. Most kind of you, I'm sure." She backed toward the French doors. "I'll just slip out this side way. No need to put either of you to any trouble, really. Thank you, ever so much."

In her haste to retreat, Agatha caught her heel on the doorsill. She came perilously close to losing her balance, but managed to recover by snatching frantically at the door handle and swinging her long limbs about in a most unladylike manner. With the two men looking on she recovered herself on the gravel walkway outside, gave them both a nervous laugh, then disappeared down the path toward her waiting Morris.

The General looked after her in disbelief. "Most extraordinary."

Crippings closed the doors to the garden, then turned to accept the dressing-down from his master, who used to command thousands.

"Good God, man. Can't you do a better job of screening than that? I am not at home to every crackpot female popinjay who passes by."

Crippings arched his full white eyebrows to display his great sorrow. "My fault entirely, General. I shall endeavor to do better in the future."

Without missing a beat, Crippings retrieved the tray of refreshments from the desk and came to attention. "If you will be needing nothing further, sir, I shall see to your lunch."

The General snorted and waved his manservant away with the back of his hand, then dropped his body into his desk chair with as much anger and disgust as he could muster.

To be sure, the appearance of the Christie woman had upset him. But right now it was the total absence of fear in the voice of his servant Crippings that angered him. It wasn't like the old days, when he was in command in the field. Not at all. Why, the man should be shivering in his boots after the kind of dressing-down he had given him. Nothing quite like a campaign against a proper enemy to shape up the troops.

He leaned back in his great chair and allowed his mind to linger on a familiar pattern of thoughts: If there were to be an extensive mobilization, no doubt he would be needed again. He knew in his heart he was still young enough to command. But the years were ticking away, and he held out only a flickering hope that the little Austrian paperhanger could do much to provide a "proper enemy." If only the blighter didn't wear that bit of a mustache. Made him look like a damn cinema comic. Nobody could take him seriously.

The General gave a great sigh and drummed his fingers on the desk.

"Whatever possessed me to think she was somehow connected with the War Office?" he asked of himself aloud. A habit he had taken up of late, when time stretched a bit long before him.

His biggest activity of the morning, a military trim on his finger nails, was already completed. Perhaps after lunch he would take a stroll to the far side of the parade grounds . . .

11

The following morning, after nearly a half-hour of trying, Dorothy had finally been able to get a telephone call through to Val Gielgud at his London office. She explained her predicament to him as best she could, in spite of a bad connection.

"Mac did not rest very well last night. But the doctor didn't want to risk sedating him. He's afraid he might slip into a coma. If he is stable enough this morning, they will be moving him to another hospital where they have an X-ray machine. They want to X-ray his head and spine for injuries. I have no choice but to stay by his side, for now."

"Yes, I was afraid you were going to say that. The Archbishop and the committee are expecting some answers before things progress any further—to what they call the point of no return, when it will be too late to put out cancellation notices. Not that I think there is any danger of that happening."

"Maybe we should let it happen."

"Dorothy. Don't talk like that."

"Oh, Val, I'm at my wit's end. At this point I don't think I could think straight enough to make any changes even if I tried. Everything is piling up on me. If Mac's injury weren't enough, I now have an American girl who has attached herself to me like a leech, asking the most personal questions."

"About what?"

"Apparently she is a mystery fan. She envisions herself

as a magazine writer and thinks I have time for an interview."

Val Gielgud laughed. "That's the price you pay for success. Why not enjoy it?"

"Please don't laugh. It is most disconcerting. It's as if the Lord or the fates were throwing everything they had to stop us."

"Dorothy, listen. Your play is brilliant. You've come too far to stop now. And it's the opportunity you've been looking for to break out of the detective fiction mold. And it's only the beginning. Remember the children's Bible story dramatizations we talked about?"

"I know. I know."

"I wasn't planning on telling you until after your play's opening, but the BBC board is most interested in the concept. It's what you want, isn't it? To carry on as your father before you in the Lord's work?"

"Oh, Val . . ." Dorothy had a handkerchief to her face for a time, too overcome to speak.

"Dorothy, are you still there?"

"Yes, I'm here. It must be the bad connection. It's what I've prayed for. But I'm not . . . I'm not the person people think I am. It's too much even to hope for. Maybe others, better qualified . . ."

"Nonsense. Modesty does not become Dorothy L. Sayers. Now listen, I'll talk with the Canterbury committee. They'll have to understand and make allowances, under the circumstances. You get some rest, now. You sound exhausted."

The hospital staff had made overnight accommodations for Dorothy on the second level of the nurses' dormitory, right next door to the hospital. She had spent a restless night in an uncomfortable bed, which she decided had been designed for a very skinny nurse suffering from narcolepsy.

After her early morning call to Val, she brushed out her short hair, put some artificial color on her pale cheeks, and started down the steps toward the front door.

She looked out the window from side to side for signs

of her new shadow. Just as she feared, the girl was seated on the cement buttress of the front steps of the hospital some thirty yards away. There would be no way for Dorothy to get by her without facing another barrage of questions, which she most certainly was not prepared to do.

Just then a group of student nurses came giggling down the stairwell behind her, and Dorothy had an idea. It wasn't as if they were perfect strangers. After all, she had shared a common bathroom with at least three of them just last night. Dorothy stepped in front of the girls, smiling.

"I wonder if you young ladies might not be willing to help me with a little joke I want to play on somebody."

"A joke, Mrs. Fleming?" one of the girls asked.

"Yes, perfectly harmless, I assure you." Dorothy stepped to the window. "You see the young lady sitting on the hospital steps over there? Well, she is a pesky newspaper reporter, waiting to ask me some questions about my husband and his accident. I simply can't face her now, under the circumstances. I'm sure you understand."

She took off her summer coat as she explained her plan: If one of the girls would put on Dorothy's coat with the large collar turned up and hurry off down the street in the opposite direction, the "reporter" would think it was Major Fleming's wife and hopefully make a dash for the coat and its contents, leaving Mrs. Fleming free to enter the hospital and go to her sick husband's side.

The girls quickly indicated their willingness, and the stoutest of them put the coat on and did as directed, making a dramatic dash down the street.

Dorothy and the others watched for the "reporter" to make the connection with the coat. It didn't take long. While Wanda ran pell-mell by the nurses' residence in hot pursuit, the other student nurses fell into gales of laughter.

Dorothy made her move toward the safety of the hospital. Once inside, she leaned against the cool hallway and caught her breath.

A childish stunt to pull, to be sure. Just a little lie and

another little deception. Done without a second thought, really. Almost out of . . . habit. But totally justified, she told herself. The little snippet of a girl had no right to her personal life.

At the nurses' station she snapped her fingers at a white-gowned figure, busy with her charting.

"Tell me, please, who is permitted in my husband's room, other than staff, I mean?"

The nurse made a quick check of another chart, then told Dorothy, "He is still on our critical list. Only immediate family is allowed in Mr. Fleming's room."

"That's what I thought. Thank you so much."

She started for the stairs and her husband's room. No one stopped or challenged her and she went directly into the room. In less then ten seconds she was back out in the hallway, cornering a passing nurse behind a breakfast cart.

"I thought I was going to be able to ride in the ambulance to the other hospital with my husband. What happened to our plans?"

The nurse stopped her cart and stared at Dorothy.

"What are you talking about?"

"Has my husband already been moved to the other hospital? He's not in his room."

The nurse brushed by Dorothy and rushed into Mac's room, Dorothy right behind. The bed was empty except for a small breakfast tray angled across the crumpled sheets. The nurse searched the bathroom next door, then came back in the room and swung open the clothes closet.

"His clothes. They're gone."

"Were they supposed to take . . ." Dorothy started.

"No. No one on staff has taken anything," the worried nurse cried, her face turning nearly as white as her starched uniform. "Not him. Not his clothes. Either someone has come in and got him or he has taken himself. He's gone."

12

Late in the afternoon Agatha arrived at a large, three-story Victorian home in Plymouth. The beautiful old wood and stone mansion reminded her of Ashfield, her childhood home in another seaside resort not so very many years ago. The main fireplace was on the wrong side, and the sun porch had too many windows to match Ashfield, but the spirit of the place seemed the same. Agatha stood by the runningboard of her car for a time, reminiscing.

Then she remembered her mission and screwed up her courage as she approached the front door. A girl of three or four answered and stood looking up at the strange lady and sucking at a pink finger.

"Hello there, my dear," Agatha smiled. "Are you the lady of the house?"

The girl laughed and shook her head vehemently.

"Does the pussy cat have your tongue?"

The girl thought that over, then announced. "My grampa is sick."

"Oh, I'm most sorry to hear that."

The child's mother came up the landing. "Bertie, I asked you not to answer the door by yourself. Now you run along."

Bertie did as directed without complaint. The mother, a slight, graceful woman in her twenties, turned her conversational face to Agatha.

"May I help you?"

"What a lively little one you have."

"Oh, thank you. She can be a handful."

"I was so in hopes there would be children in this house. It reminds me so very much of my childhood home. My name is Agatha Christie. This is the home of Colonel Husted, is it not? Colonel Algerdyce Husted?"

"Yes, it is. I'm his daughter-in-law, Rebecca Husted."

"I have come with a rather odd request. You see I'm doing some research for a new book and I was wondering if I might have a few words with the Colonel. It's about the war, you see, and—"

"Christie. Oh, yes, it finally dawns on me," Rebecca's eyes brightened. "I thought your name was familiar. You are the mystery writer, aren't you?"

"I plead guilty to that."

"My mother-in-law reads all your stories, religiously. Won't you come in?"

"Thank you."

"But I'm afraid that we won't be able to help you very much, as far as an interview with the Colonel. You see, the Colonel is not here. He was taken ill during the night and Mother had to rush him to hospital."

"Oh, I'm sorry to hear that. Anything serious?"

"It apparently is his appendix. Imagine a man his age coming down with an appendicitis attack! That's why Bertie and I are here. We actually live on the other side of town, but Mother Husted wanted us here so she wouldn't be alone."

"I see I've come at an awkward time."

"Oh, say hello to Mother Husted, all the same. The doctors are operating this evening, and we won't be leaving for the hospital for another hour yet. Please do come in. It will help Mother get her mind off things. And who knows, maybe she can answer your questions for you. I think she knows Dad Husted's stories as well as he does. She's heard them often enough. Let me just see what she's up to."

The young mother skipped into what must be the study, if Agatha's sense of architecture held true. Or maybe the sewing room. Soon Rebecca returned with a big smile on her face.

"Miss Christie, won't you come this way? Mother would love to meet you."

Agatha followed tentatively behind Rebecca into a book-lined room and found a middle-aged lady behind a large masculine desk in the process of opening letters. The older Mrs. Husted wore her nearly white hair pulled straight back and tied in a neat little bun. Agatha guessed she had been a no-nonsense military wife, and was now a doting grandmother. Evidences of children's toys and books were in a tumble on the floor behind her chair.

Rebecca made the introductions and brought forth a comfortable wooden rocker for Agatha.

"Rebecca, dear," Mrs. Husted said, "I have one of Miss Christie's books on the nightstand next to my bed. Do be a dear and fetch it for me. Perhaps I can persuade Miss Christie to autograph it for me."

"I'd be delighted," Agatha said.

"Won't be a minute," Rebecca said, on her way to the bedroom.

"I'm enjoying it immensely," Mrs. Husted said, "It is one of your more recent efforts, I believe. *Death in the Air.*"

"Oh, you have an American edition?" Agatha asked.

"Why, yes. My brother is in New York. He knows I enjoy mysteries and he sent me a copy. However did you know?"

"Oh, they change titles sometimes for the foreign read-ers. Whyever for, I am not always sure. Here at home that story is titled *Death in the Clouds.* Now isn't that silly?"

The ladies had a little laugh over this, which seemed to put them on friendly terms. Then Mrs. Husted returned her attention to the papers before her.

"I'm just trying to catch up on the Colonel's correspon-dence here," the Colonel's wife said. "What can we do for you, Miss Christie?"

"I'm doing some research about the Germans' use of

gas as a military weapon, and I understand from the
Army records your husband was in charge of the Quartermaster Company stationed at Simes during the gas attack."

"Yes, he was most certainly there. I don't know that the
company had been officially turned over to him at that
time. I rather think not. He had just been promoted to
Major, then. That I do remember."

"But he was one of the officers who suffered the attack?"

"He was one of the fortunate few who was sealed in
the supply bunker during the attack. Is that what you
mean?"

"Supply bunker?"

"Yes. Some supplies had to be kept clean and sterile, if
at all possible, and the bunkers were used. They were
portable devices that could be moved from location to
location and then buried, to protect against the bombard-
ments. As it turned out, they also proved to be excellent
protection against the German mustard gas, since they
could be sealed."

"I see."

"You know, it is strange that you should come by,
asking about the war. Just yesterday one of his fellow officers dropped by and had the longest talk with my husband about the old military days."

"A fellow officer . . . from the company? Are you certain of that?"

"Of course. The man said it was regarding a regimental
reunion. But there is no regimental reunion planned that
we know of, because they just had one about a year and a
half ago. I think he was lonely and simply wanted to
reminisce. You know how some of these old soldiers are.
They seem to enjoy each other's company more than
anything else. I should remember the chap's name, since
he did serve under my husband for a time. Square-
shouldered chap with a big mustache. Of course, there is
no earthly reason why you should know him."

"Was it Fleming? Captain Oswald Fleming?"

The lady's eyes flicked wide open. "Why yes, I do believe you are right. How on earth did you know that?"

Mrs. Husted had continued opening her husband's letters as they talked. And now, before Agatha could answer her question, Mrs. Husted turned upside-down what appeared to be an empty envelope she had just opened and watched in fascination as one small white feather fluttered out of the envelope, down onto the desk. Mrs. Husted drew in her breath in a gasp.

Agatha could not see what the scare was all about. She leaned forward and examined the feather. It looked just like the thousands she had seen on the table and stuck to the wings of the costume in Dorothy Sayers' dining room. She gave a little chuckle of bewilderment.

Mrs. Husted saw nothing humorous about it. Her face had turned ashen as she looked again at the address on the envelope. Then she called in a loud, severe voice, "Rebecca! Come in here, right this minute."

Rebecca very quickly did appear, with the Christie novel, which she handed to Agatha for signing.

"Yes, Mother?"

"Do you know anything about this?" She pointed to the feather and handed her the envelope.

The feather seemed to have the same effect on the daughter-in-law.

"Why, no. No, nothing, whatsoever."

They finally moved the envelope around at an angle so that Agatha could get a peek at it. Only a recipient's typewritten address showed. On the first line she thought she could make out the Colonel's name.

"What an odd thing to do," Agatha smiled. "Is that a new way to send greeting cards or something?"

"No, it is not," Mrs. Husted said, with heavy bitterness. "You know what it means, don't you, Rebecca?"

Rebecca solemnly nodded her head. "In the military it is a sign of cowardice. Someone is accusing the Colonel of . . ."

The two Husted ladies stood staring at the innocent-looking little feather for what to Agatha seemed the longest time. Then the senior Mrs. Husted came angrily to life. she scooped up the feather and threw it and the envelope into the study wastebasket, as if she were her grandchild throwing a tantrum.

"I'm only thankful that Algerdyce wasn't here to receive that . . . disgusting . . . hideous thing."

"You mustn't upset yourself, Mother. It may be someone's idea of a joke."

"There never, never was a more stalwart, honest, hardworking man on all the earth than your father-in-law. The very idea that he could be a coward is so . . . It is so unjust."

"Of course it is, Mother. You mustn't let it upset you. We'll say no more about it."

"Of course we shan't. The very idea."

Something knocked hard against the study door, and the three ladies turned to see Bertie come in, astride a large scruffy-looking hobbyhorse and carrying a small wooden sword.

"I'm Daddy. Look, I'm Daddy."

"Oh, Bertie," the mother scolded, "don't drag that dirty thing in here."

"Oh, leave the child alone, Rebecca. My girl Helen can clean up after her. She has nothing better to do these days."

"Well, take it out in the other room, then, Bertie," Rebecca ordered.

"Dickie is lonesome," she patted her shaggy steed. "He wants to be in here."

"Of course he does," Grandmother cooed. "He needs to eat some grass in Grampa's study, doesn't he?"

Bertie nodded agreement and proceeded to let her horse have his feed.

"You have to learn how to humor the child, my dear," Grandmother explained to her daughter-in-law.

Out of the corner of her eye, Agatha thought she detected Rebecca's eyes rolling toward the ceiling for just a split second.

"Yes, Mother, you're right," Rebecca said, pleasantly enough, without a hint of resentment.

Agatha busied herself with a nice inscription on the flyleaf of her book, then handed it over to its owner.

A telephone bell rang somewhere in the interior of the house and Mrs. Husted jumped. Her eyes froze on the door to the hall and Agatha's signed mystery, *Death in the Air*, dropped from her hands. Before long the maid gave a weak rap on the open door.

"Excuse me, ma'am."

Mrs. Husted was already on her feet. "Yes, Helen, what is it?"

"It's the hospital, ma'am. They want you to come right over. It's the Colonel . . ."

Mrs. Husted hurried out of the room toward the telephone.

"I do hope it is not bad news," Agatha said.

Rebecca gathered up her daughter and her toys, much to Bertie's chagrin, and carried them out of the room.

When no one came back into the study, Agatha put on her driving gloves and started toward the front door.

Mrs. Husted was still on the phone, but she did see her guest and called to her.

"Oh, Mrs. Christie, I'm terribly sorry. I don't mean to be rude. But there has been a change. My husband is much worse. I'm trying to get a taxi now, to get over there as fast as I can."

"My car is right out front," Agatha said. "I would be more than happy to take you there, if that would be agreeable with you, Mrs. Husted."

It didn't take her long to accept the offer. The normally self-possessed woman hurried about frantically until she had a purse under her arm and a hat to put on her head. By that time, her daughter-in-law had gotten Bertie settled down with the maid and she, too, joined them.

"There's no need for you to go . . ." Mrs. Husted started. But Rebecca was adamant about going along to the hospital with her mother-in-law.

Once they were in the car and Mrs. Husted had given Agatha brisk directions to the hospital, she then settled into a series of worried phrases, which she repeated over and over.

"I thought it was strange they would want to operate in the evening. Whoever heard of operating on a person in the evening? Just for appendicitis?"

Rebecca tried to calm her, but she was not a woman to be calmed.

"Oh, be still, girl," she scolded Rebecca. "You have no idea what I'm going through. No idea at all."

"Mother Husted," Rebecca frowned, "don't forget I'm married to Henry, your own son. I do know how I would feel if Henry were in danger."

Agatha pulled her big car into the main entrance of the hospital grounds. The very agitated white-haired lady was out of the car before it had come to a complete stop and went into the building at a trot.

Agatha parked her somewhat cumbersome auto, and a few minutes later she and Rebecca went inside, only to find Mrs. Husted sitting with a doctor near the entrance. Her eyes were already red from crying. The doctor got up when he saw Rebecca and took her hand.

"I'm so sorry. We did everything we could do."

"He's gone?" Rebecca said in disbelief.

"We didn't realize until it was too late that he had the poison in his system."

"Poison?" Agatha gasped. "You mean he was poisoned? Deliberately?"

The doctor shook his head. "We don't know anything of the kind. We don't know how it got into his system. It most likely was in something he ate. After all, this is summer. Perhaps a poison mushroom or bad fish. If it is the right condition it wouldn't take much . . ."

"Muscarine," Agatha whispered.

The doctor looked at her in surprise. "Why yes, that was it exactly. It effects the voluntary movements in the nervous system. How did you know?"

"I'm a trained apothecary," Agatha said.

While the two women cried, the doctor went on justifying the futile efforts of his staff and assuring them that everything humanly possible had been done. By the time the Colonel's stomach had been pumped and the poison identified, it was too late to do anything.

Agatha was shocked, too. But it was for another reason. She found herself stumbling out of the waiting room into the cool evening air of Plymouth. The sun was just going down behind some fleecy clouds in the western sky. It was going to be a beautiful sunset. Much too beautiful for such a sad occasion.

On the steps Agatha breathed deeply and rested against a pillar. It was the closest she had been to losing consciousness since she fainted while pregnant with Rosalind. But she must not faint. She must keep hold of herself and think what to do.

At last a pattern had started to emerge. The note in Dorothy's typewriter was like the white feather, too. Intended to indicate shame or cowardice. Did both men have something to be ashamed of? Both deaths perhaps made to look like accidents or suicide—to cover up murder?

And both connected to Dorothy Sayers. The first, killed in her house and maybe with her husband's gun. And the second: that was what had driven Agatha into the vermilion air of evening, for breathing room, that second part of the pattern . . .

She remembered distinctly that a form of muscarine had been the killing agent in *The Documents in the Case*, the murder mystery written by the masterful storyteller herself, Dorothy L. Sayers.

Agatha's head was reeling.

13

It had taken about two seconds for Dorothy to decide there was nothing she could accomplish sitting next to an empty bed in the hospital in little Shaftesbury. After gathering solemn promises from every staff member she could find that she would be notified at the first sighting of her elusive husband, Dorothy took the first available train for home.

Since she had to change trains in London anyway, she decided to help out her beleaguered staff of seamstresses and pick up three costumes that needed last-minute altering and take them back to Witham with her. Getting her mind on things as mundane as hemlines and theatrical padding was a pleasant respite, and by the time she came huffing down the causeway at Victoria Station to get her Witham train, Dorothy had almost forgotten her load of trouble.

But it was a short-lived respite, for standing before her on the loading ramp next to the first-class coaches was her little shadow, smiling up at Dorothy like the cat that ate the canary. No, that was too mild to apply to her. There definitely was an animal tenacity about the girl, but perhaps more like a fierce tigress stalking its prey on behalf of a den full of hungry cubs awaiting their first meal of flesh and blood. Dorothy mentally retracted her own analogy. Perhaps it was too strong to apply to a mere pest.

"I knew if I waited here long enough, you were bound to show up," Wanda Barton said. "Let me help you with those bundles."

"No, thank you. I can manage."

"We aren't going to be difficult, now are we?" She put a friendly hand on Dorothy's arm. "Why, what a lovely coat you have. Where have I seen it before?"

"Young woman," Dorothy barked, "I don't know how they conduct themselves in America, but this is a civilized nation, and we do not put hands on one another's person unless we know it will be welcomed."

"I just don't want you running out on me again."

Dorothy climbed into the first empty first-class compartment she came to and tried to close the door behind her. But the girl was right with her. She helped Dorothy lift her briefcase and three bundles to the overhead rack, then sat down opposite her prey and smiled her casual smile. Dorothy hoped for other passengers to come in and help curtail the girl's conversational flow, but the train begin moving out.

"I know a secret about you, Miss Sayers," Wanda said in a taunting singsong voice. "I think you better listen, before you read it in the papers."

"What could you possibly know about me from the other side of the Atlantic? I never realized before what a narrow body of water that was."

Wanda laughed, then pulled a newspaper out of her coat pocket and turned it so Dorothy could see a small article.

"It's from your Witham weekly. You're keeping big secrets from the world, it appears."

It was the same article about a dead man found in the home of Major and Mrs. "Mac" Fleming.

"How did you persuade them to use your married name?" Wanda asked. "Very clever. Before you told me, I didn't even know you were married. And I'll bet most Britishers don't know it either."

"Where did you find that old thing?" Dorothy asked.

"Oh, it's surprising how desperate you can get for reading material while waiting your turn in the . . . what is it you call your toilets over here? The 'loo'? You have such quaint euphemisms for life's basic needs. I think I really prefer 'W.C.' though. What do the initials stand for, anyway?"

"Water closet."

" 'Water closet.' How perfectly British. Even your euphemisms have euphemisms."

Dorothy took the newspaper out of Wanda's hands and stuck it in the newspaper rack next to her seat. "What is it you expect to get out of that harmless article?"

"Harmless? Listen, dear, I've got a nose for news," Wanda cooed. "I know the papers here in London would be very interested to know that one of their nation's leading mystery writers has gotten herself embroiled in some messy, unexplained death. They'll be falling all over each other trying to get exclusive stories and prying into your background. They'll have a field day. Don't forget what happened when Agatha Christie went wandering off and sent half the nation's bobbies into a wild goose chase over the bogs and moors of the countryside, in search of kidnappers and villains of all sorts. We even got headlines back in the States about it. Think of all the newspapers it sold. Such a civilized country, isn't it?" Her rude inflection gave her sarcasm a stinging twist.

"Young woman," Dorothy sighed, "you are getting yourself into things you do not understand. Why don't you leave well enough alone?"

"Oh, I have no intention of talking to any London papers. That is, as long as I get my in-depth interview with England's leading mystery writer. How about it?"

"I think that can be arranged. I'll see what E.C. Bentley is doing a week from Thursday. Would that be too soon?"

Wanda laughed. "Honestly, you should be writing for the *New Yorker*. You're so bright."

"You're too kind." Dorothy drummed her fingers on the armrest. "How can you expect me to be giving out interviews as if I didn't have a care in the world? For your information, my husband has vanished from his hospital bed."

"Oh, I think he's all right."

"Oh, you do. You are an expert, are you?"

"I know he left the hospital under his own power."

"And just how do you know that, when the hospital staff doesn't know it?"

"Because I checked with the garage where they took his damaged car after his accident. The car disappeared about fifteen minutes after you found him missing from his hospital bed. He's probably at home waiting for you right now. You left town a little too soon. I'm surprised that you, a mystery writer, didn't think to check that little detail."

"Why does everyone assume that because one writes mysteries one should automatically be the world's greatest detective?"

Wanda gave another self-satisfied laugh, then leaned forward so her face was inches from Dorothy's. "How about that in-depth interview with 'one'?"

Dorothy sighed and shook her head in resignation. "Will I have the right to read over your finished manuscript before you submit it to your editor?"

"Of course," Wanda shrugged. "There now, that wasn't so difficult for 'one,' was it?"

"We aren't going to spend the entire interview time listening to your too-cute-for-words, sarcastic Americanisms, are we?"

" 'One' promises to keep them to a bare minimum."

Just as Wanda pulled her notebook out of her pocket, a conductor opened the sliding door.

"Tickets, please."

Both ladies found their tickets and handed them over. But the conductor shook his head at the sight of Wanda's.

"So sorry, miss. This is first class. You'll have to move back two cars."

"Hey, wait a minute." Wanda looked at her ticket, then started through her handbag. "I can pay . . . You know, I think that ticket seller gypped me."

The conductor scowled. "I hardly think so, madam."

"You know, you people have the craziest money system over here. I'm running low . . ."

"If madam will come with me, please. We can adjust your ticket at the next stop, if you wish."

Wanda appealed to Dorothy with her eyes.

"So sorry, my dear," Dorothy smiled, "perhaps another time."

"Now, remember about the interview," Wanda called as she was led away, "you promised."

When the train began braking for the first stop, Dorothy hid in the W.C. She stayed out of sight until she heard the conductor's call for Witham, then quickly gathered up her possessions and edged toward the door, hoping to be off and into the Witham taxi before the girl had time to know what had happened.

The train was still gliding to a stop when Dorothy with her bundles hurried down the steps, then hurried from one side of the station to the other, frantically searching for Bantam Lapwood and his taxi. But he was not to be found. Of all the times for him to be napping somewhere . . . Then Dorothy's eye caught sight of a middle-aged woman standing next to a large, rather ancient Morris auto. And she was waving in Dorothy's direction.

Agatha Christie. Damn!

Caught between the devil and the deep blue sea, Dorothy quickly decided she was not in a position to be choosy. She hitched up her load and rambled toward Agatha and the open car door as quickly as she could manage.

Agatha started to ask if she could give Dorothy a lift, but before she could get the sentence out, Dorothy had thrust herself and her bundles headlong into the back seat of the car.

"Go. Let's drive away. Hurry, dear, if you don't mind."

Agatha, quite taken back, got herself behind the wheel without argument and ground the Morris into action.

As they drove away, Dorothy looked toward the train in time to see Wanda running in their direction. She came to a frustrated halt at the end of the platform, just as Agatha shifted her car into second gear.

"Is that someone you are trying to avoid, Dorothy?"

"Yes. A fledgling reporter trying to make a name for herself. And American on top of it."

"American? Why on earth—"

"It's a very long story." Dorothy straightened her bundles into a semblance of order and caught her breath. "Speaking of stories, what is Agatha Christie doing back in little Witham? I should think you had had enough of this town, after the dressing-down I handed you at the tea room the other day, for which I do now apologize. I was not myself that afternoon. I hope you will understand that."

For some unknown reason Agatha let out a girlish giggle. "It's quite all right. I think I understand. Better than you might realize."

"But seriously, what *are* you doing back in town?"

"I'm here to talk to you. Should I take you home?"

"If you wouldn't mind. Can you find your way?"

"Yes. It seems like only yesterday I walked to and from your house."

"Um-hum."

"As a matter of fact, it is about that same business that I'm here now."

"Agatha," Dorothy said, in a threatening tone.

"Now, please don't be upset again. I know you think the worst of me, even though there is no earthly reason why you should. I really want to help you. Please listen to what I have to say."

Dorothy was sitting with her head against the seat back, eyes closed, rubbing her temples as though she were fighting a headache. "I'm listening. I'm listening."

Agatha regripped the steering wheel for support and began, "Dorothy, do you know a Colonel Algerdyce Husted?"

"No, I don't . . . Wait a minute—my husband served with a Major Husted, I believe."

"That's the man. Dorothy, listen to me . . ."

Agatha pulled the car to a stop next to the small band-stand in the town's central park. She turned around so she could face Dorothy.

"The man is dead. I believe he was killed by the same person, or persons, that killed the Harcroft Dean."

Dorothy dropped her hands and stared at Agatha.

"What? What are you talking . . . no, it simply cannot be. You mean he has been shot as well?"

"No, not shot. He's been poisoned."

"And what makes you think there is a connection?"

"It's the military thing, you see. He was in your husband's regiment."

"That does it." Dorothy opened the door to get out. "I'm not going to listen to any more of this. I can walk from here, thank you."

"Dorothy, please listen. This isn't a game anymore. It is deadly serious."

"You have no business doing this to me. Leave the thing alone. That is what we pay the police for."

Bundles under control, she stepped out onto the grass to make her getaway.

"Dorothy, I met your son, Anthony."

Dorothy froze in place for a second, then turned back to face Agatha, her eyes narrowing in anger. "And just what do you expect to make out of that? How dare you—"

"He's a fine boy, Dorothy. I'm sure you must be very proud of him."

Dorothy was reeling from the jolt of her exposure. "And just what do you expect to make out of that?" she repeated numbly.

"Make out of . . . ? Why nothing. I only wanted you to know I understand. Dean Matthews came to your house to talk about Anthony's schooling, didn't he?"

Dorothy dumped her things on the back seat and climbed into the passenger seat next to her nemesis. She was trembling all over, as if from a winter chill. Her plump hands were turned into fists and she used them on her knees, slowly and lightly, as though searching for the right gesture that would explain everything. Suddenly her frustration gave way to tears, and she rested her head against the dashboard, sobbing.

Agatha put the car back into gear and started slowly on their way. Within a block Dorothy had recovered enough to wipe her tears away and breath more normally.

"He was born out of wedlock," she said dryly. "I suppose you had surmised as much. Not something I'm proud of, but there it is. A love child. From a love match. Not so unusual, really. There were plenty of girls who lost the great love of their lives as a result of the war. Girls who wanted to 'give themselves' in some sort of twisted concept of patriotism. Not that I'm begging excuses. My only excuse was love—and I wanted the experience. Already into my thirties and I thought I was missing out. The meaningful things of life were slipping by and I wasn't going to know what it was all about."

Dorothy went on, talking randomly, to the windshield more than to Agatha. For her part, Agatha only nodded and kept a light foot on the gas pedal. Once she opened up, it seemed Dorothy had trouble stopping, but Agatha didn't mind. Dorothy went on about how Anthony had been raised by an aunt whom she was convinced was heaven sent. How she had hoped to bring Anthony into their home in Witham, but because of Mac's drinking and other family pressures, it never seemed to happen.

"And now, finally making a change in my writing career—the change that I had struggled to make for some time—I have again put my son—my acknowledgment of my son—back in the closet, as it were. Any nation that refuses its intended king the woman he loves because she is a divorced woman is certainly not going to allow a woman of my ilk to write its religious dramas." She sighed and wiped away a lingering tear.

"Then I come home to my house, expecting to find Anthony's schoolmaster in my disheveled den, but instead I find his body. And I panic and compound my crime by lying through my teeth about knowing the man. To admit that would mean admitting everything, and I wasn't ready to do that. Foolish of me. I know now I could never have gotten away with it for long, but once I started lying I couldn't seem to stop. I thought if only I could keep up the façade until the play opened. Why I thought that would make a difference, I haven't the slightest idea. Very foolish. But then, when you come down to it, I guess I am a very foolish woman. But it is all over now."

"What do you mean, 'over'?"

"I mean, it is only a matter of time before the whole thing unravels, just like a ball of your knitting yarn. Especially since there has been no resolution about Dean Matthews' death. Things will continue to be turned over and examined. And at the bottom of that examination will be Dorothy L. Sayers and her dirty little secret. You have been able to put the pieces all together, and the press is bound to get it right in time. That American freak who hounds my every move is certainly no one's fool. I think I fear her more than any of the others . . .

"Now you understand why I had to throw cold water on the Detection Club investigation. I congratulate you, Agatha. You've proven to be quite a detective in your own right."

"Haven't you wondered why I did it?"

"I thought it was out of spite."

"Spite? Me? Why, no. Your secret is certainly safe with me."

"Well, whatever the reason, my hat is off to you."

Agatha pulled up in front of Dorothy's house. There was no sign of Mac's car. Or the American girl, for that matter. Dorothy's hand had been on the door handle for the last two blocks, and when the car stopped moving she got out immediately.

"What are you going to do?" Agatha asked.

"I'm going to ring up my friend Val Gielgud and tell him to cancel the play. Then I shall sit at home and wait for the roof to fall in. Thank you, Agatha, for the ride.

And for the use of your dashboard. I think I needed that little emotional release. Perhaps it brought me to my senses."

Before Dorothy could gather up her things, Agatha was out of the car and at her side. She took two of her packages and walked with her to the door.

"Dorothy, listen to me for one more minute. You are giving in because you think it is inevitable that your secret be found out. I don't think that necessarily has to be the case. It has been my experience that authorities, very much like the rest of us, can only follow one train of thought at a time. Now suppose, just suppose, it would be possible to keep the police and the press from concentrating on Dean Matthews and his reason for being at your house that day."

"How am I supposed to bring that small miracle about?"

"By making them think about what really did happen. By making them start looking for the murderer in another direction."

"Murderer? Are you so sure it was murder and not suicide?"

"I am."

"And you think you can solve the murder?"

"No, certainly not me. But I think I—we—can help the police enough to point them in the right direction, and away from the reason for Dean Matthews' visit."

Dorothy considered this for a moment, then shook her head. "It's impossible. I'm so very tired. So tired of trying to excel. While at the same time, to cover up . . . I feel like going to bed and sleeping for a month."

"I know the feeling. It wasn't long ago that I was at my wit's end. I've always felt, if only I had had someone to help me. A friend I could turn to . . . someone with a bit different perspective on events . . . things might have turned out ever so much differently."

"Thank you for the offer, Agatha. Very kind of you, I'm sure. But realistically, what can we do? We're a couple of stodgy, middle-aged storytelling dames."

"Well . . ." Agatha hesitated for a moment, then squared her shoulders and brought her chin forward. "We can try, can't we? If you are game, then I'm game."

Dorothy measured Agatha's words with suspicion. As usual, her moments of depression did not last long. A trace of her old pixie grin reappeared at the corners of her mouth. The grin was followed quickly by a full smile.

"The house is a sight, but would you like to come inside where we can talk?"

14

Dorothy had barely opened her front door when the four play production women gathered in the dining room stood up in unison and descended upon her like bees drawn to honey. Two of them stripped Dorothy of her bundles and headed for portable sewing machines set up on the large, disheveled table. The other two wanted immediate answers to very pressing questions. Where was the letter granting permission for the amateur performers to appear with the professionals? What was to be done about the lighting problem in the second act? The play's director and the lighting technician weren't speaking, so Dorothy would have to decide. And two of the stage actors in Act Three didn't have time to make a costume change. Would Dorothy please write a soliloquy for William of Sens to give them time? It should be at least three minutes in length.

While this was going on, Agatha wandered into the kitchen and found Dorothy's cook, Betty, once again in the midst of preparations for lunch. She seemed in much better spirits compared to Agatha's last visit. Agatha made herself useful by offering to trim the crusts off the sandwich bread. A little trick she had discovered while growing up among a houseful of domestics: servants were much more willing to talk and let young Agatha have her way if she pitched in and worked alongside them for a while.

Was Betty feeling better today? How were the Masons

next door getting along? Did Betty ever find out what had happened to the missing potato?

Betty stopped rinsing lettuce leaves and turned to Agatha in surprise. "How on earth did you know about that?"

"Oh, some friends of mine talked to one of the investigating officers, and he mentioned the house had smelled of raw potato when he came in. And then the inquest report mentioned that you had been in the backyard garden looking for an extra potato when Dorothy came home."

Betty shook her head in mock confusion, then returned to her work. "That is amazing. I don't know what it proves, but it certainly is amazing. No, I never did find the mysterious missing potato."

Dorothy appeared in the doorway. "You handle that knife very well, Agatha. If I ever need extra domestic help, I'll know where to come."

Agatha laughed. "Yes, this was my favorite job as a child. Until I sliced my finger rather badly and Mother said I was to confine my domestic work to making the upstairs beds."

Dorothy led her into the sitting room and pulled the large double doors to the dining room closed behind them. She breathed a sigh of relief and sat down heavily on the settee.

"Now, then, what did you have in mind?"

Agatha sat next to Dorothy so their voices could be kept low. "You remember in the car I mentioned about the military man's murder? Colonel Algerdyce . . ."

"Yes, yes. What makes you think it was done by the same person?"

Dorothy's mind worked very quickly and Agatha's slow, pondering manner appeared to make her nervous. As Agatha spoke, Dorothy would jerk her own head about, perhaps hoping this would hurry the lady's delivery.

"Because of the military connection," Agatha answered.

"What military connection? Just because my husband was in the same military group?"

"There's more than that. Much more. There is the matter of the odd handgun, which seems to have been unique to that one military group."

"But the newspaper said that Dean Matthews wasn't even in the Army. He spent his entire military service in the Royal Navy."

Agatha nodded. "I know. That had me stumped, too, for the longest time, but you see, that part was a mistake."

Dorothy shook her head in confusion. "I'm sorry, Agatha, but you have lost me. What was a mistake? The killing of the Dean?"

"Exactly."

Agatha got to her feet and started pacing in tight little circles. "Please excuse me, but when I get excited about a story I just have to move about a bit."

"But we're not writing a story here. We're talking about things that have truly happened."

"Yes, I know, but it seems to help if I treat it as if I were working on a story. Now that I have the faces and the characterizations of some of the players, it seems to play itself out, just as if it were a made-up story.

"Let me tell you the events that happened in your house that day. At least as I think they must have happened, because this is the only way I can get all the odd pieces to fit." Agatha began to count them off on her fingers. "The cook's story, the typed note, the potato problem, and the fact that no one heard the report from the gun."

"Just a moment. I want to get this down." Dorothy got a pencil and some writing paper out of a nearby desk and readied herself for dictation.

"Very well," Agatha began. As she made each point she used a strange downward hand movement, as if she were a carpenter pounding home a nail. "Betty lets your schoolmaster, Dean Matthews, in the front door, just as she said she did. He comes in and sits at the dining room table, or at the typewriter stand, and waits. He's expecting the woman of the house any minute. Now the cook

goes about her duties, which in her mind include helping
the elderly couple next door. The Masons, I believe. Something about moving a boiler about to prepare for canning
of fruits or something. That probably makes a bit more
noise than normal, but she thinks she can still hear everything going on in her own home, because she has her ear
out for the sound of the telephone.

"Now the murderer approaches the house. Probably he
does not come in the front door. My guess is he comes in
the back of the house, or first looks in the dining room
windows and sees a man sitting inside. This is where he
makes a big mistake. He sees a heavily built, middle-aged
man and assumes he is peeking in at the man of the
house, Major Mac Fleming—"

Dorothy gasped. "You mean . . . my husband was to be
the victim?"

"I think so. It's the only way the rest of this makes any
sense. That could explain the wording on the note—
'Dorothy, darling, I can't go on,' et cetera. That was supposed to be the husband with a guilty conscience about
something, leaving a farewell note to his wife. The note
really reads more like a husband and wife exchange than
it does a secret paramour exchange, don't you agree?
That's why it is unsigned. It was typed by the murderer
and not the dead man. You see, Dean Matthews simply
stopped by your house at exactly the wrong time."

Dorothy was so enthralled she had completely forgotten
to take notes. She started to now, but then stopped.

"But this doesn't explain why there was no gunshot."

"No, no, it doesn't. Not yet." Agatha paced again, making more of her little hammer strokes. "Now this is the
reason I feel the murderer came in by the back door."

Agatha's eyes drifted off into the distance, and she
acted out the murderer's actions as she described them. It
made a strange sight: a matronly woman in a tea party
hat, print dress, and high-heeled shoes crouching stealth-
ily in the sitting room, with one index finger being used
as a handgun.

"He has his gun ready. He has come with the specific intention of killing. He comes in the back through the kitchen. In the kitchen, or maybe on the back porch, he sees some potatoes—"

"Yes, I remember Betty telling me," Dorothy interrupted, "she had just put her groceries on the kitchen table when Dean Matthews rang the front door."

Agatha nodded. "Now this is the part that convinced me this whole thing must be connected with the military. The murderer picks up a potato and pierces it with the barrel of the automatic pistol. Then he moves into the dining room and up to the Dean, and before the Dean knows what is happening the murderer shoots him in the head, the report from the gun greatly muffled by the potato."

Dorothy laughed. "The potato? What nonsense—"

Agatha waved her to silence. "No, no. Not nonsense. There is a very sound reason for it. My brother was in several military campaigns in the Boer War. He told me that when they wanted to fire at the enemy without being detected they would spear an African beet or potato on the bayonet of their single shot rifles. Jammed against the barrel of the gun, it works just as well as the very expensive silencers. It would also explain why there were no powder burns on the body. The potato absorbed the extra powder as well as the noise.

"Now who would know such a trick except an experienced military man? The murderer used an automatic pistol as well. If they had used a revolver—you know, the kind that has the little wheelie thing with the bullets in it—why, the silencer effect wouldn't have worked because there is an air space between the little wheel and the barrel of the gun and the noise would spill out that way. I'm quite certain the murderer is an experienced military man. Probably an officer."

Dorothy was sitting listening to all of this with her mouth open and her eyes nearly popping. She was seeing "Awkward Agatha" Christie in a totally new light. She had forgotten again about her note taking. All she could say was, "Yes, I see . . . I think."

Agatha finally sat down, smoothed out the front of her dress and smiled. "Let's see now, have I missed anything?"

"Not that I can think of . . . Except, you said there was another murder."

"Oh, yes. I was out to Plymouth to visit the Quartermaster Company's commanding officer. A Colonel Husted."

"Plymouth? Mac said he was coming from Plymouth."

"Yes, I know he had been out there. Mrs. Husted described him. Her husband has been poisoned, you see. Killed by muscarine."

Dorothy's head jerked at the word. Agatha pretended not to notice and went right on.

"And the interesting thing, you see, was that on the day of his death he received in the mail a white feather, which I understand is a symbol of cowardice among military people."

"White feather . . ."

"Yes," Agatha laughed lightly, "very much like the white feathers you used for your angel wings. Isn't that a coincidence?"

Dorothy scowled. "Yes, isn't it?"

"You see, I feel the white feather and the typewriter note you found here do the same sort of thing—both are designed to make the victims appear to be cowards. Now, of course, I'm skating on rather thin ice. I'm only imagining most of this. But I feel the murderer wants to kill people he feels have done something wrong. Something to be ashamed of—and he wants the rest of the world to know about it."

Agatha waited for a reaction. When Dorothy didn't move, she went on.

"My brother, as I say, has had considerable experience seeing men under combat conditions, and he has told me our ideas of heroism and selfless bravery are . . . well, greatly exaggerated. He contends that war only brings out the worst traits in men. Could it be we are dealing with something like that in this matter?" She looked again at Dorothy and waited for her to volunteer.

"My husband has given me very few specifics about the war. Except to say it was terrible. He suffers from it still. He was gassed. Did I tell you? Primarily it damaged his stomach lining and his esophagus. Of course mustard gas is no respecter of persons. It would strike down heros as well as . . . cowards."

"Please forgive me. I certainly don't know that your husband was anything but heroic."

Dorothy patted her on the forearm. "Quite all right, my dear. We are only considering possibilities. And yet, I've had this uneasy feeling in the back of my mind . . . I wonder if you may not be right."

"What makes you say that?"

"I'm not sure. Perhaps because of the way he has been acting. He seems to know more than he is letting on. He has been making lists of his old military friends and . . . What was he doing in Plymouth, I wonder?"

"Perhaps it dawned on him that the bullet that killed Dean Matthews was really meant for him and he went to warn the Colonel."

Dorothy slapped the armrest of the settee in anger. "Oh, this is maddening. Now it is not only for myself that I'm hiding things. Now it's on my husband's behalf. I certainly can't go to the police with a story like this. Think of the terrible onus I would be placing upon my husband, if it turns out that he acted in a cowardly manner. The military was his grandest moment. The highlight of his life. He still keeps a uniform at parade-dress ready upstairs in his room. In times of trouble he still thinks first of his military comrades, as if they could huddle together against the world. A thing like this would break his heart. It would destroy him."

The two women sat in silence, studying the brown paisley pattern in the carpet and listening to the clatter of sewing machines from the other room.

"But two men have died . . ." Agatha reminded her

quietly. "What else can we do? We can't very well sit and do nothing."

Dorothy struggled to her feet. "Wait here. I have an idea."

She pushed open one of the sliding doors and went out. Very quickly, she was back, with a small leather case in her hands. She put it on the settee between herself and Agatha.

"This is Mac's shaving kit. He left it behind in the hospital when he slipped out after his accident."

"His accident?"

Dorothy explained as best she could about Mac's strange auto accident on his way home from Plymouth and the hospital episode the next day.

"Why, how extraordinary," Agatha said. "One might think he had something to hide."

"Oh, Agatha," Dorothy laughed, "you can say the most mundane things. And the next minute, you are doing something quite extraordinary yourself. I have totally underestimated you in the past."

"Yes, well, sometimes it is the mundane that has to be said first, don't you think?"

"If it helps you with your thought processes, I certainly agree."

Dorothy opened the case. On top of the two straight-edge razors and the shaving mug was a folded sheet of paper. Dorothy opened it and showed the handwritten list of names and addresses.

"I saw him compiling this list two days ago. It might give us an idea of what he has been up to. It must have some immediate importance to him. Why else would he be carrying it with him in this manner?"

Five of the names had been crossed out. Three of them with the notation "dead" scrawled next to them. Another with "Australia" and the fifth, "ment. case," which they took to mean the man had been institutionalized. General Pike's name had been checked, as had that of Colonel Husted. There was only one name not checked. That of a

Major Bruce, Queen's Hermitage, Littenbe Road, Croydon. Agatha put her finger on the address.

"Isn't that part of the large military hospital? We used to make up occasional prescriptions for Queen's Hermitage when I was with the Army Chemist Office."

Dorothy shrugged. "If you say so."

"It couldn't be far from London. Would you be interested in taking a run down there, to see this Major Bruce?"

"Yes, I would. Perhaps the Major can tell me what has happened to my husband."

Dorothy gave a lick and a promise to the production problems in the dining room, and they were on their way.

15

During the highway ride south, the two ladies had a chance to get acquainted as never before. They had known one another for several years and even worked on two of the Detection Club book projects rather closely. But this was the first time they had confided personal matters to one another, the way close friends do.

They were amazed to discover how many similarities existed between them, in spite of their different personalities. Both had brought an only child into the world from an early love union—Agatha's, of course having been done the more traditional way. Both had separated from their first loves and were now married to rather unique mature men, with similar sounding abbreviated Christian names—Dorothy's Mac and Agatha's Max.

Even their writing careers had similarities. Early on both had adopted strong-willed, brilliant, although conceited, fictional detectives in their writing. And, they were surprised to learn both had grown rather sick of their creations.

"One day he simply walked into my life," Dorothy said about Lord Peter Wimsey, "spats and all, and while I do appreciate the bread he has put on my meager table, I have grown to resent the superior tone he always takes. I've found him quite headstrong and limiting in what I am able to say as a writer. When I have wanted to branch off into a different point of view, there stood Peter with his back up, demanding that his monacle be polished or the wine be served at two degrees above room temperature."

Agatha cooed agreement. "Oh, you don't know how good it is for me to hear you say that. I thought I was being ungrateful in my resentment toward my little Belgian, Hercule Poirot. Why I made my detective a Belgian I shall never know. Well, yes I do. I needed someone, and at the time there were all these Belgian refugees living down the street, and the idea popped into my head. Have you any notion how difficult it has been to keep that silly accent of his going? And who knows how Belgian people live or what they are like? I'm afraid I've made him up more of whole cloth than I have of true Belgian."

Dorothy was laughing so much tears were forming in her eyes.

"I know, I know. And how many times I've regretted making mine an aristocrat. I thought the reading public would find him more interesting with a title. But what do I know about how the better half lives?" Dorothy paused just long enough to wipe her eyes clear. "In fact, I was rather hoping that the public would loose interest in Peter once I had married him off."

Agatha took her eyes off the road long enough to study her new friend. "You're quite serious about that? About not doing any more Peter Wimsey stories?"

"Yes, I am."

"But they've done so very well for you. Why would you want to stop writing them?"

"Oh, I don't know that I can explain it. Perhaps it is something that my father instilled in me. To excel. Maybe it is not so much that I am limited by Lord Peter Wimsey; maybe it is more that I feel limited by the genre. The mystery reader is primarily interested in finding out who did the murder. The other aspects of the book are really secondary to him. The things about people's lives, their relationships with others, with God.

"I don't mean to imply that the Almighty has tapped me on the shoulder and given me my marching orders. But I have this interest. This . . . something burning inside me that is crying for expression. I think our nation is drifting from its spiritual roots, and I want to be a part of drawing them back. To bring the godhead into their lives in a meaningful, powerful way.

"If this little Nazi character over in Germany is really going to start acting up, our nation is going to need all the moral and spiritual backbone it can find. I want to be a part of that. I want . . ."

Her normally strong voice had slipped into a falsetto. She had to wait for emotions to settle to continue. "Listen to me, preaching about God and morality. The events of the last two weeks make it clear to me I haven't any right. No right."

Agatha watched Dorothy fight back the tears again but said nothing more. She only pressed down a bit harder on the petrol pedal.

Once they reached the outskirts of Croydon their time was taken up with getting their bearings and locating the part of the large hospital complex where the Major had his residence. By the time they did it was approaching the dinner hour. Rather than knock on a stranger's door at that time of day, they decided to find something to eat first. Fortunately, in a large building a few blocks from Major Bruce's residence, they discovered a cafeteria for hospital staff members and guests of the institution's patients.

They queued up behind two older men wearing pajamas and bathrobes and waited to be served their portion of institutional food. It was a strangely quiet place. Each table that held visitors had at least one hospitalized veteran as the center of attention. Several of the men were in wheelchairs. A few were well enough to be joking and exchanging comments with family members. But most were not that well, a lingering part of war the enlistment posters somehow failed to mention. The place had a grey pallor to it, which both ladies commented on.

They found a small table by a window, where they could keep an eye on the Major's house while they ate.

The food itself was not all that bad. There had been a concerted effort on the part of the kitchen people to supply most of the basic daily requirements. Although even Dorothy, who normally held her own at any table, could not get far with the iron gelatin.

They were nearly finished when a voice at their elbows startled them.

"Well, imagine meeting you here."

Dorothy looked up into the eyes of the American girl she thought she had left on the steps of the train depot back in Witham.

"You. What is it? How on earth?"

Wanda Barton smiled with pride. "Didn't I tell you I could be tough to get rid of when I made my mind up? I'd say I was doing all right for myself, getting around in a country where they drive on the wrong side of the road and everything. You weren't thinking of jumping out on my interview, where you? Remember, you promised me."

"I hadn't forgotten," Dorothy assured her.

"That's very good for 'one' to hear. So reassuring."

She pulled a chair over from another table and sat herself down without invitation.

"Don't sit down. Don't sit down," Dorothy cried. "We're just leaving."

"Sorry. I beat you to it, didn't I. Who's your friend?"

"I don't think there is any reason why you would need an introduction," Dorothy said, defensively.

"Oh, you never know." Wanda held out her hand to Agatha. "Hi. I'm Wanda Barton, American. Here in England to do a story on the great British mystery writers. And you are . . . ?"

Agatha had opened her mouth, but nothing intelligible was coming out.

" . . . whom she has always been," Dorothy said on Agatha's behalf, then tried to change the subject. "Regarding your article, are you, ah, planning on getting up into Scotland then?"

"No, I think I'll just stay here in Britain."

Dorothy exchanged smiles with Agatha.

"Americans can be so refreshing, can't they?" she said.

"What are you doing here at the hospital?" Wanda asked Dorothy. "You know someone here?"

"Ah, yes, we're here visiting."

"Has your husband been placed here, Miss Sayers?"

"Not that I know of."

Wanda turned to Agatha. "Your husband, perchance?"

"Young lady," Agatha fluttered, "we are not used to being bombarded with questions."

"Yeah, I know. Sorry about that. But try to see things from my angle. My editor says you gotta be pushy. You gotta ask questions in this business. Otherwise you're not going to get your story."

"Would that be so terrible?"

"Yeah, terrible for me. I'm already in the habit of eating. And I've only got a few days before I have to go back. And I'm running short on cash, in case you're interested. I do wish you wouldn't travel around so much, Miss Sayers. You're costing me a bundle."

"And what about the lives of the people you are writing about?" Agatha asked.

"What about them?"

"Has it ever occurred to you that you might be doing irreparable harm to them? That they might carry the scars of what you have written about them for years to come? That families may be broken . . ."

Agatha had gone a bit too far. The quick-witted girl's eyes lit up in recognition, and she wagged a finger in Agatha's direction.

"My god, you're Agatha Christie. I can't believe it. Agatha Christie. The *Ten Little Indians* lady. I can sure understand why you carry a grudge against reporters. But can you believe this? I came across the ocean to see the two of you and here you are together in this tacky little cafeteria next to an old soldiers' home. Mr. Mencken is going to do handstands when he hears about this."

Dorothy pushed herself up from the table. "It's time we were on our way."

"Hey, where are you off to? This is just getting good."

"Miss Christie and I are going to visit our friend. And you—I would like to say where you are going."

Wanda laughed. "Are you remembering our little agreement?"

"I have not forgotten. You'll get your interview. But certainly not here. Not now."

Dorothy and Agatha started to leave, but Wanda put her hand on Dorothy's arm, which did not thrill Dorothy.

"I'm sorry, but I just upped the ante."

Dorothy cleared the air space between them. " 'Upped the Auntie?' "

"Yeah, you know. Like in gambling."

"Your American colloquialisms should be left on the far side of the Atlantic, where they have the mentalities to appreciate them. I haven't the foggiest idea what you are taking about."

"Oh, I think you do," Wanda smiled. "I want an interview with both of you. If not, I intend to phone some Fleet Street contacts I've been given and let them know about you-know-who and you-know-what."

Dorothy burned in silence. Since Wanda seemed to be loosing ground, she changed tactics.

"Sorry to be so mean-hearted about all this. But look, both of you have already made it as writers. Can't you have a little sympathy for a fellow female who's trying to make it, too?"

Agatha seemed to soften. "We will both be happy to help you with an interview," she said, "but not right at the moment. We are on a rather urgent matter. A very sick friend. I'm sure you understand."

"Okay, I can live with that. When? When can you talk? How about later tonight?"

"That is out of the question. Saturday morning would be the first time I could spare. How about you, Dorothy?"

Dorothy looked at her co-conspirator in shock. "Yes, ah, Saturday morning. Fine."

Wanda smiled and shrugged her shoulders. "Okay. At Dorothy's house in Witham?"

Dorothy nodded lamely in agreement.

"But one more thing. What's good to eat around this place?" Wanda examined the crusts on Agatha's plate. "What did you have, Miss Christie?"

"I had a tomato and cheese sandwich on white bread. Very good indeed."

Wanda made a retching sound and wiped her fingers on her trenchcoat. "The food you people eat over here. Hasn't anybody ever heard of hamburgers?"

16

Dorothy rapped on the door of the small cottage and stepped back beside Agatha to await a response. It was one in a long line of identical cottages that stood on the back side of the large military complex. Behind the cottages, a rolling stretch of manicured lawn ran all the way up to the six-story hospital buildings that stood on a rolling bluff, dominating the entire area like a Tibetan monastery. The humble thatched cottages looked somehow out of place on the grounds, as if they had been afterthoughts built by elves to house the seven dwarfs and their cousins. The evening lamps were already lit it in a few cottages, but most of the windows were dark.

When there was a delay in the response, Dorothy said, "I want to thank you for helping me out back there with the young pest. I certainly don't intend to obligate you to the torture of a long interview with the likes of her."

"Mmm. My father was American. Did you know that?"

"No, I did not."

"Yes. They are not all like your young reporter, I assure you. I think it is that harsh surly way they have of pronouncing their R's that disturbs me most about them. That and their enthusiasm. Mind you, I do appreciate enthusiasm in a young person, but I would rather like to understand what it is they are enthusiastic about. Hers seems to grow out of an ignorance of the proper order of things."

Dorothy chuckled. "You know, I don't believe I ever truly knew you before. You say the most remarkable things

146

at times. And the circuitous way you had of bending the truth back there in the cafeteria. It seemed so . . . unlike you."

"Me? Bend the truth?"

"About our 'sick friend.' "

"Yes, well, there it is, isn't it? I've always felt that phrase in the New Testament about not casting your pearls before swine applied to situations like that . . . Do you think he heard us? Maybe we should knock again."

Dorothy knocked again. This time a little louder.

"Yes. Yes, I'm . . . coming . . ." was the weak response from the other side of the door. A tall gaunt man opened the door for them and smiled out. He was so tall and the doorframe so low he had to stoop to get a clear look at his visitors. He had a long straight nose and thick grey eyebrows that moved expressively with his every utterance. The mussed grey hair on his head looked as if he had been lying down when they knocked. His cheeks were hollow and all the muscles and veins in his thin neck were well delineated, but he displayed quick animated movements at the sight of guests. He was still in the process of tying the belt of his bathrobe as he spoke.

"Oh, ladies, do come in. What can I do for you? I don't get very many lady callers."

"Major Bruce?" Dorothy asked.

"Yes, yes. Come in. I'm still getting settled in. I have just returned from a stay up the hill. You must excuse the way things look. Won't you sit down?"

He didn't wait for his guests to be seated, but dropped himself heavily into what was obviously his favorite chair. All his reading material and medications were within easy reach on a windowsill nearby. The rest of the place looked as if it were an officer's quarters in East Rangoon, full of British Army wicker. He had personalized the place a bit with old photographs. One small potted palm stood in the corner, looking sadly neglected. Next to it, his meal tray, which must have been delivered from the kitchen up the hill. It appeared he did not care for tonight's meat loaf with creamed cauliflower.

Dorothy introduced herself and Agatha by their married names. The Major picked up on the "Fleming" immediately.

"You're not Oswald Fleming's wife, perchance?"

"Why, yes I am. Did you know . . . ?"

"Of course I know him. We served in the same regiment together. You must be Dorothy, then."

"Yes, I am."

The Major clapped his hands. "You know what? I have a picture of you around here someplace. Would you believe that?" He started looking about his place without getting up. "Oswald sent it to me shortly after you were married, I believe. It was of the two of you arm-in-arm in some exotic setting . . ."

Dorothy laughed and unconsciously sucked in her waistline. "Yes, I think I remember the picture."

"He was very proud of you. Well, I'm sure he still is. No, come to think of it, it's not here. Must be over in the storage building with my other things. That's the trouble with military hospitals. Other people running your life for you."

So much excited chatter was taking its toll on the Major's endurance. He had to lean back and do nothing but breathe for a while. Dorothy took up the conversational lead.

"Major Bruce, we were wondering if we might ask you some questions about the gassing incident. I believe it was at Simes?"

He nodded. "That's when I got this." He tapped a thumb against his ribcage. He could have been thumping a drum.

"We wouldn't be doing this if it weren't of vital importance," she assured him. "I know my husband has always refused to discuss the incident so I certainly appreciate your feelings. . ."

Major Bruce's laugh was one quick burst. "That is understandable. Ol' Ozzy was out for all of it."

"Out? You mean he wasn't involved in the gas attack?"

"No, I mean he was out. Like a light. Out cold."

He paused again and took two breaths. "Have to excuse the pauses. I'll get it out, if you're patient."

"Of course. We understand. Please take your time."

"What is it you want to know?"

"Oh, just as much about it as you can recall. Who was involved, that sort of thing. We understand there was a bunker that some men were able to get into . . ."

The Major nodded his head and began. As long as he kept his voice soft and broke his story up with long inhaling pauses, he did all right.

"A lot of the men here can't remember a thing about how they got their wounds. Did you know that? But I can remember the gassing as if it were yesterday. In a way I wish I couldn't. Makes you start reliving it in your head. Thinking what you could have done differently. That sort of thing. It can make you go off the deep end if you're not careful.

"It was only April, but the weather was already hot in between the rains. April sixteenth. I was brand-new to the regiment. A year earlier I had been assigned as an adjutant to an American lieutenant colonel. One Colonel O'Rorke by name. Beastly fellow to get on with. Good enough soldier, I imagine, but not the kind of chap you'd care to have in for tea, if you know what I mean. We were supposed to be part of an integrated Allied fighting force. You probably read about it. I think it was primarily for publicity. Locking arms with our friends across the sea to fight the common enemy and all that. Looked good on paper, but it didn't work out well in the field. We have a common language with the Yanks, but they have their own way of doing things and it just wasn't working out. The unit broke up and I had been put with Quartermaster Company of the regiment, probably because they didn't know what else to do with us—my lieutenant and myself. He was put in charge of a squad of foot soldiers and I was put in the supply depot cooling my heels until they knew what to do with me. Good example of how things are run in time of war."

"Were any of the Americans involved in the gas attack?" Agatha asked.

"The Yanks? Oh, no. They had moved out en masse two days before to join up with Pershing's expeditionary force along the line farther south. They were all gone by the time of the attack. Fortunes of war, as they say. We Brits caught it all.

"I remember, I was sitting on the edge of my bunk when the first shell came in. About eight-thirty in the morning. We had heard rumors about what to expect. The canisters were noisier than the regular ninety-millimeter stuff they used for bombardment. Noisier in the air, that is. But when it hit, the canisters would spill open, sounding something like a pumpkin dropping from the top of Gibraltar. Loud of course, but not like the fragment shells they use against personnel.

"I had just gotten my boots on when I heard the first one come in. First I though it was a dud and I didn't think anything more about it. Just a stray shot to keep us on our toes. The Jerries loved to do that every half hour or so. Occasionally the shots would land well behind the lines, so we knew what they sounded like. But then I heard some women down in the street, coughing their heads off. And another canister came in. That one I heard hit just like they said, like a giant pumpkin hitting a brick wall. I didn't even bother with the helmet and my tunic. I took off for the bunker as fast as I could. I remember thinking, what if someone sees me out of uniform? We were well behind the lines and the dress code was still strictly enforced. What was I going to say? Can you imagine the silly things that go through your mind at a time like that? I was running for my life."

"What about your gas mask?" Agatha asked.

"What mask? I hadn't been issued any. No one had. I was on the top floor of a two-story book bindery we had commandeered for house officers, and by the time I got to the door I could hear people screaming and running about like wild animals, not knowing which way to run because they couldn't see what they were running from. The alarm siren was still silent, I remember that quite distinctly. Don't ask me why. You think about the strangest things when you are under pressure. I remember looking out one of the open windows and seeing a camp cook run by carrying one of the big strainers from the kitchen. And in the other hand he had an empty pillowcase. Now I ask you, where was the man going with that military apparel?

"But back to my story. I had thought ahead of time about what I might do if we came under gas attack. There had been so many wild rumors about what gas can do to you that we were all at the point of being quite irrational in our actions. But I had decided the best place to be was inside the little portable bunker they had given us for medical supplies and such. I knew the book bindery building was too drafty to keep anything out, so I made sure I knew where the bunker key was kept. I got into the supply locker that was kept in Captain Fleming's—well, your husband's—room and got hold of the key. And then at the door I took my last big breath of what I felt was the last good air I would find until the bunker, about a hundred yards from outside the door. I thought I could make it in one breath—'the best laid plans,' as they say.

"Anyway, I opened the door and went out running at my top speed. I rounded the corner of the big laundry tent and only had to make it up the service road and duck in behind the officers' mess tent. But on the far side of the laundry boilers I found"—he looked sheepishly at Dorothy —"well, I found your husband, Captain Oswald Fleming. He was lying unconscious under the wheels of our laundry cart. The two French women we hired to help with the laundry had been bringing back some fresh bedding. And, at the top of the hill, they had let go of the laundry cart when the canisters hit, and the cart had come rolling down the embankment. At the same time Ol' Ozzy had come out of the tent to see what the excitement was all about. The cart pinned him up against the fire boilers. I thought at first it had smashed his chest.

"Anyway, I stopped and got him hoisted up on my shoulders—I was quite a few pounds heavier then—and carried him with me to the bunker. Needless to say, I had to take quite a few breaths by then. Just one of those things you do without thinking. A friend is in danger and you help him. It's as simple as that. There was the distinct smell of mustard, but I didn't notice anything about my lungs during that time at all. That all hit later.

"When I got to the bunker there was someone else already going inside. I didn't have to stop to fumble with the lock after all, but of course I didn't know that at the time I went for the key—wasting valuable seconds, you see. If only I hadn't stopped for the key or for . . . well, it's water over the dam. Water over the dam."

The defeated expression with which he told the story came complete with hand gestures, as if he had delivered it hundreds of times before.

"I barged right in after the chap ahead of me and put my load on the first stack of boxes I could find. It was a crowded area. small in the first place, but a lot of new boxes had been brought in recently, leaving barely enough space for us to turn around. The other chap closed the door behind us and we were in total darkness. I called for him to strike a light, but he said we should stay in the dark."

"Who was the man?" Dorothy asked.

"Didn't know him at the time. But when he closed the door I got a good look at him. Later on I found out it was Major Husted. Algerdyce Husted.

"The place had a dank smell to it, or at least that's the way it seemed to me. Like somebody's bad breath, only really fowl. I suppose now, looking back, it must have been coming from inside myself. It must have been the damage that was being done to my own lungs. The next thing I knew my chest started paining me and I couldn't stop coughing.

"Then other men were outside the bunker, pounding on the door begging to be let in. One of the voices I could recognize. It was my own lieutenant, Gerald Dennis. I had told him of my plans about the bunker, and he must have been nearby when the canisters hit. I called to the other chap as best I could. 'That's my man out there. You've got to let him in,' I screamed in a hoarse voice. But he said no. There were too many. Once that door opened it would never get closed again. They would all be clawing to get inside. We could all end up dying.

"Of course he was right, you know. Hard to understand, I know, but he was right." Major Bruce slammed a tired fist on the arm of his chair, as if he were still trying to convince himself. "In basic training we pose certain questions to our men. Things such as, 'What would you do if you were driving a truckload of your own men along a mountain road and you were suddenly confronted with a child playing directly in your path? Do you run over the child or do you drive off the road and risk killing the truckload of men?' The kinds of questions that don't have any good answers. But the kinds of questions you get called upon to answer in wartime. And then you live with the answers for the rest of your— But fortunately for us, we made the right decision. Right decision."

"And your lieutenant?" Agatha asked. "What happened . . ."

The Major brightened. "He pulled through, would you believe it? Of course he's got the lung problem rather bad, and most of the men in his squad were lost. I still wake up in the night listening to them at the door, scratching with fingernails and pleading . . . but he pulled through. It's some consolation."

"Did you ever see him afterward?" Dorothy asked.

The Major seemed not to hear. "He had a wife who stuck by him. Raised a family, I believe. Family is some consolation, I always thought. Lives up in Oxford. Have a picture of them around here someplace, clipped from the newspaper. Oh no, must be in storage. Everything's in storage . . . I wrote to him several times. Finally got a short note from his wife saying it wasn't a good idea to bring up the memories. Set him back a peg or two. You'd think he could have signed his own name or she could have told me how he was getting on, but no. Just her name on the letter . . . " The Major looked out the window, off into the twilight, seeing things only he could see.

Agatha blew her nose and dabbed at her eyes, then leaned forward in her chair. "I was wondering, Major Bruce, is there the possibility that someone else was in the bunker, other than you three officers?"

"Someone else?" he frowned at the new idea. "Why, I never thought of that. I suppose that is a possibility. But if there was, I never heard them. Why do you ask?"

"Oh, nothing. I was only wondering if you were sure."

"I can't be sure of very much from then on. The next thing I knew I was in a field hospital, well behind the lines. I must have passed out, either from the pain or lack of oxygen.

"Lost track of Oswald after that, too. I suppose this is what you wanted to know about your husband's war record. Wish I could tell you he had a more heroic part to play. But then, keeping supply records and the like can be vastly important, can't it?"

Dorothy cleared her throat. "Actually, it wasn't so much that I wanted to know about my husband's war record. It was another matter that brought us here."

She looked sideways at Agatha for a clue as to how to proceed, but Agatha only smiled back benignly.

"Major Bruce," Dorothy went on, "there has been an attempt on my husband's life, and Colonel Husted is dead. He was poisoned. It appears that both acts were committed by someone with a military background. By someone who thinks my husband and the Colonel did something to be ashamed of."

She waited for a reaction. Major Bruce stared at her and breathed.

"So you are thinking of the bunker . . . "

"Yes," she said. "Unless you can think of any other reason why someone would be after them."

His eyes seemed to cloud over and loose their sense of community. His bony hands found their way into the pockets of his robe.

"No. No reason I know of."

"Has anyone been by to see you? Has anything happened here of a threatening nature?"

"I've been in hospital. Four days in hospital. Lungs backed up on me. No. There has been no one to see me. I don't have visitors, as a rule."

Agatha asked, "Do you remember if your lieutenant carried a side arm?"

"I imagine so. All the line officers would be issued side arms, I believe."

"Did he choose to use the Berten-Wellar automatic, do you think?"

The Major shook his head. "Don't know. Was someone shot with a Wellar?"

"Yes."

"Gerald Dennis was not that sort of man. Not revenge. Not him. Even if he did blame me. Not a bitter, resentful bone in his body. Just because he did not answer my letters . . . You have the wrong man."

"Major, may we ask you if you have received anything like a white feather in the mail or—"

Major Bruce let out a cry and started to get out of his chair, but quickly dropped back in place. He was trying to say something but had to wait.

"I was a career officer. Served honorably in India. Good record. Gave my life to His Majesty's service. All my life. Now, I've given even my health. And my wife. Am I now to give up even my honor? By God, I will not do it. I threw . . . damn thing in . . . fire. I will not have it, do you hear? I am an honorable member of His Majesty's—"

He struggled to get to his feet. Beads of sweat had formed on his face and his eyes were livid with anger. The spirit was certainly willing, but the lungs were no longer equal to the task. His lips turned blue and his legs started trembling, as if under a great weight. The two women sensed that he was about to topple and managed to get hold of him, at least enough so he didn't hurt himself in his slide to the floor. He was surprisingly light. It was more like handling a giant rag doll than a human being.

Dorothy started for the door with the thought of going for help, but Agatha called her back when she noticed the Major pointing toward the corner of the room where a bellpull hung.

"That must be connected to the hospital. Why don't we try it?" Agatha said.

While they waited, the Major's eyes slid silently behind his half-closed lids. Dorothy felt his pulse to make sure he was still with them.

Ten minutes later the lights of an Army ambulance could be seen bouncing along the service road in their direction. The ladies had the Major propped up slightly and resting on blankets. Color had returned to his face and he seemed to be resting quietly.

Agatha went over to the Major's desk and started shuffling through some of his effects.

"What on earth are you doing?" Dorothy demanded.

"I'm looking for Lieutenant Dennis's address in Oxford. Yes, here it is. I've got it."

She had the address book safely back in its drawer by the time the attendants came in the door.

17

Dorothy and Agatha waited outside the large ward until the two male attendants working on the Major came through the double doors. One of the men came over to them to talk.

"Are you ladies relatives?"

"No. Only friends," Dorothy said. "He was in the same unit as my husband."

The attendant nodded and looked back through the windows with a worried glance. He was a small man, probably in his sixties. The heavy furrows in his brow were a measure of the concern he felt for his charges.

"He can use all the friends he has, now. We have him on eighty percent oxygen. He'll rest through the night all right, but I don't think it will be much longer for him. He's gone on pretty well with only a quarter of a lung, wouldn't you say?"

"A quarter of a lung?" Agatha asked. "He has lived like that since, since the war?"

The attendant nodded. "They have their good days and their bad days. Those that manage to keep their weight down and avoid catching colds—like the Major, here—get along quite well. He has been able to be on his own quite a bit. But we get so we can tell when the end is near. You can see it in their eyes or something. Like watching a fine old clock run down. He had been doing quite well. Eating his meals and all. That's a telltale sign, when their appetite starts to tail off. But then last week, we found him on the floor of his cabin, very upset about something. Going on about feathers and his bravery. We brought him up here and got him calmed down again. At least I thought we did . . . Well, thank you for your help, ladies. You can visit with him starting at nine-thirty in the morning."

The man gave them a good-bye salute and followed his fellow attendant down the corridor. The ladies started toward the exit.

"I must have been out of my mind, mentioning that damn feather business," Dorothy growled, under her breath. "Why, oh, why, didn't I keep my mouth shut?"

"I think we were both too wrapped up in what we were doing," Agatha consoled. "I don't think there is any way we could have anticipated this."

"Yes, I could have. I should have. Knowing my husband's feelings about the honor of the military, I should have anticipated. It's that blasted war. Are we never to be done with it? Is it always to be on our minds, muddying our every thought and action?"

When they reached the doors of the hospital's main entrance Agatha stopped with her hand on the handle to get Dorothy's undivided attention. "We had better put our self-incriminating thoughts in the back of our minds right now. We have something more pressing to consider."

"What are you getting at?"

"Has it occurred to you that the mere appearance of the white feather in this poor man's mail could have been an attempt to kill him? If the murderer knew the kind of response it would generate—"

"I know, I know. I can't think about that, now. I need some breathing room. Let's get out of this place." Dorothy took Agatha's hand off the door and stormed out, angrily.

Agatha didn't try to talk with her again. She would bide her time until the lady was ready. They got back to Agatha's car without any sign of the reporter pest. The girl seemed to appear and disappear at the strangest times. Like a locust. Or was she out there somewhere in the dark, writing her exposé, waiting for the most embarrassing moment to make another appearance?

After Agatha had driven off the hospital grounds, she pulled her car over to the side of the road behind some shrubbery, just to see if they were being followed. She waited several minutes before proceeding, but there was still no sign of the girl.

When they had covered several miles along the highway to London, Dorothy was in a calmer mood. She apologized for her actions earlier and Agatha quickly accepted, taking much of the blame upon herself.

"It's a comedy of errors, you know," Dorothy sighed.

"What do you mean, a comedy of errors?"

"This entire charade we are witnessing. The German artillery gunners erred in their target area. They no doubt intended their shells to land much closer to the front. Probably a miscalculation on how far the mustard canisters would travel. Then my husband stumbles out of the tent like an innocent and gets himself knocked silly by a laundry wagon.

"And now, twenty years later, someone with a misplaced grudge against an unconscious man comes into my house and shoots the first pair of pants they see. It's unbelievable."

"Yes, I see," Agatha nodded. "It is almost as if there have been too many mistakes to be believed."

"And to top it all off, you know what must have been in those new boxes in the bunker that made the place so crowded?"

"I have no idea."

Dorothy snorted a laugh. "My husband told me that gas masks had been delivered to the regiment, but no training on their use had begun. Those boxes must have contained gas masks. Can't you see it? The men cowering in the bunker on top of boxes containing gas masks— afraid to open the door for fear of dying. We humans can be unbelievably stupid when we put our minds to it. If it weren't so tragic I could split my sides laughing."

"Yes, I see what you mean. As if it were a comedy of errors. I know from personal experience that I do not perform very well when I am under a good deal of stress. But I don't know if that is universally true of others. It would seem to me . . ." Agatha's voice trailed off without completing her thought.

"What is it? What are you thinking of?"

"I think you may have hit on it yourself, Dorothy. I think there are too many errors. Maybe something that has happened, which we think is an error, was not really an error at all. Or perhaps there is another reason for the error that we do not understand right now."

"I'm not sure I follow all that."

"I'm not sure I do, either," Agatha laughed. "Oh, I do wish I were back home in my comfortable sitting room chair, where I can think best. A nice cup of tea at my side, a good crackling fire in the fire box, and Max puttering about in his study. Then perhaps I could puzzle this . . . *puzzle* out. Oh, heavens, I just can't think right this minute. The characters don't seem to be acting properly."

"Characters?"

"Yes. The characters in our story."

"Agatha, need I remind you again, we are not writing a story here. We are observing life. Life in the raw, if you will. We can't manipulate the actions of our characters as if this were a work of fiction."

"Oh, but you can, I feel. Once you know your people—know them clear through to the bone—I think you can let them loose in your imagination, just as if you were writing them into a story, and they will lead you to the logical solution. I frequently do that when I am having plot problems."

Dorothy watched her out of the corner of her eye, to make sure she was being serious. It seemed she was.

"I think the problem with that line of reasoning," Dorothy said, "lies in knowing people clear through to the bone. We all have our secrets—as you know, I speak from experience on the subject. And we all try to hide them.

Can we ever hope to know people well enough for that kind of analysis?"

Agatha tapped the steering wheel while she mulled over Dorothy's words. "Yes, of course. That's it. Someone is lying to us."

Dorothy rolled her eyes in frustration. "Yes, dear. Murderers have been known to exhibit that slight character flaw."

Agatha was oblivious to the sarcasm in Dorothy's comment. She was too deep in thought to notice and too far removed from Dorothy's urbane cynicism to understand the barb had been intended for her.

Dorothy suddenly let out a healthy yawn and stretched her shoulders. "Excuse me, Agatha, I think my late nights of play preparation are catching up with me. I can't seem to keep a train of thought."

Agatha seemed not to hear. She was not too tired to keep on the subject. While Dorothy tried to rest her eyes, Agatha kept at the mental problem at hand. Like the proverbial English bulldog just getting her teeth set, she ground it over and over in her mind, rejecting one thought and trying yet another.

As the car rolled on into the night, the drone of the engine put Dorothy into an uneasy sleep. She woke with a start at Agatha's sudden call.

"I'm not sure it is a revenge thing at all, do you see?"

Dorothy sat up and tried to focus her eyes. "See what?"

"If it is a revenge killing, then why did it wait for twenty-odd years? Why wasn't it done sooner? Why the twenty years?"

Dorothy yawned and tried to get on top of the subject at hand.

"Perhaps it has taken that long to fester to a boiling point. Remember what Major Bruce said about letting memories prey upon your mind. It can start to twist your thinking after a while. I'm thinking of that young Lieutenant Dennis outside the bunker, pleading to be let in. If he brought his men along with him, he no doubt had to stand helplessly by and watch his men drop like flies. How many nightmares has he had about that scene? And if he was injured, too, think about him lying about, imprisoned in his own damaged body for twenty years."

"Yes, that's true. But he must be well over forty-five by now. A time when people turn more conservative in their thinking."

Dorothy wasn't so sure. "My husband still carries a torch with a good flame on it for all things military."

"You think his feelings are so deep-seated that he would be willing to kill over an old grudge?"

"Now that's a loaded question, isn't it? Very well, let's say for the sake of argument this was not a revenge killing. What other motive could be involved?"

Agatha wiggled to readjust herself behind the wheel. "What about secrecy? I have been wondering why there was no formal investigation into the incident."

"Perhaps there was."

Agatha shook her head. "I did some reading in the military library in London about all the activities of your husband's regiment during the spring of 1916. Even if it had been done in secret, the results would have been made known by this time. But I couldn't find anything in the records about it."

"I don't know that that proves anything," Dorothy said. "Perhaps they simply felt it wasn't called for. There is also the possibility the high command felt it would be demeaning to the military to look into a case that would place in question the bravery of their officers. In wartime you need stories about heroes. Not . . . others.

"We still do not know how the bunker people were discovered, do we? We've talked to only the two people who lost consciousness. And we can't very well talk to the poisoned Colonel. Which brings us back to the Lieutenant, doesn't it?"

"You still feel Lieutenant Dennis is our most likely suspect, don't you?"

Dorothy nodded. "I certainly would like to know if he carried one of those automatic handguns."

"Would you like to take a trip up to Oxford with me to find out? We could stay overnight at my flat in London and get an early start first thing in the morning."

It was tempting, but Dorothy thought of a thousand reasons why she should not. Not the least of which was her concern for her husband. Was she helping or hurting him by all this probing they were doing on their own?

"There have been enough errors made already," she said aloud. "I've already contributed my fair share. I don't want to be the one making any more."

"I think most of the errors we have talked of were made because the people were ignorant of certain facts. Perhaps if we don't go to Oxford we will be guilty of the same kind of ignorance. Have you considered that, Dorothy?"

Dorothy had no answer.

18

During the night in her London flat Agatha managed to sleep the sound sleep of the innocent. But it was Dorothy—after her catnap in the car and finding herself in a strange bed—who tossed and turned through the night. Her restlessness was not without its benefits. About three in the morning it finally dawned on her that Lieutenant Dennis, if he was the deranged killer they were thinking he was, could certainly be dangerous to anyone who came snooping about. Especially to two middle-aged "mystery ladies" with no apparent business, examining other people's miseries.

All this Dorothy brought out during their hurried breakfast of toast and tea. She saw no way around it and was prepared to cancel their plans to visit her old university town.

Agatha was also not without her familiar mental resources, and before they made it to the highway, she had formulated a plan that might get them what they wanted, without unduly exposing them to any possible dangers.

It was an elaborate plan, fraught with traces of the famous Christie imagination. They would appear on the Dennis doorstep as sisters, Lela and Lila Dennis. The tale they would recite ran as follows: they were in search of their long lost cousin Gerald Dennis. Their uncle, Commodore Harold Foster Dennis, had died leaving his entire estate to his nieces and nephews, having no direct issue of his own, and the estate could not be settled until cousin Gerald could be found. Agatha went on in great detail about the size of the estate, how it had built up in value as the result of expanding sheep herds in New Zealand and excellent market prices for copper mined in western Australia. Agatha even had worked out her story with an added touch of verisimilitude, having the sisters argue over differing versions of the old Commodore's honesty.

Then, if and when the real Gerald Dennis would disassociate himself from the Commodore Dennis estate, which was to be a test of his general honesty, the ladies were to inform him that the last news the family had had of Gerald was that he had been adopted by another distant cousin of the Dennis clan—that the parents who raised him were probably not his real parents after all. Had Mr. Dennis ever had the feeling he might have been adopted?

Dorothy thought this last Dickensian twist was going a bit too far. The entire plan was merely to gain them access to the household. Not get the Dennises's hopes up about some fictitious inheritance or destroy the man's sense of family.

"But how are we going to find out about his choice of side arm?" Agatha reminded. "Or about his traveling itinerary for the past two weeks? We have to get into their confidence in some manner . . . I know," Agatha's eyes brightened in mid-sentence with another thought. "We could be two sisters doing a series of articles on handguns used in the Great War."

Dorothy was already shaking her head on that one. "What we know about handguns wouldn't fill a thimble. They'd smell us out in an instant. Let's stick with our first plan. It sounds at least slightly plausible. Then we can see where we go from there. I only hope they haven't read too many of your books."

"Very well. Although I might feign a problem with a sore bunion if the lady of the house is not of a mind to let us in for a chat."

Dorothy looked at the chameleon sitting next to her, as if she had just suggested robbing the Bank of England. "You are having fun with all this, aren't you?"

"Why, no, quite the contrary. But one must do the best one can with the talents one has."

"Your talents being outlandish plot contrivances."

That hurt Agatha. "Not so outlandish, I should say. Imaginative perhaps . . . but not so outlandish."

Using the address Agatha had copied from Major Bruce's address book, they made their way toward Creademont College in the southern part of the university complex. Oxford had not changed all that much from Dorothy's student days, and she was able to guide them directly to the place. Fully expecting to find a house, they were both surprised to see their destination was an ancient four-story sandstone building, obviously a part of the college's large quadrangle. Judging from the looks of it, it was probably last repaired in the late thirteenth century. The door facing them seemed to be serving as the back door for one of the college's societies. Several young men in student apparel and impedimenta came running or biking up to the building from their early morning classes. Others, in less of a hurry, were on their way to classes, or tennis lessons, or rowing exercises, judging from their casual dress.

"This can't be right," Agatha said. "I must have got the numbers wrong."

Dorothy stepped up to one of the students as he dismounted his bicycle.

"Excuse me, young man. We're looking for the Gerald Dennis residence. Could you direct us?"

The student hiked his load of books from the back of his bike to his shoulder and thought a bit.

"Sorry, ma'am, we don't have a Gerald Dennis in our house. Is he an upperclass man?"

"No, no. He must be forty-five or fifty years old. Not a student, of course. Perhaps we have the wrong address."

"The only Dennis I know of is Mrs. Diana Dennis, who does for us as matron. She's probably sorting mail about now." He pointed with a copy of Tennyson's light verse toward the busy entrance. "The poor old dear just lost her husband. Gas victim in the war, I understand. Don't know how ready she is to talk to strangers."

Dorothy's face was drained of color. "His name . . . was his name Gerald?"

"I wouldn't know. I didn't know she was married until after the services, when some of the chaps were raising some money for her. Too bad about some of those old chaps, isn't it? You must excuse me now. I'm late for squash."

Dorothy thanked him woodenly, then turned to Agatha. She spit out her words in startled desperation. "Another death. What are we doing?" she cried, her voice literally trembling. "What are we going? We aren't helping this situation at all. This is terrible."

When they began drawing inquisitive stares, Agatha steered Dorothy toward a nearby bench where they could watch the passing parade and regroup. Dorothy's condition was not improving.

"We are out of our minds. We expected to come up here and find ourselves a murderer and all we find is another victim. We are out of our depth. I can't go on like this. If we had told the police what we knew in the first place this might not have happened. There is blood on our hands, Agatha."

Agatha consoled her as best she could, speaking in a soft voice and hoping Dorothy would start doing the same.

"Now we don't know that, do we? We don't know how he died. Or when . . ."

"This is all my fault, isn't it? If I hadn't been the head-strong rebel. If only I had kept my life in order. I thought I was only hurting myself. But the deception starts and the lies get bigger. Lies, lies, lies."

Agatha almost touched Dorothy's mouth with her own hand to quiet her. With her other hand she fumbled about in her purse for a clean handkerchief.

"Yes, I agree. Please don't carry on, now. There is nothing to be done about that now. We can only go forward. We can't go back, no matter how much we would like to. We've got to make the best of what we have left, and we've got to think for ourselves. Think for ourselves. This feminine wailing isn't going to help us one bit. Believe me, I speak from a good deal of experience."

Dorothy started getting control again and they sat in silence, waiting for the students to get to their mid-morning destinations. When the area was at last quiet, Dorothy labored to her feet. But Agatha stayed put, her shoulders rocking back and forth while she tried to absorb the news.

"If the Lieutenant was on the outside of the bunker, and still he has been killed . . . that seems to put our theory about a revenge killing in a cocked hat, doesn't it?"

"Your penchant for stating the obvious is a wonder of our age. I think we should get ourselves directly to a telephone booth," Dorothy announced, "and let the Police Inspector in Witham know about this entire military connection."

"And what are we to say when he asks about the connection with the Dean from your son's school?"

"As a last resort, I am prepared to fall back on that little-used but usually reliable shocker—the truth."

"I think we should at least talk to the widow, here, first."

"What good will that do? Remember, my husband was gassed as well. I've heard all the sad tales about old soldiers and their internal problems that my system can tolerate for a lifetime."

"I want to know the circumstances surrounding his death, don't you?"

Dorothy slapped her thigh with her heavy purse. "Yes, of course I do, I suppose. I'm just carrying on. You seem to have a greater tolerance for this sort of thing than I. But I don't see what it will possibly change. All we are doing is delaying my exposure. We aren't avoiding it. However this business is to be resolved, the question of the Dean's appearance in my house is going to be pressed. What is the point of delaying the inevitable?"

Agatha pushed her driving glasses up her nose a bit more snugly, a move she frequently used while looking for the right words.

"I'm not sure what the point is. I simply want to avoid the confrontation as long as we can, and hope we can think of something when the time comes."

The two ladies stood on the uneven walkway, one pulling toward the street and a telephone booth, the other tugging to see the new widow sorting mail in the alcove nearby.

"We are already this close. What can be the harm?" Agatha asked.

She finally had her way. Dorothy followed along behind, a new, passive role for her, which did not sit well with her aggressive nature.

19

Agatha looked through the small postal window and saw the back of a middle-aged woman. She was wearing a green eyeshade and a grey smock and was tucking letters into the series of cubbyholes surrounding her. She did her work almost without looking at the destination for each letter.

"Mrs. Dennis," Agatha called.

"Can't talk while I'm sorting. You know that," Mrs. Dennis snapped.

"Yes, well . . ." Nonplussed, Agatha stepped back, and prepared to wait until the sorting was finished.

Dorothy had already had enough of her passive role. She stepped up and said, "See here, Mrs. Dennis, we are not students waiting for our mail."

The startled matron turned around and peered out.

"Oh. Yes, ladies. What can I do for you?"

"We have just driven up from London, hoping to have a few words with you."

"With me? Whatever for?"

"It is a matter about your late husband, Lieutenant Gerald Dennis."

Agatha tugged at Dorothy's sleeve, hoping to soften her approach. It didn't work.

"My husband? Why, whatever for?" Mrs. Dennis whined.

"Is there somewhere where we might might talk, other than this academic version of a confessional booth?"

Mrs. Dennis seemed not to understand, then called to an assistant in still another small workspace to take over

170

the mail filing for her. She took off her eyeshade and pointed a way for the ladies.

"Come through the far door there. We can use my sitting room, if you like."

They followed her directions and a door opened up for them at the end of the causeway the students traversed. Mrs. Dennis was a medium-size woman with brown hair that was once blond. She had large doe eyes that she used to search her guests for further explanations.

"Are you ladies with the government? I was meaning to notify the pension board about his passing, but just haven't got to it yet."

"No, we are not with the pension board, Mrs. Dennis. Did I hear you say we might use a sitting room?"

Mrs. Dennis bowed slightly and led the way along a dim corridor. "Watch your step along here, please."

She continued past the kitchen, where the kitchen crew was still sorting breakfast plates. The steamy air that drifted by their faces cried out kippers and dried eggs. Down another three steps and they turned into a small sitting room. Mrs. Dennis was to be complimented. She had done a very nice job of making an uninteresting ᵤpace quite livable. Needlepoint pillows and mottos in crewel reminded the visitors they had entered a loving home, neat and tidy all around. The only object that seemed out of place was a large photograph of a clown or court jester, which hung on the wall opposite the entryway. No windows, though, except for some sort of overhead skylight in the adjoining room. Not the most healthy environment for a man with lung problems, Dorothy thought.

Mrs. Dennis pointed them toward a rather nice sofa with a colorful crocheted afghan draped across the backrest.

"Now then, how can I help you?"

As usual with strangers, Agatha only opened her mouth slightly and looked about for help. She was leaving the talking up to Dorothy, who by now had completely forgotten about their carefully planned grand deception involving the long lost "uncle."

"We understand that your husband was a mustard gas victim at Simes. Is that correct?"

"Yes, it is."

" . . . and that he and several men, ah, men under his command, were outside a sealed bunker trying to get inside at the time of the attack. Is that also correct?"

Mrs. Dennis didn't move. But moisture started forming along her lower eyelids.

"I am most sorry to be here at this time," Dorothy said, "and I assure you I wouldn't be, except this matter is of the utmost urgency."

"It's all right. Go on. The other gentlemen should have heard about that, too, you know."

"Other gentlemen?"

"Why, yes. The two that said they were with the Army, although they weren't in uniform. I suppose you are here about the same matter?"

"Two gentlemen . . . they talked to your husband about this . . ."

"Oh, no. They were only here two days ago. Gerald was already . . . gone away."

Agatha spoke up. "What did they look like? Can you describe them?"

"I thought at the time they reminded me of Don Quixote and his little friend. One quite tall and gaunt, and the other short and plump. The taller one had an eye that was odd. Sort of looked off at an angle. I don't think he could see from it, to be honest about it."

Dorothy and Agatha exchanged looks of confusion.

"And they came here asking you about Simes—" Dorothy began.

"Oh, no. They came to talk to Gerald. They didn't know about his passing. They were embarrassed, to say the least. They said they wouldn't have come if they had known."

"But they told you they had come here to ask your husband about the bunker business?"

"Well, no, not exactly. They said they were questioning

different people who had served under General Dana
Pike. Or Colonel Pike, was what he was when my husband was under him. They were interested in what kind
of an officer he had been and if there had ever been any
trouble under his command. That sort of thing. They
tipped their hats as polite as you please and said they
wouldn't trouble me further. I stood there like a ninny
with my eyes full of tears, as they usually were then, not
having sense enough to speak up.

"That was when I should have put in my own two
cents worth about the bunker. Daddy had told us all
about it. I will not understand until my dying day why
nothing was ever done about that whole business. Why
hadn't the men been issued gas masks? There had already
been one gas attack along the line. They knew what terrible weapons the Germans had, and they were not above
using them. And why did the men inside the bunker
where the gas masks were kept not open the door to their
friends and comrades outside? There are just too many
questions. But they didn't seem to be interested in what a
lowly widow had to say on the subject."

"Did your husband, during his lifetime, ever try to have
those questions answered?" Agatha asked.

"Daddy? No. I used to ask him about it when he first
came home. But he would only shrug his shoulders and
smile. "There are two kinds of soldiers, my dear," she
started mimicking her husband's voice. He must have
been something of a raconteur, from the sound of it.
" 'There are the fighting men. And there are the gentlemen. And the fighting men learn not to disturb the gentlemen merely because there happens to be a war going
on.' "

"But your husband was an officer, Mrs. Dennis," Dorothy said. "Didn't that qualify him as a gentleman?"

"Oh, I suppose it did. But he never felt a part of it.
People here at school got him in with the commission and
all. He was a drama major at Creademont. Did every-

thing from Shakespeare to the Spring Frolic. He could make a statue laugh, that man could. That's the kind of person he was. More of a court jester than a soldier. Born for the stage. Bound for London's West End, that man was. I wish you could have heard him mimic Noël Coward. That man could mimic just about anyone, but Noël Coward . . . 'Mad dogs and Englishmen go out in the midday sun . . .' well, it was something special. Very popular with his fellow students. So he got his commission as a lieutenant and he was to be in charge of camp programs and that sort of thing. Building up morale and the like. Well, as the Army does things, it doesn't always mean your plans are going to stay the same. Suddenly there was a need to put together an All Allies fighting force and Daddy was called upon to serve as an aide to one of the senior British officers . . ."

She paused and pressed her lips together, as if to force herself to stop talking. Agatha took a fresh look at the happy-go-lucky face looking back at them from his place of honor on the wall. What was it about smiling pictures of the deceased that always made her want to cry?

Mrs. Dennis went on. "I don't suppose you came here to listen to me jabber on about Daddy's problems, did you? I'm sorry. I seem to have lost track. What *did* you come here for?"

"There have been several peculiar deaths," Dorothy said, "involving people who were in the gas attack with your husband. Deaths that seem to have been caused by . . . I don't know why it is so difficult for me to say this. I've written about it often enough. It seems there have been murders committed involving the gas victims as . . . victims. We had come to talk to your husband about the matter and naturally we are quite shocked to learn that he, too, has died. Would you mind telling us how he . . . expired?"

"You mean, you are wondering if my husband didn't die a natural death, but was murdered?"

"Yes, we are wondering if there is that possibility. Sorry to be so blunt about it."

Mrs. Dennis relaxed in her chair for the first time. "Why, how very strange. The doctor did assure me his passing was a result of his condition. But still, all the same . . . It is true, he had been failing terribly the last year. The doctor wanted him in hospital, but Daddy wouldn't hear of it. He wanted to be here with his family, he said. If it meant he would go a bit sooner, so be it. I wasn't about to argue with him. He had gotten a head cold, you see, and we were doing everything we could to keep it from going to his lungs. We had oxygen tanks brought in to use when he would have an attack. Corps Hospital was very good about that. We did as best we could for him, and for the last day or so he was doing much better. Truly he was. Sitting up and acting like his old self. But it happened pretty much as the doctor said it would. Said it was heart failure brought on by . . . Is that what you wanted to know?"

"Then he died here at home?"

"Yes, he did. Right here on the sofa where you ladies are sitting. It was . . . peaceful. As though he just went to sleep. I came in and found him here. I thought he truly was asleep, since he frequently managed a morning nap, and when he didn't call back to me or tinkle his bell when I came in to ask if he was ready for his tea, why.. . ."

"So you were in the other room?"

"No. I was sorting the post down the way there, just as you saw me do this morning. I finished that and came back, as I always did to fix Daddy his tea . . ." Her chin started vibrating, but she quickly got hold of herself. "Amanda Jo had already left for class and she waved to me as she went out. She had been reading to him."

"Amanda Jo, I take it, is your daughter."

"Yes. 'The apple of me eye,' Daddy used to call her."

"So . . . there really was no one here with your husband when he actually . . . left us."

"Well, no, not literally. But as I say I was just down the

hall. Surely you don't think that he could have been . . .
Oh, no. I don't think that for a minute. I have no reason
to think it was anything but a natural death."

"And the attending physician? I suppose he felt the
same."

"Of course."

"So he felt no inclination to investigate the matter of the
death."

"Whatever do you mean?"

"I mean there was no autopsy."

"Why, of course not. There was no need."

Dorothy grunted a knowing sound, then got to her feet
and looked out into the corridor that had brought them
there. She turned back to Mrs. Dennis.

"Someone could have come in through the student's
kitchen, without your knowing about it."

"Yes, I suppose that is possible. But the cook, Mrs.
McCurdy, would have told me. She keeps a close eye on
us. Helps me lift Daddy when necessary. Helped me, I
mean to say. It is still hard sometimes for me to think he
isn't here waiting for his tea or waiting to tell me some
joke or funny story he read in one of his books."

"And the other end of the hallway," Dorothy persisted,
"where does that lead to?"

"It leads to the dormitory rooms upstairs if you follow it
far enough. And there is a door to the street level just
beyond the corner out there. I suppose that is what you
are getting at."

"Could someone have come in that way?"

Mrs. Dennis shook her head. "The idea is too ridiculous
to consider. Who in their right mind would want to do
away with a kind, loving man who had only a few months
to live? It doesn't make any sense at all."

"No, it doesn't seem to make sense," Dorothy agreed,
"but as you say, we may be looking for someone who is
not in their right mind."

Agatha finally took a turn. "Mrs. Dennis, you have
been most kind to put up with these trying questions. I

wonder if I might ask one more of my own? Precisely when was it your husband passed away?"

"It was two weeks ago last Friday."

Dorothy and Agatha looked at one another. They were both starting to do mathematics in their minds. Agatha got her sum first.

"That means he died three days before—"

"Yes," Dorothy marveled in surprise, "three days before the man in my house . . . That means he was the first."

"He was the first, as far as we know," Agatha corrected.

"The first to die? Is that important?" Mrs. Dennis asked.

"The sequence of deaths might be important," Agatha said. "We really don't know at this point. Mrs. Dennis, might we ask one more, somewhat unusual question? Had your husband received anything unusual in the post that you know of?"

"What do you mean, unusual? Naturally I bring in our mail, and I don't recall anything. He doesn't receive many letters."

"Anything of an upsetting nature. Anything—"

"What she means to say is," Dorothy put in, "has your husband received any white feathers?"

Mrs. Dennis frowned. "White feathers . . . you don't literally mean white bird feathers, do you?"

"Yes, we do," Dorothy went on. "Most of the regular Army people seem to consider a white feather a sign of cowardice."

"Why, I never heard of such a thing."

"Apparently it is common knowledge among the military establishment. At least two of the other men involved have received white feathers. Is there any chance your husband might have got one and not told you about it?"

Mrs. Dennis reached into the sewing basket next to her and refolded a piece she had been working on, then turned back to her inquisitors. "Well, I suppose it is possi-

ble he could have. I didn't hover over him while he read
his mail."

"I suppose you have already gone through all your
husband's effects and would know if there had been a
feather tucked away anywhere," Dorothy said.

"No, I haven't touched his things. Everything is just as
it was. I haven't had the emotional strength . . . too many
memories connected with everything."

"Yes, of course," Agatha said. "We understand."

"I do want to be helpful." Mrs. Dennis suddenly got to
her feet. "Perhaps if I had some company . . . Why don't
you come this way? We can look in his room together."

She led them through the next room, which served as
the family dining area and kitchen. Daylight was stream-
ing in from one long narrow window near the ceiling.
They were in a basement apartment that looked out to the
east from ground level. Then they were moving down
another corridor lined with the same large stone blocks
that formed the exterior walls of the building. No place for
a person with claustrophobia. The place was built to serve
people who stood approximately five feet tall, which made
it difficult for even moderate-size modern people to move
about gracefully.

But quite soon they were standing in a good-size space
with a window of its own. Besides a double bed and a
desk and a wicker-backed wheelchair, two walls were
lined with shelves crammed with books and doll-size
wooden figures in different dramatic poses, fit for the
stage.

"This was Daddy's room. He slept alone in here, the
last year. I slept in with Amanda Jo. It was easier for him
that way." She picked up a wire cage from the desk and
pushed it over near the door. "That's not supposed to be
in here. Some of my daughter's schoolwork," she explained. "She had mice or rats for a biology experiment
that didn't work out very well. I hate cages, don't you? I
remember my mother used to keep a canary and I always
thought it was so cruel, keeping a beautiful songbird

caged up that way. But now, here I am living out one of those strange tricks that life plays on us. Here I've been spending my days taking care of my own songbird that had to live inside the cage of his own body."

She moved over to the desk and straightened a few loose papers. "Would you like to look through his things here? I don't see anything resembling a feather."

She started going through drawers, with Agatha and Dorothy looking on over her shoulder. In the large drawer on the right side was a motor-driven wood etching tool, covered with fine sawdust and wood chips.

"One of Daddy's hobbies," Mrs. Dennis explained. "He did all the carved figures you see up on the shelves there."

Simply to be polite, Agatha started looking them over carefully. But one immediately drew her attention. She picked it up and offered it to Dorothy.

"I believe this is an acquaintance of yours."

"Oh, good heavens." Dorothy took it with a smile of surprise on her face and turned the object over carefully in her hands. It was a seven-inch-high figure of a dapper gentleman standing very erect, with a painted monacle in one eye and a walking stick under one arm. He wore grey gloves and spats, and on his head, a very stylish homburg.

Mrs. Dennis saw her guest's interest and quoted the words that had been etched into the base of the statue: " 'As my whimsical Lord takes me.' That's the motto for the crest of Lord Peter Wimsey, the detective Dorothy Sayers uses in her mystery stories—are you familiar with her work?"

Both Dorothy and Agatha had to laugh.

"Indeed I am," Dorothy said. "I am the one who created this conceited popinjay. I am Dorothy L. Sayers in the flesh."

It was Mrs. Dennis's turn to laugh. She raised her arms to Dorothy as if she were her long lost sister and would have embraced her had her station in life permitted. But just as quickly as her expression had turned joyful, she now resorted to tears and dropped down on the desk chair.

"Oh, if only . . . if only . . . Daddy would be so tickled to see you. He was so fond of a good mystery and you were one of his favorite writers."

"And what about Agatha Christie?" Dorothy asked.

"Oh, yes, of course. He loved most of her things, too. He was an avid reader."

"Well, the lady with me here is Miss Christie."

Dorothy had intended the introduction to please, but it only brought on more tears from their host. Mrs. Dennis found a tissue buried in a pocket of her smock and tried to clear her eyes.

"If only Daddy could be here. He so loved to read a mystery and then talk about them. He'd weigh the different clues and the blind alleys the writers would lead people up. And we would stop before the end each of us would try to decide who had done it. He made it like a parlor game. Amanda Jo and I would argue this way and he would argue that. And more often than not, Daddy would be right. But not always, of course.

"Near the end we would take turns reading to him. He couldn't sustain his reading for long, but he could follow along when we read to him. We read everything you two ladies wrote, of course, and most of the other big English writers. Then we would start with the American writers. The 'hard-boiled chaps,' Daddy used to call them. But he didn't like them as well as the English. All that shooting and violence just didn't interest him. He had had enough of that sort of thing, you see."

It seemed to give her pleasure to reminisce about happier days, and her guests had sense enough to let her ramble on. She got back on her feet and found a small painted figure that bore a strong resemblance to Mrs. Christie's Hercule Poirot, complete with waxed mustache and dark, tight-fitting suit. He even looked foreign, Dorothy thought.

"We spent so many happy hours, here in our strangely shaped little home. Of course, we didn't know we were happy then. We only thought we were . . . simply living. But books and good talk can make such a difference. We are so indebted to you. Both of you, for so many happy hours . . . Oh! And we are doubly indebted to you, Miss Sayers, for something else. You know what that is?"

"No, I don't. What do you mean?"

"Because you led the way for all English women. You were in the first graduating class for women at Summerville College. And now my daughter, Amanda Jo, is following in your footsteps. If it had not been for you and your successful work as a student, why, we might never have been able to get her admitted. Oh, I do wish she were here. She's sitting for an early exam now. Won't be home till late, because this afternoon she drives Mrs. Murdock, a very rich lady here in town, about. Amanda has been working so very hard. What with my little pay here at the school and Daddy's pension it's been hard to keep a university student going. She has had to help out with her driving and errands. School does not come easy for her, what with her father passing and all. Oh, I do wish you could meet her. It would be such a pick-me-up for her. I will have so much to share with her, won't I? If only I could hold you here some way to make this day go on and on for us."

"Perhaps you would like us to autograph one of our books for you," Dorothy suggested.

"Oh, would you? That would be so sweet of you both."

She had no trouble finding copies of each of their works on the crowded shelves. From Christie's work she selected one of her short story collections; from Sayers, *Have His Carcase.* But there didn't seem to be a proper fountain pen nearby that could develop a decent thread of ink.

"Oh, look in the nightstand next to Daddy's bed," Mrs. Dennis suggested. "He always kept his good fountain pen in there."

Dorothy opened the nightstand drawer and easily located the pen.

Very quickly, however, her mind was brought back to the seriousness of what their visit was all about. Right next to the pen were two white feathers, just like the ones back home on her dining room table.

20

It was near noon before Dorothy and Agatha could free themselves from Mrs. Dennis and her home full of memories. When they did get back to Agatha's Morris they had trouble getting the normally reliable auto started. A local mechanic had to be called in who spent several minutes rummaging about under the bonnet before deciding Agatha needed a new magneto, whatever that was.

The upshot was they did not get back on the road to Witham until late afternoon, and by then both ladies were quite tired. But the noise and movement of the car had different effects on them. Dorothy it seemed to put to sleep, while it acted to rejuvenate Agatha and get her thinking on her special "story level," as she called it.

They were several miles down the road when Agatha tapped Dorothy on the arm.

"I think I know why they came to see her," Agatha smiled.

"I'm sorry, I must have dozed off," Dorothy said sleepily. "Why who came to see whom?"

"The two government men. The tall one with the strange eye and the short stout one. I think I know why they came to see the Lieutenant and his wife."

"Yes, all right. Surprise me. What were they doing there?"

"I think General Pike is trying to have his commission reinstated. I was at his house not long ago and he was most certainly making noises to that effect. He thinks the Hitler business is going to lead to another war. The Army was sending investigators around to see what kind of leader he was."

"Wouldn't they already know from their own records?"

"You would think so, wouldn't you? But perhaps records were lost. Or perhaps so many of his superiors are gone now, they would have no way of knowing firsthand."

"What were you doing at General Pike's house?" Dorothy asked.

"It seems so long ago, now. I was trying to determine who might have had access to the automatic handguns that his regiment used."

"Oh, yes. I'd all but forgotten about that handgun. Too many details . . ."

"I thought at the time that the use of that particular handgun limited the scope of our suspects. It had to be someone from the regiment. But now I'm not so sure. Someone else may have got hold of the gun and used it, simply to throw us off the track. I remember there was a rather good American mystery a few years back that involved a series of killings. They were all military people, too, as I recall. The murderer killed two military people simply to throw the police off the scent. Then, when he killed his own uncle, who happened to be a military man, naturally suspicion was thrown off the nephew because he had no military background that would connect him to the earlier killings. The police were too busy looking into the military connections."

"You mean some of our murders were simply deceptive tactics?"

"I'm only guessing, of course. It is certainly a possibility," Agatha pondered.

Dorothy shook her head. "Who could be so cold-hearted, to kill innocent people that way? It is also a possibility that the murderer didn't know the significance of the military handgun—he used it simply because it was handy. Have you considered that?"

"No. No, I haven't," Agatha said.

"It goes on and on, doesn't it? And we are no closer to

a solution than when we started. I appreciate what you have tried to do for me, dear, but we have to admit we are at the end of the proverbial tether. I am going directly to the police station when I get back to Witham. I can't stand having this over my head a moment longer. At least then it will be someone else's worry."

They drove on in silence for several miles. Even though Dorothy had given up, Agatha was still on the case. She interrupted Dorothy's rest a second time.

"Consider this. Let us examine the case as best we know it. We might be overlooking something."

"Oh, very well, if you insist."

"Lieutenant Gerald Dennis died first. Two weeks ago. It could have been foul play, although there is no evidence. He was the only one on the outside of that bunker to have died recently. At least that we know of. But the thing that troubles me is, why was he awarded *two* white feathers? Not one, but two? Second point: If indeed he was killed, the most logical method of killing him would have been asphyxiation. Perhaps a pillow over his head, since there were no signs of a struggle. That was the only murder that could not have been committed by an invalid."

"Meaning the shooting of the Dean and the poisoning of Colonel Husted could have been done by anyone. Including invalids."

"Precisely. And now we come to Major Bruce. I have a question I would like you to ponder: Do you think he could have been faking the attack that sent him back to his hospital bed?"

"I don't see how that could be possible," Dorothy said. "You saw how he acted when he started talking about the white feather. He had all he could do to bring himself to his feet. His knees were quivering and his lips were turning blue."

"You or I could turn our lips blue if we held our breath long enough."

Dorothy thought about it for a moment. "No, I don't believe it. Not unless he is one of the great actors of the world. What would be his motive? He's all alone in the world, as far as I can see. And why would he send himself a white feather? Where is his motive?"

Agatha nodded in agreement. "I think you must be right. But someone is lying to us and it is driving me insane trying to determine who."

"What do you think of the family members of Colonel Husted, the poison victim?"

Agatha looked confused. "What do you mean, what do I think of them?"

"Earlier you discussed the possibility of the military connection being only a red herring. The real murderer may only have committed most of murders to throw us off the track. What about the Colonel's family? The wife and the daughter-in-law? Did they get along well, et cetera?"

"No, I don't think they did. The daughter-in-law showed a bit of resentment at being dominated by the Colonel's wife. But that certainly doesn't qualify either of them as mass murderers, does it?"

"Which brings us down to the only other major players . . ." Dorothy sighed heavily. "Myself and my dear husband. You might as well run through our portfolio as well."

"Yes, well, I didn't know how you might take it. Why don't you do the honors?"

"Very well. What of myself? I have been so busy with my play I have not had time to think of any major crimes, much less perform any. I certainly cannot establish an airtight alibi for the time span in which Dean Thornton Matthews must have met his end. But I certainly had no motive to do him in. That may sound a bit jaded, after I make my confession about going in my own front door, finding the poor man, and deliberately hiding his identification. But there it is. And, since Mrs. Dennis has told us the time of day and the date on which her husband died, I do believe I can manage an alibi for that entire evening. My calendar back home should show I was meeting with the BBC people that very morning, down in London town. The other death—the poisoning thing—would prove a bit more difficult, since the poison could have been administered in a pill or a bottle, some hours, even days before the colonel ended up taking it."

Agatha nodded. "Yes, I see. We should learn more about that poisoning, shouldn't we?"

"No, dear, we should not. We are hanging up our amateur detective badges, remember? We are only having this conversation now to pass the time of day at the end of a tedious trip. We are most definitely not looking into any poisoning."

"Very well, if you feel that way."

Agatha drove on in silence for several miles. Then, just as Dorothy's head was beginning to nod again, she said, "Did you notice the obituary statement on the Colonel in the *Times*, Dorothy?"

"No, I did not."

"I believe the poison used was muscarine. Are you familiar with that type of poison?"

"Muscarine? You know I am. Please don't toy with me. I used it in one of my books. It should also be noted that muscarine often appears naturally in certain foods, if not managed properly. That is what makes it such a sinister poison: it is hard to determine the source. And it also means there is the possibility that the Colonel ingested the poison naturally."

"And the white feather?"

"What about it? Perhaps only an ugly insult. Remember, the other recipient, Major Bruce, is still alive. Let's face it. The only death we can point to as a provable murder is the shooting of the Dean. Perhaps we are only jousting at windmills. Has that thought occurred to you?"

"And your husband's accident? How do you explain that?"

"I've thought a good deal about it. I'm afraid he has a very large drinking problem which can no longer be ignored.

His stories to the contrary were simply his attempt at a cover-up, I'm afraid."

"And his subsequent disappearance from his hospital bed?"

"Perhaps he wasn't through with his binge."

"Has that ever happened before?"

"No," Dorothy answered with a note of surprise in her voice. "He always did his drinking at home. Or at our local pub. Disappearing that way is new to his pattern, I must admit. You see what I mean about it all going on and on. Oh, Agatha . . ." Dorothy rubbed at her temples, as if to let the demons out. Then looked out the window to the west, where the rolling green countryside was being treated to an amber wash from the retreating sunlight.

"How I would love to find a nice quiet home in the country, somewhere where I could tend my garden and start to recover just a trace of my sanity. Start afresh, without all the emotional baggage we acquire in the course of our lives. Do you suppose every new generation assumes it and it alone has discovered sex for the first time, Agatha? I think ours did."

"Yes, I felt that. But I never . . ." It wasn't in Agatha's makeup to finish the statement.

Dorothy laughed. "No, I don't suppose you did. I doubt if there is a rebel bone in your body. So silly, really, when you look back on it. All that intellectual freedom. Questioning the Old Guard. It had to manifest itself in some form, I suppose. And my poor parents—I must have put them through hell on earth."

Dorothy sighed and watched the countryside race by. "I'm talking too much, aren't I?"

"No, no. Not at all."

"Never in my wildest dreams did I imagine I would be talking basic girl talk with the likes of you, dear."

"I'm glad you feel comfortable enough to do so."

"You know, I had a most unusual dream during the wee hours of this morning in your guest bedroom. I dreamt that I was a juggler, of all things. There was a large audience of women before me, most of them weeping or at least on the verge of tears. And I was doing my best to keep their minds off their troubles and on this spectacular act I was performing for their benefit. I must have had twelve different objects going in the air at one time. Me, who has trouble keeping three oranges going for more than two seconds."

"What were the objects?" Agatha asked.

"Yes, the objects. An interesting selection, I must say. Many of them were common objects most jugglers work with. Dumbbells, candlesticks, long knives. Then there was my play script with swatches of costume patterns tucked in the pages, which for some amazing reason didn't fly about when I tossed the script. There were probably two bottles of Scotch. There was also a handgun, such as my husband . . . but you know about that. And, of course, a miniature version of the cradle Anthony used to sleep in. I was tossing that about, too, with apparent ease."

"Were you managing to keep the weeping ladies happy?"

"Not happy. But I was keeping their attention. I was certainly working hard enough at it. Do you believe dreams are trying to tell us something?"

"I am open to the idea."

"What do you make of the weeping women?" Dorothy asked.

"Well, we've certainly seen our share of tears, lately, haven't we? I could imagine them being all the women that have been injured by the war results. Certainly their wounds have far exceeded the war years, haven't they?"

When the Morris chugged into Witham's quiet streets after dark, Dorothy asked to be taken directly to the police station. Agatha reluctantly did as directed. But there was no light in the small station house and no response to Dorothy's knock. She finally caught sight of a small handprinted sign in the front window:

If you are in need of a Constable's services after
hours, please ring 239, or come to Mrs. An-
drews' boarding house and ask for Sergeant
Whitecomb.

Dorothy put her hands on her hips as a measure of
disgust. "Not a very professional way of handling things,
is it?"

"Do you know where the boarding house is?"

Dorothy shook her head. "Haven't the foggiest."

"May I make a suggestion?"

"What's that?"

"Why not wait until morning when you've had a good
night's sleep. Your mind will be fresh then."

"You wouldn't be trying to dissuade me from my course,
would you, Agatha?"

"No, I wouldn't. I can see you have your mind set. I'll
not try to dissuade you again."

"Perhaps you are right about the night's sleep." Dorothy ambled back toward the car. "At this point, I don't
suppose a few hours could make that much difference."
She dropped back into the passenger seat. "Would you
care to stay overnight? We have a spare bedroom, if some
of my play people haven't commandeered it in my
absence."

"That's very kind of you. No, I think I'll press on."

There was no sign of life at Dorothy's, except for a dim
glow from the kitchen, a low-wattage bulb that Betty often
left on for her. And there was still no sign of Mac's big
roadster. Dorothy hoisted herself out of the car.

"Well, it has been interesting, if nothing else. I think we
could write a pretty good mystery together, if it ever came
to that."

"Dorothy, I have a question, if it is not presuming too
much."

"Yes, of course."

"In your play, I presume the sins and shortcomings of
your William of Sens are found out . . ."

"Yes, they are."

"Then what happens to him?"

"He is open to public ridicule. He eventually loses his position as Chief Architect for the Cathedral."

"Was that really necessary? I mean even after he was sorry for his shortcomings, was it necessary for such a heavy blow to fall?"

"I think it is dramatically correct. I feel the theatre demands measurable justice for evil doing. I think the public demands it."

Agatha opened her mouth to protest, but then thought better of it. "Good night, Dorothy. I shall be thinking of you. You can be sure of that."

"Thank you, love. And good night."

Dorothy went into the dark house alone, and Agatha got her car back on the road to Witham's main street.

At what appeared to be the largest inn in Witham she pulled her Morris into a parking spot reserved for guests. She got out and found her emergency overnight bag in the boot, then went up to the main entry.

A small, foreign-looking gentleman was sitting behind the reception desk.

"Excuse me, my man. Do you have accommodations for a single party for this evening?"

"Yes, madam, we do." He turned the registry for his guest to sign in.

"And how is your telephone service? I will have several trunk calls to make tonight, and I will require a room with a telephone."

"Oh, our telephone service is very modern. We have our own telephone lady to connect your calls. I will tell her to keep a sharp ear out for your ring."

"And the local switchboard—how long do they stay open?"

"I believe the town switcher is on duty until eleven. And after that, she is only sleeping in the next room. The switchboard too, is very modern."

"Very good."

Agatha signed in and went directly up to her room.

Her first call was to E. C. Bentley. She got through to his home without a problem, just as the desk clerk predicted. After the phone rang six times a tired voice answered.

"Hullo?"

"Oh, Edmund, I'm sorry. I've gotten you out of bed, haven't I?"

"Yes, well . . . who is speaking please?"

"This is Agatha. Agatha Christie."

"Yes, Agatha. What is it? What's happened? Are you all right?"

"Yes, Edmund, I am perfectly fine. I am calling because of your suggestion the other day in the library. Do you remember saying you would like to help our friend Dorothy Sayers if the opportunity presented itself?"

"Yes, of course I remember."

"Well, I think the opportunity is presenting itself. Are you still willing to help?"

"Of course. What can I do?"

"My second question, Edmund—do you recall when we took the train to Witham, you and young Mr. Breen were willing to masquerade as officials of the law from out of the area?"

"Yes, of course. Silly idea, I suppose . . ."

"Well, Edmund, I was wondering if you might not be willing to do something like that now?"

There was a pause on the line. "Why? Do you think that is necessary?"

"Yes, I do. You would be helping Dorothy out of a very tight spot. I'm sorry I can't be more specific at the moment."

"All right, Agatha, I'm in. What is it you want me to do?"

"Thank you, Edmund. This will be rather lengthy. I would like you to get a paper and pencil and write down what I tell you."

"I'll have to go downstairs. Please hold the line."

"Yes, of course."

She could feel her own heart racing as she thought of what lay ahead. She had to force herself to remain calm, for Edmund's sake if nothing else.

It had been that dream of Dorothy's that did it finally. That had gotten her onto the right track. Now, she was almost certain she knew who had done the killing.

21

The next morning Dorothy was up at quarter to six. She felt she had a stack of letters of apology to write. Several old friends from her advertising and publishing days had gone to work for her when the play opportunity presented itself. Labors of love, really, since the Festival's budget was so minuscule. And now she was letting them down in a most ignominious fashion.

But try as she might, the letters were not flowing. What could she tell them? Please excuse me for being the person I am and not the person you thought me to be. Perhaps in another lifetime we might get together again for another try at my being who people really think I am. Everything had a trite, hollow ring to it. Not the kind of note she could feel comfortable writing.

Her problem, unquestionably, was she was too assertive. Her natural writing style was too positive and self-confident, and switching to a contrite tone was too severe a change for her so late in life. Whatever the reason, she finally had to give up the idea of letters of apology. At a bit after seven she heard Betty moving about in the kitchen below.

She carelessly dressed herself in one of her black dresses—after reaching a certain proportion she had discovered it really didn't matter what outfit she wore since they all had about the same overall effect. She was getting to be a very large lady.

At the head of the stairs she found a dustrag in the hall closet and managed to dust the banister and generally pick things up as she descended. Perhaps sensing she wasn't going to be around for a while.

"Oh, good. I did hear you come in then, after all," Betty laughed at the first sight of her mistress. "The kettle is on the boil. Shouldn't be a mo."

Dorothy marched solemnly into the kitchen. "Have you seen or heard from the Mister, Betty?"

"No, not a word. But your play people have been in and out of here, like to be the death of me, they are. I put your telephone messages on the shelf here in the kitchen. You want them?"

"Yes, I suppose I had best look them over."

Dorothy seated herself at the worktable and Betty got down the handful of notes she had made. Dorothy thumbed through them, listlessly.

"Betty, you mentioned the other day that your brother, I think it was, would like to have you come and 'do for him' as you put it. Is that still an option?"

Betty looked injured. "Well, he did say it to me, one time. He meant it as when we got old and tottery, you understand."

"I see. I rather got the impression it was a pressing request. But now I see . . . it was your way of gracefully backing out of a difficult situation."

"Why, whatever do you mean?"

Dorothy held her breath for a moment, then let the truth out with full force and in her formal voice. "I mean you knew in your heart I had come in the house by way of the front door and found the dead man, before I showed myself in the backyard to you. That I was lying through my teeth to the police."

Betty blushed and busied herself at the sink.

"It's all right, Betty dear. You don't have to be upset about it any more. I'm going down to the police station and make a clean breast of it."

"Oh, Miss Sayers," Betty sobbed, "I would never do a thing to hurt you. You know that. I, I . . ."

"Oh, gawd, woman. Please don't cry about it. I've got

women crying at me in my sleep. Very soon I'll have people queuing up to cry at me. Don't you be doing it, too. Come on, now. You're a better woman than I'll ever be. There's no need for all that."

"Does this mean you want me to be leavin' your services?"

"No, no. Not at all. I simply thought . . . oh, never mind what I thought. Why don't you do up some toast for me? And don't spare the marmalade."

Dorothy marched to the telephone in the front hallway and requested the number she had seen posted in the police station window the evening before. After three rings she heard the Inspector's sleepy voice on the other end.

"Hullo?"

"Inspector Petry, this is Mrs. Fleming calling."

"Yes, Mrs. Fleming. What can I do for you?"

"That should be reversed. It is a question of what I can do for you. I have not been entirely honest with you about the shooting in my house. I would like to make a new statement."

She thought she heard the telephone drop from the Inspector's hands, but she couldn't be quite sure.

"Hello, Inspector? Are you still there?"

"Yes, of course. I was rather expecting to hear from you, eventually. I did not think for a moment that you had told me everything that you knew."

"You are most perceptive."

"I think, under the circumstances, I would like to see you at the station. Where are you calling from?"

"Is that really necessary? I would rather not be hauled off to Old Bailey like a common criminal, if I can avoid it."

"I hardly think this is the time to be considering such matters, do you? I shall be right up to your house to pick you up."

"Too bad, for I shall not be there."

"Oh, where will you be?"

"In five minutes, when I finish my breakfast, I shall be

walking south on Bellhorn Lane until I reach the town square. At which time I shall turn right and proceed to your station. If you wish, you may drive along Bellhorn Lane and pick me up."

She hung up crisply, without waiting for his response. This was not going to be easy. Her sense of independence and her tendency toward belligerency when cornered would somehow have to be held in check.

Betty had overheard most of the conversation and was of little use in getting something together for her mistress's breakfast. Dorothy tried keeping their parting on a casual basis and managed to get out the front door with only a few tearstains on the front of her dress.

It seems the Inspector had not been dressed when she called him, or he had trouble getting the town's police car into service, for Dorothy was almost at the town square before she spotted him slowing up in the street next to her. He got out and opened the passenger door for her.

"The reason I asked that we take your statement at the station, Mrs. Fleming, was so that it might be typed and witnessed," the Inspector explained, formally. "Sergeant Whitecomb should be right along."

He didn't bother speaking the rest of the short trip, but nervously and quickly got his passenger into his office and seated opposite his desk. He was going to get this done properly if it killed him. He got out five sheets of white paper and four blue carbons and pressed them into place in the office's one typewriter.

Sergeant Whitecomb came in the back way, with his uniform jacket half buttoned.

"Yes, sir. Ready to go, Inspector. Oh, Miss Sayers. Nice to see you again."

"Hello, Sergeant."

"Mrs. Fleming is here to change her statement, Sergeant," the Inspector barked. "I would like you in here to hear it. I'm going to try to take it down."

The Inspector started putting a few words on the paper with a very slow hunt and peck system.

"Inspector, is that the best you can type?"

"We'll get the job done," he said, defensively.

"We're going to be here all day, at this rate," Dorothy groaned. "Here, get up. I'll do the typing."

She shooed him away from the desk and Dorothy sat down in his place. She rattled off the day, date, and the location. Then turned back to Petry.

"You want me to do this on my own, or should I be responding to questions?"

Inspector Petry scratched at his sideburn. "I think a statement in your own words would be best. Then I will ask questions, as needs be."

Dorothy whirled back to the machine and set up a new paragraph. Then, speaking as she typed:

"I, Dorothy L. Sayers, a.k.a. Mrs. MacDonald Fleming, do hereby wish to recant and change the story about my involvement in the death of Dean Thornton Matthews. The earlier version I did willfully give to Inspector Petry over the past fortnight was in error. The reason will become apparent . . ."

There was a rap on the front door in the adjoining room.

"Sergeant, will you see who that is? Put them off if at all possible," Petry directed. He turned back to Dorothy. "Please go right on."

" . . . reason will become apparent . . ." Dorothy repeated to prime her mental pump for her lost train of thought.

"Sorry, sorry, ma'am. The Inspector is busy right now," Sergeant Whitecomb was explaining in a loud voice to someone at the front door. "Perhaps if you can tell me your trouble . . ."

"So very kind of you, Sergeant, I am sure."

Dorothy's ears perked up. It was Agatha Christie's voice she heard. She and the Sergeant seemed to be having a misunderstanding about what her business was about. There even seemed to be some shuffling of feet, as if they were dancing or moving about together.

"I want you to know I have lost track of my friend, Miss Dorothy Sayers—"

"Lost track? The Inspector is busy right now. Lost track, you say?"

"She isn't on the premises, perchance? Is she in with the Inspector?"

"The Inspector can't— I say, you can't go in there."

The next thing Dorothy knew, the door to the Inspector's office had flown open and the Sergeant and Agatha Christie, both trying to enter the room at the same time, had wedged themselves into the opening of the narrow doorway.

"Ah, Dorothy, so good to see you," Agatha called out.

"Sorry, sir, but she . . . she . . ." The Sergeant, still wedged against Agatha, was looking for a safe place to put his hands.

Petry got to his feet. "Didn't you hear the Sergeant say we were busy?"

"Why, yes, of course, I'm sure you are," Agatha fluttered. "Busy with the murder case, aren't you? That's what I am here about. Isn't that a coincidence?"

"Fine, ma'am. The Sergeant will be happy to take your statement in the other room."

"So very kind of you, I'm sure."

Agatha finally got out of the doorway by backing up slightly. Then, when the Sergeant did the same, she did a graceful pirouette against his midriff and found herself back in the Inspector's office.

"You see, Inspector," she rattled on, "I am most interested in the story that Miss Sayers may have told you. You haven't told them anything yet, have you, Dorothy?"

Dorothy's mouth was agape at the unusual acts being performed by the normally retiring Agatha Christie. It took her a second to respond.

"I was . . . we were just getting started here . . ."

"Oh, how fortunate . . . for me, I mean."

Petry came around the corner of the desk to usher the strange woman out, but during that split second, Agatha

managed to ease herself into a nearby chair, all the time
jabbering like a magpie to keep the conversation going. The
Inspector was reaching the end of his patience.

"Who are you, woman?"

"But Inspector, Dorothy here knows me. Why don't
you ask her who I am?"

He looked frantically to Mrs. Fleming.

"Yes, ah, this is my acquaintance, Agatha Christie,"
Dorothy stammered. "We know one another, you see—"

"Yes, you see we've been working on this murder business together," Agatha went on. "We have done rather
well with it, actually, and we want you to know—"

"Christie? Did you say Agatha Christie?"

"Yes, Inspector. Perhaps you know her," Dorothy said,
"she is a write—"

"Indeed I do know the infamous Miss Christie. I know I
spent one cold winter month in 1926 as a rookie officer,
walking up and down the snow-blown hills of Central
England on a wild-goose chase searching for the lady in
question. While all the time she was cooling her heels, or
warming her heels, in some comfortable resort hotel
somewhere."

"Oh, I am so sorry, Inspector."

"Indeed you should be. You gave me a case of chil-
blains that almost put me in hospital, I'll have you know."

"Oh, I am *so* sorry. Please except my belated apology."

"I will be happy to entertain your efforts toward an
apology. Only in the other room, if you please. Mrs.
Fleming and I are in the midst—"

"Yes, I know. Trying to put together the puzzle about
the murdered man."

"Mrs. Fleming was in the midst of changing her story
regarding—"

"Exactly. That's what I am here about, too."

"Changing her story?"

"Yes, you see we have some new information for you. I
now am almost certain I know who killed the man in
Dorothy's house."

"Oh you are, are you?" Petry scoffed. "And just what makes you think that you—"

"Inspector, Inspector," Dorothy interrupted. "I think it might be wise if we listened to the lady. I know her, and she wouldn't be carrying on this way without good reason."

Petry took time to measure the seriousness in Dorothy's voice. Then he sat down on the edge of the desk and narrowed his eyes at Agatha. Sergeant Whitecomb stepped into the room again and quietly closed the door after himself.

"Very well. Who killed the man?"

Agatha hesitated for the first time. "You don't know the murderer. That is why this is going to be rather difficult to explain. You must be patient."

"But you do know the murderer, is that it?"

"Yes, well, indirectly, I know. We haven't been formally introduced—that is, properly, by rightful names and all."

"But you do know?"

"Yes, that is correct. I do know who killed the Dean and who did the other acts—"

"Wait a minute. Wait a minute. What other acts?"

Agatha put her hand to her brow. "Oh, dear. Where does one begin? It's so rather complicated. You see, the Dean was killed by mistake. The murderer took him for someone else. A military man about the same age. You see, this is all a military matter, held over from the Great War when people were gassed in France and the truth about matters was never made public."

Inspector Petry shook his head. "Wait a minute. You do have some proof to back up all these allegations you are making, I presume."

"Yes, we do," Dorothy put in. "We have been working on this approach together and we do have certain evidence."

She went on to explain in capsule form what the two of them had learned. That the handgun was quite unique in the way it was connected to Mac Fleming's regiment. That other people in the regiment had received white feathers and one man was dead from poisoning after receiving the feather. That all the people who had been threatened were regimental officers who had hidden in the sealed bunker during the mustard gas attack. Agatha had had the presence of mind to bring along a copy of Colonel Husted's obituary as well as a copy of Lieutenant Dennis's obituary from the Oxford paper, which she had dug up from some place.

Judging from his manner of questioning, Inspector Petry had finally started to lose his disbelief and take the two women seriously.

"Why didn't you come forth with this information before?" he asked.

"We only last night got back from seeing Mrs. Dennis up in Oxford. There really hasn't been time," Agatha said. "But now you have it. You being in charge of the matter, we thought you should be the first—"

"Thank you for that belated vote of confidence. It is unique in its singularity. I am no longer in charge of the case."

"You are not?"

"No. London is sending two men up. They should be here this afternoon. Or tomorrow at the latest. County people are not happy with the lack of progress, apparently. Why don't you wait for the afternoon train? Perhaps you will find someone at the depot with whom you can share your news."

"Then why are you taking Dorothy's deposition?"

"I was hoping . . . this might give us a bit of help. A leg up, as it were."

"Wouldn't it be interesting if you could manage to solve the entire case before the London people showed up?"

Petry grunted. Agatha thought his eyes sparkled just a bit at the thought. But then he frowned, formally.

"I don't think there is much hope of that."

"Oh, but there is," Agatha smiled. "There is a very good chance."

"Miss Christie, you still haven't given us a name. Is this thing a conspiracy or what?"

"It is . . . you see, it is rather difficult to explain, sitting here so far removed from where things could—how shall I say it?—would be so much better. So much safer if we could all be out . . . outside where I can explain better."

"Safer? Explain better? What the devil does that mean?"

"I wonder, Inspector, if you would indulge me just a bit more. I wonder if we all might not drive just a short way out into the country?"

He shook his head. "There is nothing wrong with the atmosphere right here in this room. We are all perfectly safe."

"Oh, I see. Well . . ." Agatha didn't move.

"Oh, this isn't getting us anywhere. Off with you, now." He waved at Agatha to make herself scarce, then turned back to Dorothy: "You were about to type your statement . . ."

Getting to her feet, Dorothy pulled the pages from the typewriter carriage.

"I think, Inspector, that we should do as the lady says. If that is what she wants, let us take a ride out into the country."

22

Once outside on the street Agatha took Dorothy by the arm. "Why don't you get into the passenger seat of my car?" she encouraged.

As soon as the ladies began to move toward Agatha's car the Inspector called after them.

"I say there, what are you doing? Why don't we all ride in the police car? We have plenty of room."

"You'll be able to follow us just fine," Agatha called, hurrying to get behind the wheel. "I promise not to drive fast."

The frustrated Inspector ordered his Sergeant to get into the driver's seat of their own vehicle and follow along behind the women.

Once inside her car with the doors shut, Agatha breathed a deep sigh of relief.

"What on earth are you up to?" Dorothy demanded.

With her right toe, Agatha pressed down hard on the self-starter button until the car groaned to life, then explained, "I had to get you out of there. I just couldn't have you telling them everything. Not now."

"Oh, Agatha, this isn't solving anything. Where do you think you are taking us?"

"Just as I said. Out in the country a little way. You'll see."

"This is embarrassing. We are only delaying the inevitable. You promised me last night you would not interfere with my wishes anymore."

"I know, but this is different. This is ever so much

different. Where do you think I got the nerve to come charging into the station the way I did and rescue you from yourself?"

"I was wondering about that. You are acting very much . . . unlike yourself."

Agatha tipped back her head and laughed. "It gives me such a feeling of power, of devil-may-care nerve. You see, I really do know the identity of the killer."

"You do? Who?"

"You know, of course, if I said 'who' and then it turned out to be wrong, why I could be sued, don't you?"

"I thought you said you knew, definitely."

"Well it is almost definite. I only have to . . . get two things together. Then I really will know, definitely. Can you trust me? Just for a few miles?"

As they talked Agatha had been driving up Bellhorn Lane, approaching Dorothy's house. Dorothy wasn't paying attention until Agatha pulled into her front drive.

"What on earth are we back here for?"

"Oh, I thought you would want to let Betty know you may not be back in time for lunch," Agatha explained innocently.

"Nonsense. There's no reason to do that. She doesn't expect me until she sees me these days. I don't even want to go in."

"Are you sure?"

"Of course I'm sure. It will only upset her more than she already is."

"Very well," Agatha said, and put her car into reverse. Back at the street she stopped to look for the police car. They were waiting patiently, halfway down the block. Then Agatha used a nod of her head to point at something else.

"Do you see what I see?"

Dorothy followed Agatha's eyes and saw the young would-be reporter, Wanda Barton, standing next to a tree across the street.

"Good heavens. The pest is back. I'd completely forgotten about her. Hurry, get going before she gets any ideas."

"Yes. Good idea."

But when Agatha tried to let out the clutch for a fast getaway she only succeeded in killing the engine.

"Oh, do please hurry," Dorothy begged. "I think she's coming this way."

Agatha ground and ground the starter, with nothing happening.

"What's the matter?"

"I think I flooded the engine."

The American girl hesitated in the middle of the road, then, after watching Dorothy jumping up and down in her seat, decided to come over to the car. Agatha continued to try to start it.

"Maybe it's the magneto again," she said.

"Oh, do something, do something," Dorothy begged. "I shall die if that woman gets on to us."

But come over Wanda did. She got into the back seat and made herself comfortable.

"No, miss, don't, please . . ." Agatha stammered.

"Well, hello, ladies. Remember me?"

"Only too well," Dorothy groaned.

"You wouldn't be trying to run out on me again, would you, Dorothy? After all we've grown to mean to each other? Why I'll bet you've already forgotten your promise, haven't you? It's Saturday morning. Remember?"

"Saturday . . . oh no," she sighed. "I promised to grant you an interview. And I will. But we have an emergency situation here. This is impossible."

"Sorry, dear, but I'm not budging," Wanda smiled. "You've run out on me twice now. You're not going to do it a third time."

The police car had pulled up. The Inspector was waiting to see what Agatha was going to do.

"They're waiting for us, Dorothy," Agatha whined. "What'll I do?"

"Let's call the Inspector over," Dorothy barked, "and
have her thrown out on her ear."

"You do that and I'll turn nasty, too, Mrs. Fleming,"
Wanda threatened. "I've dug up plenty of dirt on that
drunken husband of yours. And I won't hesitate to publish some choice little items about you that I've uncovered."

Dorothy and Wanda exchanged hard looks until Agatha
put the car back into gear.

"I'll just have to leg her tag along."

Dorothy groaned as Agatha pulled out and headed for
the highway west of town.

"Well, now, where are you girls taking me?" Wanda
asked. "I do hope it'll be a nice long drive so we can get a
little work done on our interview."

She flipped open her secretarial pad and crossed her
legs, as if anxious to get down to work.

"It so happens, young lady," Agatha started, "we are
working with the police. Helping them with some details
on a real murder case."

"You're kidding."

"No, we're not 'kidding.' See the police car following
along behind us?"

Wanda looked out the back window and her eyes
widened.

"Holy smokes! You mean this is about the man who
died in the Fleming house?"

"Yes, partly—"

"No kidding? It really was a murder, then? Not a suicide as I heard first?"

"Yes, that's right. It was murder."

Wanda forgot about her pad and leaned forward, her
elbows firmly hooked over back of the front seat.

"My gawd, do you have any idea what kind of story
this will make? Agatha Christie and Dorothy L. Sayers
working with the police to solve a genuine murder? My
gawd, do you have any idea what I can sell this story for?
It's mind-boggling. That's what it is."

"How nice," Dorothy said through her teeth.

"Ah, please don't be upset, dearie," Wanda said. "Think what this will do for my career. Don't you think women should have a place in journalism? This will give me a name in the States. If you two help solve a genuine murder case I can write my own ticket. Do you really think it will ever get solved?"

Dorothy looked at Agatha, who nodded slowly.

"I think it will, before the day is out. If not sooner."

Wanda clapped her hands in joy. Then she looked about for her writing pad. "Let's see, now, what was that man's name? If I'm going to be a reporter, I'll have to start doing better at remembering names . . ."

Agatha supplied the name of the dead Dean and the answers to several other general questions the girl had about the case.

All the while they headed west on the nearly deserted highway. Only a few farmers, out with their hay mowers or other horse-drawn implements, slowed their early morning progress. Twenty miles out of Witham Agatha turned north off the main road and continued on for several more miles on a narrow secondary road with heavy hedgerows on either side.

Finally they came to a broad opening in the countryside where an ancient roundabout had been created to accommodate the junction of five separate roads. Agatha went halfway around the large circular loop and pulled to a stop on the outer side of the road so as to be out of the way of any continuing traffic that might come by. The police vehicle settled in right behind Agatha's car.

When Agatha switched off the engine they realized just how much into the country they were. The only sound they could hear at first was the cooing of some mourning doves in a grove of poplar trees near a river bank about a quarter mile away. One field, to the northwest, was under cultivation of some kind. It looked as if it might be barley. The adjoining fields appeared to be untended pastureland.

"Now what are we supposed to do?" Dorothy demanded.

"Why don't we join the officers?" Agatha suggested.

The two ladies and their shadow got out of the car and walked back to the police. Inspector Petry was already standing on the gravel road, looking about.

"Is there something supposed to happen out here?" he asked.

"Oh, yes, indeed." Agatha smiled and looked at her wristwatch. "It shouldn't take much longer.

"Inspector, I don't believe you and the sergeant have met our guest from America, Miss Wanda Barton. She is a budding reporter, interested in . . . our police procedures."

The three of them nodded and shook hands all around, Wanda being the most ingratiating.

"This is so exciting for me. Being from the States and all, I feel it a great privilege to be a part of the investigation. Let's see now. You're called an Inspector, is that it? That must be like a captain in the States, wouldn't you say? And 'Sergeant' I know. We have them in our police, too."

The Inspector cleared his voice vociferously. It hadn't taken him long to get his fill of the girl.

"What, exactly, are we waiting for, Miss Christie?"

She checked her watch again. "Oh, it won't be long, I don't think. Then all your questions will be answered."

"What are we to do in the meantime?" the Sergeant asked. "This isn't going to be dangerous, is it?"

Agatha considered that seriously. "I—I'm not sure. I don't think so."

A slight breeze wafted in from the southwest and brought with it a refrain from a distant military band.

Petry whirled in that direction. "What's that? I heard something. What was that?"

"Nothing, sir," his Sergeant assured him. "Just the drum and bugle corps from the Army camp over yonder. Must be time to review the troops."

"Oh, is that all? That's over a mile away from here, isn't it, Sergeant?"

"Just under, I should say, sir."

The Inspector took off his hat and wiped at the sweatband with his handkerchief. "I must be getting jumpy. Listen, folks, why don't we make ourselves comfortable? I think there is room enough for all of us in the back seat of our car, there."

"I think that might be a good idea." Agatha said.

The Sergeant got in the back of the large car first, and folded down two small jump seats so that they faced the large back seat. Then all five of them got in.

"How exciting," Wanda Barton cooed again as she snuggled up next to Sergeant Whitecomb in one corner. Agatha got on the jump seat opposite. Dorothy was next to the Sergeant and the Inspector was last in, taking the jumpseat next to Agatha. They all sat looking rather foolishly at one another for a few minutes. Finally, Agatha noticed the Sergeant removing something from the breast pocket of his tunic.

"I say, are those real handcuffs, Sergeant?"

The Sergeant showed off a pair of unlocked handcuffs. "Yes, I thought I would keep them handy, just in case."

"Oh, how exciting. I don't believe I have ever seen a pair of handcuffs in real life before. How do they work?"

"Quite simply, really. They're the new snap-lock style. So you can have them open"—he demonstrated by swinging at his own left wrist—"and by one quick stroke you can have them locked in place. You can have a prisoner under lock before he even knows what's happened to him."

"Why, how interesting. May I see them?"

"Well, I suppose . . ."

"Sergeant," the Inspector admonished his man, "let's not be showing off department equipment, if you please."

"Oh, certainly. I understand. I was merely curious," Agatha assured him. She already had the cuffs in her hands when the order to return them came forth. But in her rush to return the handcuffs she inadvertently connected one loop on the Sergeant's wrist as he reached out to take them from her.

"Er, ma'am, don't do that."

Sergeant Whitecomb had to fumble about in his pants pocket to find the key to extricate himself. Wanda laughed at his struggles.

"Honestly, you English are so funny. I can't believe a citizen doing something like this to cops in the States. They would be all over you just for trying."

"Yes, well, we over here," Petry said with a good deal of chin showing, "try to maintain a more civil relationship with the public."

"That I can believe," she laughed some more. "I can't for a minute see Baltimore cops letting civilians lead them around the open countryside with nothing but a promise of rounding up some famous desperado or what have you. She hasn't even told you what we're out here for. I honestly can't believe real policemen would act like this. You *are* real bobbies, aren't you?"

"Miss, you are coming very close to abusing our hospitality—"

Wanda interrupted him with more laughter. "I won't be able to put this part in my story. I swear, nobody Stateside would believe it."

"Miss, you do grate on a person's . . . sensibilities. Do you know that?" the perspiring Inspector told her.

"Okay, okay, I'll be quiet."

The Inspector ordered his man to roll down some windows to let in more fresh air and they all sat in silence for another stretch of time.

"As long as we are waiting here with nothing apparent to do," Petry said, "I have a question for you, Mrs. Fleming."

"Yes, Inspector?"

"Since you say the Dean killed at your house was actually killed in error, I was wondering if you could tell me what it was he was doing there in your house in the first place."

Dorothy rolled her tired eyes in Agatha's direction and groaned. "I knew it would come down to this. Inspector, he was there—"

"He was there," Agatha interrupted, "for a very specific reason. And we will all, no doubt, know that reason in a very short time. You see, this business is all tied together somehow, and it is difficult to explain one part without explaining it all. Do you see?"

It was the Inspector's turn to groan. "No, Miss Christie, I do not see. Please try to make that clearer, if you please."

"Yes, well . . . someone will be coming." Agatha sat staring out the window, without offering further explanation.

"How soon?" Dorothy asked.

Agatha looked again at her watch. "Very soon."

"Well, who is this someone we are waiting for?" Dorothy pleaded. "Won't you give us a hint?"

"There's a hint right out the window." Agatha pointed. "I'm surprised you haven't picked up on it before now."

"What? Where?"

All eyes in the car searched the barren surroundings for traces of a clue. Finally, their eyes zeroed in on the road sign that stood in the middle of the roundabout.

"That sign?"

Agatha nodded.

Dorothy got her pince-nez into position and read the signboards. "Anson's lane, Road to Dellcort, Twin-Oaks Road . . . Twin-Oaks . . ." She looked at Agatha, her eyes widening.

"Ever seen that road address before?" Agatha asked.

"Yes. Yes, I have. On my husband's list of officers . . ."

"Of course," Agatha encouraged. "I thought the sound of the military band would tell you . . ."

Dorothy smacked her thigh with a resounding slap. "That's it. Now I've got it. I know who did the killing."

"You do?" Petry leaned forward. "Tell us all, then."

Dorothy looked at Agatha again, to see if she wanted to take the lead. But Agatha was smiling slightly and watching her own hands, which she held quietly on her purse in her lap.

"Very well," Dorothy began. "It wasn't a revenge killing at all. That's what we thought it was at first. But now I can see it was a killing—or killings—to keep people quiet. You see, twenty years ago there was a badly managed regiment near the front lines in France. The gas masks that were scheduled to be passed out to the troops sat unused in a storage bunker when—"

"Excuse me. Not so fast," Wanda called. "I'm writing this all down as fast as I can."

"—when the gas attack struck," Dorothy went on, ignoring the girl. "Somehow or other, the matter of the bungled gas mask training got hushed up and nothing was ever done about it. But now, twenty years later, when the commander of that regiment is looking to get his commission reinstated, he doesn't want anyone nosing about, asking his old officers embarrassing questions. We know for a fact that the Army has had men out asking what kind of officer he was. They came to question Lieutenant Dennis, only he was already dead when they arrived. The same is probably true about Colonel Husted and Major Bruce. You see, they were all men who knew about the bungled gas mask training. They all knew the masks had arrived at the regiment, but nothing had been done about deployment." Dorothy had so warmed to her task she was almost shouting, in spite of the close confines of the police car. Now, her theologian's index finger went up in the air, as if a final authoritative pronouncement was on its way.

"You see, our murderer is none other than General John Dana Pike, retired Commander of the Old Regiment. It so happens he lives right down that road over there, on Twin-Oaks Road. I remember reading his address on my husband's list of regimental officers. We are sitting here, waiting for him to come along in his car. Is that the way you have it figured, Agatha?"

Agatha looked up with a startled expression, almost as if she hadn't been paying attention.

"What? Oh, yes, well, that certainly is a possibility, isn't it?"

Dorothy blinked. "What do you mean, a possibility?"

"Oh, yes, I agree. For quite some time I thought he was our murderer. And it might very well be correct, still . . ."

She let her sentence drift off unfinished and the others sat staring at her in disbelief.

"Agatha, you're going to be the death of me yet," Dorothy stormed. "Do you or do you not think General Pike is our murderer? Why in God's Holy Name else would we be sitting out here in the middle of cow pastures twiddling our thumbs, if it isn't that we are waiting for the General to drive along that road?"

Agatha stammered. "Honestly, Dorothy, there is no reason to carry on so. I'm doing the very best I know how."

"Then why are we sitting looking at country road signs, may I ask?"

"Oh, yes, the road sign. Don't you know of anyone else who might be along that road. Twin-Oaks . . ."

Dorothy looked again at the sign and had to give up. "No, I do not."

"Oh, I see. Well, it so happens the General does live down there. You see, he lives just off a post that used to serve as the regimental headquarters. Other people live down there, you see. Other military men. In fact on the old camp there is an old soldiers' home . . ."

Dorothy frowned. "So what does that mean?"

"Well, you said it yourself, dear. You said that the veterans of the Great War like to get together when things go bad for them, or words to that effect. And I have been racking my brain, trying to think of where your husband, Mac Fleming, might have gone to. And then it finally dawned on me. He would probably go to his old regimental headquarters. They have established an old soldiers' home down there. Did you know that?"

"No, I did not. You mean Mac has been staying there, down Twin-Oaks Road, at an old soldiers' home . . ."

"Just temporarily, of course, until all this trouble passes

over. Then he planned on coming back home. I talked to him last night, by telephone."

"You talked to him?"

"Yes, I did. He said he would be willing . . ."

The sound of a distant auto could be heard approaching the country junction. Dorothy must have recognized the sound of the roadster's engine, for she started to get out. but Agatha reached across and put her hand on the door and looked at the Inspector.

"Sir, may I suggest we all stay here, inside the car, for the time being?"

The Inspector nodded agreement and craned to see the approaching car.

"By the way, Dorothy, I've been meaning to ask you," Agatha said in her soothing way, "why did your husband change his name after the War?"

"What?" Dorothy's head jerked violently back and forth between calm and sedate Agatha and the open road out the window. "Oh, he told me there was already an Oswald working for the *News of the World* when he went on staff there, so the paper asked him to change his name. That's what he told me. Why do you ask?"

Agatha patted her arm. "Just tying up loose ends. Please try not to upset yourself, Dorothy."

"You mean my own husband, Mac . . ." Dorothy cried. "No, no, I don't believe it. It can't be."

Major Fleming's old yellow roadster came north on the Twin-Oaks Road and slowed as it approached the round-about, the badly damaged front fenders wobbling and banging against the bonnet as it came. The car pulled to a dusty halt several feet from the police car.

Major MacDonald Fleming was alone. He got out, read-justed his white sling to carry his injured arm and started toward the police car.

23

"So very nice of you to come, Major Fleming," Agatha called from her place in the car. "I am Agatha Christie. We spoke last evening by telephone, I'm sure you recall . . ."

"Mac, Mac, how are you?" Dorothy called and reached out to her husband. Besides the sling, he still wore a small bandage across his head, but otherwise he seemed in good health. He had even started a fresh mustache for his naked upper lip. Grey stubble could be seen when he got close to the car.

"I'm all right, old girl," he reached out to his wife's open hand. "Now then, what's this all about?"

"Very simple, really," Agatha said. "We only need the answers to two questions. You no doubt remember your accident on the Exeter road, when your car was forced into the ditch and you turned over?"

"Yes, what about it?"

"I would ask you now to look about in the car, here, and see if you see the face of the boy that forced your roadster off the road."

"Inside this car?" the Inspector said. "What on earth are you talking about?"

"Please, Inspector . . ." Agatha asked.

The group all exchanged dumbfounded expressions, then stared at Mac Fleming, while he in turn stared back at each of them.

While this was going on, Agatha surreptitiously "bor-

215

rowed" the open handcuffs from the lap of the Sergeant, who was otherwise occupied.

Mac looked over each face at least twice. Then he did a strange double-take and suddenly pointed a straight finger inside.

"There. That's it, right there. Him. I mean her . . ."

Quickly as she could, Agatha reached out with the open handcuff and looped one end over the wrist of the person Mac pointed to—Wanda Barton. Then she handed the other loop to the startled Sergeant.

"Here you are, Sergeant, for safekeep—"

But that was as far as she got. The girl let out a blood-curdling scream and started thrashing about like a wild animal in the crowded confines of the car. The men were doing their best to subdue her, but she had twisted her body about so that they had to contend with her flailing legs. The Inspector, seated diagonally opposite her, caught a particularly vicious kick from her sturdy walking shoe square on his nose and blood started squirting about, adding to the general mayhem.

Sergeant Whitecomb was still managing to hang on to his end of the handcuffs, but finally the girl, spinning like a wild banshee, twisted herself out of the window head first, which forced the Sergeant to relinquish his grip. The girl tumbled headlong into the ditch.

Dorothy was out of the opposite door like a shot and, in spite of her bulk, circled the car like a fullback. Just as the girl was righting herself in the ditch, Dorothy, with sheer abandon, took a leap into the air as if she were going into the deep end of the pool feet first. She landed on top of the girl, sending her back down in the ditch on her stomach.

By then the two policemen were out of the car watching the proceedings, not knowing exactly what to do. The Inspector was holding his head to one side, trying to keep his flowing nose from totally drenching his uniform.

"Help down there, Sergeant"—he waved a bloody finger at the women—"give Mrs. Fleming a hand."

The sergeant eased down into the steep ditch, trying to

look underneath Dorothy for something a gentlemen might grab onto.

Dorothy was wiggling and jumping about, as if she had suddenly become infected by ants.

"Do something, man. Oh, do something. She's biting and pinching my backside something fierce."

The Sergeant finally found the empty end of his hand-cuffs and managed to loop it around the first limb he could get hold of, which happened to be the girls' ankle.

"There, that should at least slow her down a bit." He helped Dorothy back to her feet and the two of them stepped back to see what kind of wild animal they had captured.

For her part, the girl had been mostly incoherent with her screams of hatred and desire to kill. The only thing discernable was that her American accent had disappeared. She tried to scale the ditch to get back up on the road, but her crablike configuration forced her to sit down. She was cuffed left-wrist-to-right-ankle and her wild movements only acted to throw her off balance. The party from the car now formed a semicircle around her and watched. With her twisted shape and long dark hair she could have been Richard the Third, scanning the empty horizons for his horse.

Now that she realized her predicament she slumped over and began to cry and swear at no one in particular, her hair plastered in ringlets against her sweaty head.

Dorothy, with the Sergeant's help, got back to the road and to her husband's side. She looked down at the girl and shook her head.

"The American? She is our murderer?"

Everyone looked at Agatha, who nodded her head solemnly.

"I don't get it," Dorothy panted. "How could she possibly be the murderer? I don't understand this at all."

"Remember I told you someone was lying to us? She was the one."

"Lying? About what?"

"About what and who she was. You were the one who put me on to her, Dorothy. You and your silly dream. All those women mourning for their men who suffered in the war. I got to thinking about those mourning women and wondering if we had considered them all. That was when I started reconsidering all the women we knew and what they had told us. I should have caught on to her much earlier, but her convincing American accent and the rude manner had me totally confused. She was very good. Her father would be very proud of her. She must have inherited his talent for the stage."

"But you told us she was a reporter from Baltimore," the Inspector said.

"Yes, that's what she told us," Agatha said, "but I doubt if she has ever been across the Atlantic, much less anybody's reporter."

"How do you know?"

Agatha turned to Dorothy, who was still busy brushing herself off from her roll in the ditch.

"Remember at the cafeteria, where I first saw her—do you recall what she said to me when you introduced her?"

Dorothy frowned. "Didn't she make some snide remark? 'My gawd, if it isn't the *Ten Little Indians* lady—or words to that effect?"

"Exactly. She called me the *Ten Little Indians* lady. I should have known right then she was not the genuine article, but her blunt sassy ways completely put me off balance."

"Why should that tell you anything?"

"My American publisher didn't care for the title of that book. He felt there wouldn't be enough Americans familiar with the nursery rhyme it was based on. So for the American market the title *Ten Little Indians* was changed to *And Then There Were None*. If the girl had just gotten off the boat as she claimed, there could not have been no way for her to know the *Indians* title. Not unless she was British. Which she is."

The girl made a sideways movement, as if she were going to try to get up on the road and away from her tormentors. The Inspector, who had finally gotten his nose problem under control, was keeping a close eye on her and issued a quick warning for her to stay where she was.

"Good heavens. She is British?" the Sergeant marveled. "God save the Empire."

"Indeed she is. As a matter of fact, she is a student in good standing in Dorothy Sayers' old school, Summerville College, Oxford."

Dorothy clapped her hands. "Of course. Lieutenant Dennis . . . had a daughter."

"That's right. Amanda Jo Dennis. The young lady who used to read detective stories to her ailing father. Who had to sit helplessly by watching day by day as her father got weaker and weaker. Until at last he died."

Agatha's quiet explanation was interrupted by more mournful sobs from the broken-hearted girl in the ditch. When at last they subsided, the Inspector called, "Are you ready to behave yourself, young lady?"

Amanda Jo wiped at her tear-streaked face with her free hand and nodded her assent. The Sergeant went back into the ditch and undid the cuff around her ankle and helped her to the roadside.

All the others, still not sure of her intentions, gave her plenty of room. The back seat of the police car was equipped to handle violent prisoners. She was recuffed and a chain was linked from the handcuffs to a secured place on the floor of the car.

"You comfortable now, Miss?" the Sergeant asked.

She made no reply. Mac Fleming leaned forward to get another, better look at her.

"It's amazing . . ." he started to say. But the girl spit into his face.

"You pig, you!" she screamed. "If it hadn't been for you and your two buddy officers my father would be alive today. You selfish pig."

"No, girl, it wasn't our fault," Mac cried. "It wasn't our fault. We didn't know . . ."

"Never mind, dear," Dorothy said "I think any explanation now would fall only on deaf ears."

"But she wants to kill me. And Major Bruce. And the Colonel—she must have killed the colonel. She's insane."

"We know, dear. We know."

Inspector Petry finally started acting as if he were in charge of the situation. He ordered the others to stay clear of the prisoner and rolled up the car windows to help the separation. He wanted to get everyone back to Witham as quickly as possible in order to get the whole story into a report. He started planning how the move was to be accomplished.

It was quickly determined that Mac's roadster, with its crumpled fenders, was not roadworthy and would have to be left behind, to be retrieved later by a towing service. That left two cars and six people. After several suggestions for arrangements, sometimes resembling a country version of musical chairs, it was finally determined that Sergeant Whitecomb would drive the police car, with the prisoner safely secured in the back seat. The Inspector and the Flemings would come along behind, riding with Agatha in her car.

Petry sat in front, beside Agatha, where he could keep a sharp eye on the police car ahead. But once on the main road he soon got more interested in his note taking as the explanation of events started spewing forth in Dorothy and Agatha's rapid-fire discussion.

"The poor thing must have gone completely insane, once her father died," Dorothy was saying.

"I'm not so sure," Agatha said. "She must have done some planning during her father's last days. Preparing the poison, finding out the addresses of the three officers in the bunker. I think she did a good deal of calculated planning."

"Preparing poison?" Petry asked.

"Yes, I believe she did. Remember, Dorothy, the empty

rat cages we saw at the Dennises's? I think those were probably for experimental poison tests and not for her college work, as her mother thought."

"So the poisoning came first, you think?" Petry asked.

"No," Agatha pondered, "I think the ill-fated visit to the Fleming household came first. More than likely that was where she picked up the white feather idea. She saw all of Dorothy's feathers for her angel wings, took a handful with her when she left, and stared mailing them to the next victims."

Dorothy grunted a sound of recognition. "So that's why there were the two feathers in her father's nightstand. They were simply left over from her mailing efforts."

"That's the way I see it, yes."

"But when and how did she get into my house?" Dorothy asked.

"I think she probably came to town dressed as a boy. All that hair of hers would fit nicely under a cap. We know that was the costume she was using later on when she ran your husband off the road. I think she may have done the same thing when she came to Witham. I recall one of my Detection Club fellow sleuths said something about a bicycle being taken from a nearby house and found later in someone else's yard. I think she must have pinched the bicycle and driven about the neighborhood until she found your house. Then she went in the back-yard, as if she were a delivery boy, looked through a window and saw a middle-aged man in the dining room and assumed it was the man of the house. Then she went in the back way, picking up a potato from the table where Betty had left her shopping things—remember, her father had about twenty years to tell her of his war experiences. He could very easily have told her about the potato working as an effective silencer on his automatic handgun, which she had brought along.

"And remember she is very quick with her tongue, it would have been a simple matter of saying she was there to pick up something, then walk over to the unsuspecting Dean and shoot him point blank in the head."

"Oh, no," Dorothy moaned, "that could have been you, dear," she told Mac.

"I know. Lucky we had an argument that morning and I was still out driving about like the Mad Hatter," he chuckled.

"And the suicide note?" Petry asked.

Agatha nodded. "Written by the girl, of course. She wanted it to appear that Major Mac Fleming had killed himself in shame. I think her intentions were that all the deaths were to look self-inflicted or natural. That way the men would be properly humiliated because of what she assumed was an act of cowardice, but the deaths could not be traced back to her. Unfortunately for her, she shot the wrong man.

"It was so silly of me, not to have picked up on that before. It could hardly have been one of Mac's fellow officers who shot the Dean. They would most certainly have seen who they were aiming at and known it was not Mac. Only the girl who had heard of Mac Fleming but probably never seen him in person, could have made a mistake like that. Or possibly General Pike, of course, who didn't seem to remember his line officers very well. But I ruled him out, primarily because our murderer seemed to be so active and so very resourceful. Both attributes that didn't seem to fit the retired General, who was used to having things done for him."

"But I don't understand," Dorothy called from the back seat. "Why did the girl make up that cock and bull story about being an American and following me about begging for an interview?"

"That was pretty clever of her, wasn't it? That was her cover. Her father, a born actor, probably mimicked the blunt Americans he had soldiered with during the war. And the girl obviously has some of her father's traits and picked up on the idea of being a foreigner to throw suspicion away from herself.

"You see, she wasn't following you about at all. She was waiting for a second chance to kill your husband. That's why she hung about in front of your house. And that is why she showed herself at hospital after Mr. Fleming's road accident, and again at the cafeteria near Major Bruce's home. I think she was at the Major's to find a way to poison him. Remember that dinner tray of virtually untouched food we saw at the Major's? I just wonder if it had been tampered with."

"How did she manage to get around so well?" Dorothy asked. "I thought she was the poor struggling student, trying to make ends meet."

"It would be my guess she traveled about in a borrowed car. Remember, her mother told us she got pin money by chauffeuring some lady about the town of Oxford. She was quite the sly one, wasn't she?"

"Yes, she was," Dorothy said. "You're a pretty good actor yourself, Agatha."

"Why, whatever do you mean?"

"I mean that business this morning about your car stalling. That was just an act to get the girl into the back seat."

Agatha giggled nervously. "Yes. I had driven by earlier and saw her standing there, no doubt waiting for Mr. Fleming's return. For a minute this morning, I didn't think she was going to take the bait and come over to the car. But it worked out, didn't it?"

"And what would you have done if the girl had not still been there?"

"Well, I suppose we would have had to think of something else, wouldn't we?"

Agatha noticed a heavy frown on the Inspector's face. "Is there something still troubling you, Inspector?"

"It is all still a bit much for me. So the girl thought the three officers in the bunker had locked the door on her father and kept him and his men from getting to the gas masks?"

"That's right, Inspector," Mac Fleming said. "I had decided it must have been something like that as soon as I read the strange suicide note. But we three men inside knew nothing about any gas masks. Actually, I thought the murderer was Lieutenant Dennis, for I knew of his bitterness. That's why I headed for the Colonel's house as fast as I could, to warn him. But I was too late. Then I tried reaching Major Bruce and found out he was already hospitalized. I assumed the murderer had already gotten to him. So after the two attempts on my life, I headed for cover to protect myself. The only cover I could think of was the regimental home."

"I suppose this Major Bruce and Colonel Husted business can all be verified?" the Inspector asked.

"Of course," Agatha smiled. "When your detective friends come up from London perhaps they would like to do some legwork for you in order to prove that part of the story."

"What? Oh yes," he smiled back, "send them packing, as it were. I see your point. Good show."

He kept busy for the next several miles, getting his notes in order. But then as they neared the outskirts of Witham he began his frowning and sideburn scratching again.

"There is just one problem I still have . . ."

"Yes, Inspector?" Agatha asked.

"This business of the Dean . . . I still have no logical explanation as to why the man was there in your house in the first place, Mrs. Fleming."

The Inspector turned about and directed his attention to the back seat, where Dorothy and Mac sat without speaking, and went on. "You see," he chuckled, "the way I had it mapped out, he really was your, er, lover, Mrs. Fleming, and your husband had killed the chap in a fit of jealous rage. Silly, that, wasn't it?"

"Yes, silly." Dorothy smiled as best she could.

"But since that obviously wasn't the reason he was there—" the Inspector continued to bear down—"what was the reason for his presence? Miss Christie, you said earlier that you had an explanation. I would like to hear that explanation now."

Agatha slowed her car because of the traffic ahead and smiled at the Inspector.

"I was hoping you weren't going to persist with that line of questioning, Inspector."

"I'm sorry, but I must. All the loose ends will have to be tied up. The London people will certainly insist upon it. I'm sure you understand."

"Yes, of course." Agatha cleared her throat, as if she were about to take the plunge. "You see, Inspector Petry, it was this way . . ."

Dorothy and her husband both leaned forward to hear what Agatha was going to say.

". . . you do recall our telling you about the two government men who had come to see Lieutenant Dennis, in order to ask him about General John Dana Pike?"

"Yes. Something about his war record, you said."

"Exactly. Now, doesn't it sound logical to you that the same government agency would also send an agent to interview other officers from his regiment?"

"You mean the Dean from a public school . . ."

"It would be logical that he would have a decent cover, doesn't it? I mean if he were working for . . . Whitehall, for example?"

"Yes. Certainly. Most logical. You mean to say that Matthews was a government agent?"

"Something like that could not be confirmed or denied in public, could it? They must keep their work ever so quiet, what with foreign agents and provocateurs ever on the watch."

"Oh, yes, I see what you're driving at."

"And the cover for such an agent should most certainly not be exposed by anything as mundane as a local investigation about an entirely different matter, now, I'm sure you agree."

Petry only scratched at this sideburn and frowned inquisitively.

The police car, still ahead of them, pulled to a stop at the side of the Witham police station. As Agatha pulled into an adjoining space, she noticed a familiar figure make its entrance from the doorway of the station. It was E.C. Bentley, looking very businesslike in his best dark suit. Agatha brightened at the sight of him. Thank heaven he had left his deerstalker cap at home.

"Why, whoever could that gentleman be, Inspector?" Agatha cooed. "Do you recognize him?"

Petry squinted. "Yes, I think I've seen him before, somewhere. Although I'm not sure . . ."

"You don't suppose he is here about Dean Matthews, do you?"

Petry got out of the car without answering and approached Bentley.

From the back seat of the car Dorothy leaned forward: "Agatha, what's Edmund doing here?"

But Agatha hushed her and slid over to the open window of the car to hear what was said.

"Good morning, Inspector," Edmund Bentley began officiously, "My name is Cremmel from the Army."

Petry took his hand. "Yes, Mr. Cremmel. You're here about one of your fallen comrades, the Dean, I believe."

Edmund was taken back. "Fallen Dean? Oh, why yes . . ."

"Don't worry yourself about it, sir. We may be a small station here in Witham, but we know our national duty when we see it. Not a word. Not one question will be asked about Dean Matthews' part in this matter. Now, if you will excuse me, sir, we have a prisoner to attend to."

He saluted Edmund and hurried over to the police car where the Sergeant was already unshackling the prisoner.

Edmund seemed hurt. He walked over to the car window where Agatha sat. "He already knew what I was going to say. I didn't even get a chance to give my speech."

"Yes, Edmund, I noticed. We had more or less gotten him prepared for the sight of you."

"But I was up all night, memorizing that blasted storyline

you gave me on the telephone." He took his hurried pencil notes from his pocket and showed Agatha. "And now I don't get to play my scene?"

"You already did. We all agree you played it beautifully, Edmund. It was just a bit shorter than we anticipated."

"Did it do any good, you think?"

"Oh, it did, Edmund. Most assuredly, it did."

"Good. I'm pleased. Now, kindly tell me what the duce this is all about."

Agatha suddenly developed a hearing problem. She smiled benignly at the inquisitive Edmund, got out, and opened the back door of the car for the Flemings.

"Well, there we are, now. That's that."

24

On opening night the play ran quite long. There were a few amateur gaffes showing here and there—lighting that missed its target once and a delayed entrance by some townspeople because of some recalcitrant scenery. But the quality of Dorothy's writing overcame all barriers and carried the story along with remarkable ease. The sympathetic audience sat enthralled throughout the evening.

Just as Dorothy had predicted, when her central character saw harsh justice meted out to him, and he was brought low from his haughty place on high as Architect to the Church, the audience seemed to accept his fall with understanding and approval.

At the end, the audience stood in unison and applauded wildly. Cries of "Author!" finally brought Dorothy from the wings, complete with her large fur coat, parson's hat, and walking staff. She gave a short speech, very modest for her, in which she gave major credit to her unflagging staff and her priceless performers. She concluded with an obvious genuine thank-you to the public. She would do her best in the years to come to bring drama back to the Church in which it started so many years ago. If Dorothy had not chosen to be a writer she could very easily have made her way in the world as an actor. By the time she took her final bow she had the cast and audience eating out of her hand.

Agatha and her husband had to wait for nearly an hour for their chance to talk to the laureled author. She was surrounded by so many well-wishers it was hard to see

her, much less talk to her. But Dorothy had made Agatha
promise to be there and had sent tickets to their London
flat by special messenger.

A goodly number of the Detection Club members were
present backstage, bubbling over with prases for their
beloved Dorothy. She was not to go "high-hat" on them,
they lectured, but was to continue her energetic leader-
ship at the monthly meetings of the Club. Much to their
pleasure, she promised that she had every intention of
doing precisely that.

When the crowd finally thinned out and only a few of
the backstage people remained, Agatha put her head into
the room and called Dorothy's name.

"Oh, come in, dear. I have been looking for you. So
glad you could be here." Dorothy got to her feet again for
the hundredth time that evening and gave Agatha a big
hug. Agatha introduced her husband, Max, freshly back
from his archeological dig, and complimented Dorothy on
her play's success.

"I suppose by now you are tired of hearing it, but we
truly did enjoy the play. Max was quite surprised that a
mere mystery writer could do anything so poetic and
moving."

Dorothy laughed. "Ah, Mr. Mallowan, you'd be surprised at how deep and obtuse we mystery writers can be
at times." She winked at Agatha. "And let me thank you
again, Agatha, for being my friend in need. This evening's
success is as much your doing as mine, you know."

"Oh, no, that's ridiculous," Agatha scoffed. "This is
your evening. Your success. We're all so very proud of
you."

"I only hope the Almighty is as pleased. I still can't help
but wonder if in the long run we have done the right
thing. Perhaps I should have taken my medicine, as it
were. I feel a bit . . . I don't know, duplicitous this way."

"Nonsense. That's not the way to look at it at all."

"It isn't?"

"Why, no. I've come to feel the Lord in his wisdom

gave mankind a wonderful mechanism for forgiveness and a second chance. It's hardly our fault that English society is not ready to do the same. All we have done is help the Lord have his way with the world until society has had a chance to evolve properly."

Dorothy laughed heartily. "Agatha, you have an amazing way of looking at life. A truly marvelous way with words."

"Me? Oh, mercy, no," Agatha blushed. "You are the author. I am only a puzzle maker."

Dorothy only patted Agatha's hand and smiled. She had learned not to argue with the lady.